P9-DHR-751

The Hidden World
The Age of Tolerance: Book One

by Schuyler J. Ebersol

© Copyright 2013 by Schuyler J. Ebersol

ISBN 978-1-938467-67-7

All rights reserved. No part of this publication may be reproduced, stored in a retrieval system, or transmitted in any form or by any means – electronic, mechanical, photocopy, recording, or any other – except for brief quotations in printed reviews, without the prior written permission of the author.

This is a work of fiction. All the characters in this book are fictitious, and any resemblance to actual persons, living or dead, is purely coincidental. The names, incidents, dialogue, and opinions expressed are products of the author's imagination and are not to be construed as real.

Published by

köehlerbooks™

210 60th Street
Virginia Beach, VA, 23451
212-574-7939
www.koehlerbooks.com

Publisher
John Köehler

Executive Editor
Joe Coccaro

The Hidden World

The Age of Tolerance: Book One

Schuyler J. Ebersol

VIRGINIA BEACH
CAPE CHARLES

This book is dedicated to my mom,
who is the strongest person I know.

Table of Contents

*The imperfection of the human mind is that which makes
the human race all the more beautiful*

The Before

THE YOUNG BOY staggered wearily through the woods. His dark-brown hair was tangled and his gray eyes were heavily shadowed and deep set from exhaustion. He hadn't slept in days. His clothes were tattered and dirty, covered in dark stains that looked like blood. As the boy staggered onward, an owl hooted, a rodent rustled noisily through the leaves, and far in the distance, a lone wolf howled mournfully. The boy gazed up for a minute and then looked back down at the path that only he could see.

The freezing night shrouded everything in a black blanket; the only light—a tiny sliver of moonlight—shone through the trees. The wind hurried through the valley, taking whatever it could carry on its way. Leaves were caught in its fingers as it pulled and pulled at branches, trying to wrench them from the trees. The Moon followed the wind at a slower pace, nonchalantly traveling across the sky until it reached the next horizon where its journey would begin again.

As the Moon neared the far horizon, the woods began to brighten—very subtly at first. The shadows grew from the encroaching darkness, captivating the land in their eagerness to precede the sunlight.

The boy stumbled over brooks and fallen trees. He passed

cliffs of unimaginable heights. Every now and then the lights of a large city could be seen glimmering through the trees. The boy kept going, mindlessly pressing forward with no clear end in sight. Every step was painful, but he did not hesitate or stop.

The Sun had found its place in the sky long before the boy had reached the last cliffs, which towered over the waking city far below them. It sat nestled against their protective natural wall. The boy stared at the city longingly. His eyes drooped as he tried to focus. He turned to head back toward the forest. The boy took several steps, and then collapsed. The leaves rustled and settled over his body.

The wind, on its relentless path, clawed at the boy's clothes. Finally, it ceased and stillness settled in. Not even the birds stirred as the Sun moved gradually across the sky—exactly as the Moon had before it, endlessly repeating the age-old pattern.

The sound of footsteps crunching through dead leaves and laughter preceded a young girl stepping out of the forest. She stopped mid-laugh when her blue eyes caught sight of the boy. She stared at him for a minute and then darted back into the woods. She returned several seconds later dragging a man by the hand. The lines on his face seemed to change, and he looked young and old simultaneously.

The man rolled the boy over and jolted back when he caught sight of his face. A hint of recognition showed in his eyes, but he mentioned nothing of it to his daughter. Instead, he said softly, "Sofia, darling, go and fetch the water, please."

Without hesitation, Sofia nodded and ran off, returning several minutes later grasping a canteen of ice-cold stream water. The man gently took the water from his daughter and tried to force some into the boy's reluctant mouth. He managed to get a few drops in, and at the taste of the cool water on his lips the boy's eyes shot open.

"I am Desmond," said the man. "Are you all right?"

"I'm Nate," the boy said in a whisper. "I am so tired."

Desmond stood and turned to his daughter. "We'd better get

him back to the car. He doesn't look well."

"Yes, Dad."

Desmond handed his small daughter the water canteen and then carefully lifted the boy into his arms. The two of them made off into the forest, Sofia running to keep pace with her father's much larger strides.

Chapter 1
The Fight

NATE SLOWLY DESCENDED the spiral staircase. He felt the smoothness of the stainless steel beneath his right hand, which was lazily trailing the circular railing. The temperature dropped with each step. Everything was silent and unnaturally clean.

Every morning since he had arrived in the Williams household, Desmond had sat in his favorite chair by the floor-to-ceiling windows reading the newspaper, yet his chair was empty today.

Emma greeted Nate with a smile as he entered the room.

"Where's Dad?" Nate asked.

"Good morning. He left early for L.A. He will be back tonight," said Emma. Nate's foster mother was beautiful. Her hair was straight and fell gracefully on her shoulders. It had once fallen several inches farther in waves like her daughter's, but her role in an upcoming movie required the haircut. Her eyes were blue and shimmered with kindness. She never missed a chance to dress extravagantly, and her good spirit preceded her everywhere she went.

"Long day." Nate took Desmond's usual seat by the window in an attempt to fill the gaping hole. "What's for breakfast?"

"I am so sorry, Nate. I have to leave in five minutes for a meeting with my manager. There is pancake mix in the fridge. Would you mind making breakfast for your sister?"

"Of course not." He often took the responsibility off his mother's shoulders so that she could relax or study her lines.

Nate Williams was shockingly extraordinary, in addition to having a financially privileged life and striking looks. He struggled with the problems and reveled in the joys that one would expect of someone his age. He had his faults, like anyone else, though it was difficult to see them under the mask of his popularity and confidence. From the look of him, it was impossible to guess his past. He was of average height for seventeen, and his clothes were unremarkable. He was most often seen in simple dark jeans and a faded T-shirt or polo. He cared about how he looked, but did not overdo it. His eyes were the only thing about him that might hint at his true identity—they were gray and guarded, locked gateways into a place bursting with the amazing and the unexpected.

Nate's foster father, Desmond Williams, owned half the city in which they lived. His foster mother, Emma, was a very talented actress and his younger sister, Sofia, had inherited her mother's angelic beauty and ability to charm.

Desmond had stumbled upon Nate's unconscious body when he and his young daughter had been hiking above the city. Desmond, being of the belief that his daughter should see the city that she was to inherit every year until it was hers, had chosen one formidable autumn day to take her to his favorite viewpoint. Nate had been only six, and Desmond and Emma had immediately adopted the young boy. Very few people knew of it, and those who did didn't talk about it much. Desmond was the most powerful man in the city, and therefore, no one objected.

Nate's recollection of that fated night was as shrouded as the dark woods where he had wandered and ultimately collapsed. The cold and loneliness of that night were preserved in his memory, but to this day Nate kept secret how he had come to be all alone in the forest. He had a nagging feeling that he was forgetting some crucial aspect. This mental omission had driven him crazy. That changed one day when he sat down at the piano at the age of twelve and found that he could play through his stress and express himself through the music. Ever since that day, Nate had played religiously and daily.

Emma was arranging her things by the doorway. She never rushed; she always had everything done before it needed to be. Even if she was late, she would always take her time and make sure she had everything that she needed. Nate admired that skill, for it was one he would never have, and he knew it. He was often late and even more often, disorganized and forgetful. Emma went upstairs to say goodbye to Sofia and returned a minute later with her purse in hand. She grabbed her short white coat and then kissed Nate goodbye.

"Dad left you the Rover. I didn't get a chance to say goodbye to Sofia. She was in the shower. I swear she spends more time in the shower than the rest of us put together. Tell her goodbye for me, will you?"

"Sure, Mom," Nate said, then struck by a sudden thought he ran to the door and shouted, "Where's Gatsby?"

"Check underneath the piano," called Emma from the driveway.

Nate smiled. He should have known. His dog, Gatsby, had a favorite spot to rest and relax—right underneath the Steinway in the formal living room. Nate entered the room and sure enough found his dog lying under the piano looking questioningly up at him, almost as if asking, *Aren't you going to play?* Nate smiled, knelt, and pet his Bernese Mountain dog. Gatsby had been a gift for his sixteenth birthday, and he loved him. Gatsby had huge paws that were more white than normal for his breed. He was generally fun-loving, if not occasionally lazy, but he was always a great companion.

Nate returned to the kitchen, got the pancake mix from the fridge, and began making breakfast. While he was warming up the pan he turned on the TV, which rose out of the counter. He flipped through the channels until he settled upon SportsCenter, then listened to the debate about a young football player retiring while still in his prime.

When Sofia entered the room, the table was set with two piles of buttermilk pancakes on white plates, each with two small pitchers of steaming maple syrup and a plate of butter. Nate was proud of the whole setup. No matter how much he cooked, he could never seem to get it right. Thankfully, the only thing he had to do was flip a pancake. If he'd had to make the batter, he would've almost certainly forgotten some crucial ingredient. It had happened before. He grimaced as he remembered pancakes without milk.

"Where are Mom and Dad?" was the first thing Sofia said when she entered the room.

"Good morning to you too. Dad left early for L.A., and Mom just left to meet with her manager. She went up to say goodbye, but you were still in the shower."

"Oh. Did you make breakfast?" She looked slightly impressed at the table laid out before her. Sofia's hair had not yet dried and hung down around her face, but she looked beautiful.

"Yup."

"I'm impressed. It looks ... normal."

"You should be. Mom did the batter."

Sofia grinned. "I should've known."

They sat down and for several minutes, all that could be

heard was the clink of silverware on plates and the sound of chewing. Nate looked over at his younger sister. She was just as beautiful as her mother and very similar looking. Lighthearted and carefree, she studied hard and smiled often. Locks of brown hair cascaded down her shoulders like so many waterfalls, and her eyes were light blue and kind, like her mother's. She never said more words than were necessary; rather she conveyed emotion through facial expressions and the tone of her voice. She knew she was very pretty and took care to make sure she remained that way, but she was not arrogant.

"Did you know I was dating Xander West?"

Nate dropped his fork and spluttered for a full minute before finding his voice. "You're dating him?" he exclaimed, half as a question and half as a blatant display of disgust.

"Was ... for several weeks. I could have sworn I told you."

Nate shook his head, still looking shell-shocked, and clasped his hands tightly in front of his plate to silence the urge to flip the table over.

"Well, we split up yesterday," she said with a nonchalant shrug.

"Why?" His tone sounded pleased yet reserved, as though he suspected the very worst of Xander West.

"He was cheating on me the entire time, with some senior slut."

Nate swore so loudly that Sofia jumped. He took several long deep breaths and then spoke. "Did you honestly like him?" Nate was trying to say this in the kindest possible way, but he was having considerable trouble managing it.

She laughed, and it was this laugh that made Nate breathe steadily again. "Not exactly. However, I am not at all happy that he would cheat on me."

"Nor am I." He kept the details of his plans for Xander West to himself. He knew when it was time to drop something, and even though Sofia had just laughed, he felt they had reached some unknown line that, if crossed, would mean a silent car ride to school. When they had both finished, Nate took their plates to the dishwasher and cleaned the pan.

The car ride to school turned out to be silent anyway, but that didn't bother Nate. He could tell the difference between a fuming silence and a pleasant one.

When they arrived at school, the parking lot was full of cars but almost completely devoid of students. On rainy days like today, no one wanted to risk getting dirty or wet. Watson Academy was an exclusive and expensive college prep school, the kind of place where just about every one of its four hundred and fifty students was a stickler for how they looked. This might be considered slightly conceited at most schools, but Watson students took it in stride. Nate wasn't among this group. He cared how he looked when it was important, but when he was wearing jeans and a T-shirt, he couldn't care less about the state of his clothes.

Once inside, Sofia melted away into the crowd to find her friends. Nate admired how she could do it; he knew that skill was something he would never be able to even attempt, let alone master. Nate looked around and saw Baako Clark sitting in an armchair to the side of the circular hallway.

"Baako!" shouted Nate just loud enough for him to hear.

Baako looked in his direction and smiled, his perfectly white teeth cutting a stark contrast with his dark skin. He was the star of the football team, tall and muscular. He usually wore jeans and a button-down shirt. Baako was an intimidating figure to strangers, but those who knew him well found him to be kind and considerate.

In the last couple of years, he had shattered all league and state records for wide receiver. His father was a renowned banker who jumped back and forth from his true home in Desmond's city to New York. Desmond and he were almost as close as their sons and frequently ended up working together.

Nate took a chair next to Baako and brought out his flashcards for today's third-period math test. He had made the flashcards the previous night, and it would only take one look to memorize most of them. He was almost as good as his friends in academics, but tended not to study much. To him, there were always more important things to do.

"What do you want to bet John spent two hours studying?" Baako looked up from his notes, grinning.

Nate was looking at a beautiful girl several feet away and answered distractedly, "A lot."

John caught up with them five minutes later with his messenger bag slung over his shoulder. He looked disdainfully at the two of them studying their cards. "I have no idea how you remember things that you don't even pay attention to."

John Reynolds was a better student than Baako and Nate, mostly because he worked harder. His wavy blond hair, bright-blue eyes—a scar from a biking accident was stamped above the right one—and mischievous smile put him almost on par with Nate Williams. The difference between them was that Nate didn't follow the rules as strictly as John, and most students admired him for it.

"Oh, John." Baako had very recently taken to sighing when speaking to John on this very subject. "It's a skill you have yet to develop. One day, maybe you will have the wonderful ability, as Nate and I do."

Nate laughed and looked up from his cards. "We can teach you and make that day come a little sooner, if you want."

"I do fine on my own, thanks." John scowled.

They packed up and joined the crowd moving up the circular hallway to the next floor. Nate had turned a deaf ear to his friends, for they had left the topic of grades and had moved on to listing off the people who wished to be Nate Williams.

The three of them set off down the curving hallway lined with floor-to-ceiling windows and on to Mrs. Jones's history class. She was a very pretty, young teacher, and many of the boys paid more attention in her class than any other. Baako and Nate stared blankly at the Smart Board while John drank in every single word, as he did religiously. He had always been fascinated by history and paid close attention as the lecture turned from the Church's persecution of scientists to the wider persecution of believed werewolves.

Nate, on the other hand, gazed at the long brown hair cascading down a white-shirted back at the desk in front of him, lost in its beauty. It reminded him of Sofia's hair. He also thought about the soccer game that was coming up in a week against their rival, Bell Academy, the best team in the league. Nate and his teammates were aching to beat them. He was jolted out of this revelry by Professor Jones's words and turned his ear to hear her clearly.

"In the early fifteenth and sixteenth centuries, the Church was cracking down hard on anything that did not fit with their interpretation of God and the Bible. Believers in science were persecuted mercilessly. Accused witches, vampires, werewolves, and many others who had a different view or look were burned at the stake. They destroyed things they didn't fully understand.

"Bloodless bodies were found with teeth marks on their necks, and accounts of men turning into wolves during the full moon were widespread across early Europe. There were stories that once boys turned a specific age, they would die and come back to life. Upon seeing moonlight, they would become wolves and would remain as such until they saw the sunlight once again."

At this, there was some scattered muttering among the class. Nate looked at Baako and rolled his eyes. He nodded toward John, whose face was upturned attentively.

"There have been stories of other were-animals, but for some reason, wolves have been the most popular, and the legend has lived on throughout many church burnings and biblical denouncements."

Mrs. Jones spoke about how legends have carried on throughout the centuries, like the oldest of Greek mythology. Legends were often concocted to explain the mysterious. Tales of fierce dragons guarding gateways to other countries would repel foreign invaders. Stories of monsters lurking in the forest would keep strangers from snooping around. "Some still believe in the existence of creatures like werewolves and vampires, and they have dedicated their lives to researching and finding them."

The bell rang just as Mrs. Jones finished her lecture, and the entire class breathed a barely audible sigh of relief. They packed their bags, and John caught up with Baako and Nate as they left the classroom. He always sat apart from his friends because he knew they distracted him from his studies.

"You know, it would do you good to listen to a bit of what she says." John's irritable tone coincided with Baako's sighing whenever they spoke.

"You listen?"

"Of course I listen."

"Oh." Baako's face fell comically. "I was always under the impression you were just entranced by her beauty."

"Shut up, Baako."

Nate punched him playfully. "Come on, John, lighten up. I actually did listen near the end. I always wondered about the werewolf thing."

Baako and John looked at Nate, surprised. Baako spoke: "Really?"

"Yeah. Anyway we have more important things to think about today."

"Like what?" asked Baako.

"I don't know. I'm hungry."

"It's second period, Nate," John pointed out.

"I know. Isn't that odd?" Without further explanation, Nate strode off toward the dining hall. John and Baako stared after him for a minute then ran to catch up.

"Nate, French starts in two minutes." John gestured to the large clock on the wall.

"Yeah, but I need something to eat. French can wait a couple of minutes. There are more important things in life."

"Like unnecessary eating?" asked John.

"Pretty much." Nate entered the cafeteria and poured himself a bowl of cereal. He walked over and grabbed a glass of juice then sat in the very middle of the deserted dining hall and ate leisurely without a care in the world. Baako looked at John incredulously. John's face mirrored Baako's, but they both shrugged and headed to get some cereal. If Nate wanted something, he got it immediately, and to hell with the consequences.

"Nate Williams, why are you late?" Mr. Acton asked some minutes later. He was not amused at Nate's tardiness.

"Sorry, Mr. Acton. My friends and I missed our breakfast and needed to grab a bite to eat. It won't happen again. I promise."

Nate's French was flawless. He boldly smiled and surprisingly, the teacher smiled back. He gestured for them to take their seats without another word. Baako and John exchanged disbelieving looks as they sat down. French passed a little faster than history, but only by a small margin. Baako and Nate played several games of Hangman in the back of the classroom while John paid close attention at the front, as usual. Soon, they were flooding back out into the hallway for break.

"Nate, I will never understand how you get away with stuff like that. I would never dream of pulling that, let alone get away with it."

Nate smiled broadly at John. "Just charm."

"Whatever. I still say you were born with an extraordinary amount of whatever 'it' is," said Baako.

"I feel like a Gatorade," John said in a remarkably good imitation of Nate. He strutted off toward the vending machines.

Baako and Nate caught up with him just before he reached

the blue Gatorade machine, "John, it's break. You can get a Gatorade."

"Dammit. Ah, well. Wasn't too bad, was I?"

"I don't know. Nate wouldn't make that mistake." Baako laughed. "But I have to admit, the strut was pretty good."

"Oh, come on. Nate makes mistakes. He never thinks anything through. He's impulsive," said John defensively.

"Hey! Let's not go that far."

"I guess you're right." Baako grinned. They continued with their increasingly common and heavily annoying habit of talking about Nate as if he weren't there. At least this time, it was about one of Nate's impulsive flaws and not mocking his popularity.

Break and the next two classes passed quickly enough, and soon Nate and his friends were in the middle of the rapidly growing crowd pressing toward lunch. The math test had gone as well as Nate could've hoped, and he put it from his mind. He ate lunch with John and Baako on the far right table of the dining hall. They were an imposing and well-known group.

Xander and Harry West soon joined them. The West twins were thin and pale. Their smiles never quite reached their cold black eyes, and their hair was just as black and closely cropped. They often sat with Nate and his friends, but never spoke much.

"What's good, Twins?" asked Baako as they simultaneously set their plates of pasta on the table. Nate shivered—it always creeped him out how everything they did was in unison.

"Stuff's all right." Nate shivered again. The way they spoke at the same time was the worst. He had no idea how they always managed it. The table was relatively quiet until John turned to Nate.

"Hey, Nate."

"Yeah."

"Jenna White has been looking over here quite a lot since

we sat down."

"Really?" Nate tried to act uninterested. He was, however, unable to resist a quick glance over to the next table where a very pretty, brown-haired girl sat talking with her friends—the same brown-haired girl he had been admiring earlier. Nate was suddenly struck by a similarity between her and the twins. He shook his head and put the disturbing thought from his mind. She looked up and caught his eye for a second before they both turned their attention back to their plates and friends. Sofia sat among Jenna's friends, chatting animatedly. Jenna glanced at Nate again and smiled. Nate returned the smile and caught his sister's eye briefly.

Everyone else at the table exchanged smirks.

"Isn't she with Rob Anderson?" Baako had caught the not-so discreet look at Jenna. Everyone else had noticed too, but Baako was the only one who had the nerve to say anything. Nate had a tendency to be very touchy when it came to girls.

"She was," said Nate slowly. "They got in some fight— something to do with him being overprotective."

"Mmm, the usual." John grinned at Baako.

"You seem to know a lot about it." Xander's cold coal-like eyes shifted to Nate.

"I might." Nate glanced up from his food and glared at Xander.

Xander lowered his gaze, but Nate knew he wasn't smart enough to stop talking. Every time he spoke, Nate wanted to bash his head into the table.

"You do? Prince gonna hook up with the whore? She isn't the only whore in that group."

Sofia was sitting right next to Jenna. They all knew what Xander was implying.

"Easy, Xander." Baako's eyes flashed a warning. "He likes her. And that's Nate's sister who sits next to Jenna every day."

"Yeah. Your sister fits in so well, doesn't she?"

"Shut up, Xander!" Nate's face had become a white sheet of rage.

"Take the advice." Baako had been friends with Nate for years, and Sofia was practically his little sister. Nate could also pack a powerful punch when he wanted to.

"Cool it, both of you." Xander remained cool. "I'm just saying she doesn't exactly wear the clothes that say 'no'."

Nate's plate went flying as he dove across the table. He hit Xander, and the two hit the floor with a crash. Nate's fist slammed into Xander's face. He managed to land several punches before John and Baako pulled him off. Xander was cowering on the floor, his face covered in blood and his nose clearly broken. Nate shook his aching fists to get the blood off them and relieve the tension.

"Easy, Nate. Not that I don't approve, but this isn't the place." Baako glanced around the dining hall, which was full of silent, awed faces.

"I'm sick of the twins. Why do we sit with them?" Nate's fists were still tightly clenched.

"Don't know." John's constant smile was etched on his face, but his eyes were not looking all too kindly at the twins.

"Did a teacher see that?" Nate's eyes held curiosity rather than fear. His question was answered before John or Baako could open their mouths.

Mr. Pike strode toward the boys. His face looked much like Nate's had only a minute ago. The whole dining hall had gotten up from their tables and were now crowded around the broken-up fight. Mr. Pike had trouble getting through all the students. No one really liked the twins and most people were attempting to hide smiles at the sight of one of them whimpering on the floor. Mr. Pike stomped past them.

Nate was well-liked by most of the students. He was an idol, but he wasn't arrogant about it. They also liked nothing better than seeing the twins get what had been coming to them for a long time.

"Nate! Follow me. Harry, take your brother to the infirmary."

"He was provoked, Mr. Pike." Baako tried to be a voice of reason.

"He deserved it." John's comment prompted laughs from the bravest among the onlooking crowd. One person cheered.

"I don't care."

"But—"

Mr. Pike cut John off before he could utter another word. "Enough! Nate, come with me. Now!"

Nate rolled his eyes to the ceiling then left his friends and followed the teacher.

Mr. Pike led Nate through the dining hall and down the crowded hallway. Nate smiled and greeted students as he passed them. He treated it like a casual walk to get a drink. Luckily, Mr. Pike did not look back or else he would've been a good deal angrier. The two finally reached a small, cramped office, and Mr. Pike held open the door and gestured Nate inside.

"Mr. Williams, what was that?" Mr. Pike sat behind a desk that seemed to push him right up against the wall. There was barely enough room for his chest to move as he breathed.

"Sorry, sir. He was insulting my sister."

"Nevertheless—"

"Do you have a sister?"

"I do."

"If someone was insulting her in front of you, would you just try to resolve it with words?"

Mr. Pike sat there for a second, staring at Nate. Nate held his gaze. He seemed to be considering what Nate had said. He tried to speak several times, but the words didn't come.

Finally, Nate asked, "Can I go, sir?"

Mr. Pike seemed caught off-guard. "Yes, make sure it doesn't happen again."

"Of course." Nate smiled politely and left the office. He

walked nonchalantly back to the dining hall and sat down to finish his bowl of cereal. Half the school stared on.

"How the hell did you get out of that one?" Baako was as startled as everyone else to see Nate back so soon, looking completely unabashed. He and John were used to Nate getting away with careless acts, but those were along the lines of skipping class and being late. Fighting often ended with suspension.

"Just got lucky. Twins gone?"

"Yeah. Harry took Xander to the infirmary. Don't expect to see them for a while," said John.

"Xander's just jealous and can't hide it as well as everyone else. He can't fathom how you get away with everything. It eventually went to his head, and I imagine he was happy to see you so worked up. That was until his nose was broken."

"Are you defending him? The son of a bitch deserved it!"

"Calm down, Nate." Baako laid a hand on his arm.

Sofia stopped by their table. "You all right?"

"Yeah, fine."

She looked at Nate, her eyes boring into his, then simply said, "Thanks." She hugged him quickly and went back to her table.

After several minutes, John glanced around at the other two. "Time to clear?"

"Yeah, let's go." Nate nodded and they all stood and carried their plates over to the quickly growing line by the dishwashers. People moved aside, casting Nate admiring looks as he passed. He treated the whole thing casually enough, and they dropped their plates off then headed out onto the fields.

The Sun had finally won its battle with the clouds and now shone brightly over the fields, still glistening with miniscule specks of water. The warmth and light had only recently managed to reach the ground.

"I think I'll talk to Jenna later." Nate looked for the third time in five minutes to where she was sitting on the grass with her friends.

John punched him playfully on the arm. "About damn time too. I was starting to think you'd never get up the nerve."

"Ha, right. That'll be the day," said Baako.

"Who is the Saturday game against, Baako?" Nate tried vainly to change the subject.

"Eastern. Can't stand them. But anyway, Nate, has there ever been a time you didn't have the nerve to ask out a girl?" Baako looked toward the pristinely groomed football fields.

Nate raised his eyes to the heavens. It was worth a try. "Yeah, first grade. Sarah Presley."

"It wasn't like you had a choice." John laughed. "She got the chicken pox late. Right, Nate? Nate?"

John looked around. Nate was nowhere to be seen. "Baako, where's Nate?" John's voice trailed off.

Baako turned slowly in a half-circle before answering, "There!"

"Nate!"

Nate was lying on the field behind them. His face was buried in the grass, and he wasn't moving. Baako and John ran back to his side.

"Nate?"

Baako shook his friend violently. "Nate!"

Nate didn't stir. His heart was barely beating, and they could see no other signs of life.

John looked unfocused. "I didn't even know he wasn't with us." His voice was riddled with shock.

Baako looked up. People on the field were now staring in his direction. Screams rent the air as several girls nearby, including Jenna and Sofia, noticed Nate's still form in the grass. More students came running over and encircled him. Sobs could be heard, and a teacher plowed her way through the mass of students.

"Baako, what happened?" Ms. Auburn's voice was laced with

fear.

"He just ... fell. While we were walking."

Ms. Auburn called frantically to the two other teachers who were outside. They both shot over in a matter of seconds. The football coach and a young math teacher lifted Nate and carried him back to the school.

John and Baako stood, watching as their friend was hurried through the doors. A second later, Baako felt a force hit his chest and looked down to see a mass of wavy brown hair covering a face buried in his shirt. Sofia was crying uncontrollably. Baako held her and guided her back inside. At the entrance to the infirmary, however, the football coach stopped them.

"Sorry. No one in to see him until Mr. Williams arrives."

"But—"

"Sorry. The headmaster is with him now. Return to your classes. You may see him when classes have ended. Sofia," his voice softened, "come with me. I'll get you something to drink."

Baako and John sat through the rest of their classes in a daze. They didn't quite follow Ms. Auburn's explanation of the periodic table and both failed their English quiz. When classes ended, they rushed back to the infirmary, only to find a grim Mr. White exiting. The headmaster looked deathly pale.

"Mr. White, can we go in?"

His unfocused eyes shifted to the two boys, his gaze almost going right through them. "I'm sorry. Nate was moved to the hospital over an hour ago. It seems he had a heart attack and has slipped into a coma. The doctors are at a loss. He was a healthy boy. I just don't understand it. A perfectly healthy boy. I'm so sorry."

Mr. White strode off. Baako and John stood, shocked, outside the infirmary for several minutes. Sofia ran up to them as Mr. White was leaving, but Baako just shook his head. She hugged him and for a long time, none of them spoke until, quite suddenly, they realized there was no reason to be there, and turned and walked silently out to their cars.

Chapter 2
The Dangling IV

AFTER ATTEMPTING SCHOOL the next day, Sofia didn't return. She sat beside her brother throughout the day and night, refusing meals and waiting patiently. Desmond and Emma sat with her, looking for any sign that Nate might awake. Emma had delayed the shooting of her movie for a month, and Desmond had left control of his business to his deputy for the time being.

Floods of doctors and nurses came and went. Mornings brought the unbearable horror of a clearly confused doctor who would come in, shake his head for the fiftieth time, and sigh upon learning that Nate's condition had not changed. The afternoons were filled with silent friends leaving gifts, flowers, and words of consolation. Nate's family barely noticed the latter. The vital monitor that was still dubiously pinging a faint heartbeat entranced them. Not much else mattered.

Every day after school, John and Baako rushed from the locker rooms—Baako not even bothering to change from his dirty football pads—to check on Nate. They both sat on Nate's bed and told him the goings-on at school, however inconsequential they might be. Talking gave them something to do when they were with him, and it seemed to help the two. When a nurse kindly told them that Nate couldn't hear anything they were saying, Baako gave her a murderous look that made her leave in a hurry.

On the Saturday after the attack, late in the afternoon, Nate's eyes sprang open. He sat up, looking around at the sea of flowers and gifts that overflowed onto the floor. Sofia was dozing beside his bed, tear tracks framing her nose. In the corner, his parents were also asleep. A glass door slid open, and Nate turned his head slightly to see a young doctor enter the room.

He glanced up from a clipboard as he neared the bed. Locks of curly brown hair framed his thin face, and he had to push it out of his eyes every couple of seconds, but he had kind eyes and an intellectual air about him. He was wearing a lab coat, which immediately made Nate feel better. If there was one thing that he couldn't stand, it was doctors in scrubs.

"Ah, you're awake. About time too. We were beginning to worry." His face reflected more relief than his words and after a couple of seconds had passed, he added, "Sorry. I'm Dr. James Harper, and I've been looking after you for the past few days."

"Days?" Nate's gaze shifted from the doctor to staring in wonder at the gifts that lay like mountains against the wall.

"Five days to be specific. We were beginning to think you might never wake up. But here you are." He smiled.

"Five days? What happened?"

The doctor began to speak then paused for a minute, as if wondering whether to tell him the truth. Nate was only seventeen, and it was usually the parents' job to tell the patient, but he seemed to settle upon breaking the rules. "Heart attack. The youngest age I've ever seen with such severe symptoms." He shook his head. "I'll wake your parents." He walked over to Desmond and shook him gently. Desmond's eyes shot open immediately, and he sat up, blinking. His gaze fell instantly upon Nate. His face lit up, and he jumped out of his chair.

"Nate!" He rushed over and embraced his son. Handsome and in his mid-forties, Desmond displayed an unbelievable resemblance to Nate. His eyes were brown and bright. His hair was short and close cut. His style could not be more different from that of his wife—he never wore a suit when he could avoid it. He was often found in jeans and a suede jacket. Desmond Williams was a cheery man, and it took a considerable downer to dampen his spirits.

At the sound of Desmond's voice, louder than the doctor's, Emma and Sofia began to stir. Sofia shifted in her chair for several seconds before opening her bleary eyes and looking around.

"What happened? Is Nate all right?" She stared at Nate sitting up in bed looking happy and healthy and shook her head several times to make sure she was really seeing him. "Nate! You're awake!"

She leapt up, bounded to his bed, and hugged him. Emma came last, walking in a kind of trance, kissed her son on the brow and then hugged him dazedly.

"I will let you be. Desmond, I'll be back shortly to discuss what's next." The doctor backed quickly out of the room, but the family barely noticed. They were deep in conversation around Nate's bed.

"I swear, every student from your school has been here this past week, Nate." Desmond smiled proudly.

"Yes," chimed in Sofia. "And that includes every single crying girl wanting to know how you were doing and refusing to leave the room. We had to get security for one of them. Pretty sure you know who *that* was."

Nate rolled his eyes and smiled, but Sofia nodded vigorously.

"No, it's true! It happened on several occasions, actually."

"Whatever you say." Nate turned to his mother. "Mom, if my math is correct, the movie should have already started."

"Oh, it can wait. You're more important, and I think I impressed that pretty well upon the studio."

Nate was about to ask whether or not they had begun filming at all when he happened to glance at the door and caught a glimpse of two boys headed toward his room. The tall, black one was drenched in water and mud and still in his football gear. The nurses looked on with displeasure as Baako tracked muddy footprints throughout the building. John walked beside Baako, looking just as wet, yet without the mud and football padding. They both looked tired, but their expression changed completely at the sight of Nate sitting up in bed, awake and grinning. They ran the rest of the way to the room. Baako almost slipped as he pulled open the door, grabbed Nate's hand and shook it.

"You're awake!"

John roughly pushed his hand aside and hugged his friend in the type of hug teenage guys do so well—quick and loose with an extra pat on the back.

"We won, Nate!" John was smiling from ear to ear.

"The team played for you, Nate. The school hasn't been the same this past week, and everyone felt it. Not a single point was scored against us. Thirty-five to zero."

None of them could stop grinning. "Looks like it did something then, didn't it?" John laughed. "We can't leave out the most important statistic: three touchdowns by this one here," he said, clapping his hand on Baako's shoulder. Baako smiled but shrugged off the praise.

"Nice, Baako. Eastern, that's awesome. So, how's everything else?"

"The twins have been shut up. They don't talk much, like they ever did, anyway. You're lucky they didn't have time to start a hate campaign, seeing as ..." Baako's voice trailed off. "Well, not lucky."

Nate smiled. "I know what you mean. When they did talk, though, who failed to shiver?"

"I'm shivering just thinking about them," Sofia said, joining in.

Nate, John, and Baako looked at each other quizzically, then they all smirked.

"Oh, shut up." Sofia smiled.

"So, what else is new?" Nate knew Sofia did not look back on her relationship with Xander fondly, and he did not want to help her dwell on it.

"Jenna is pregnant," John chimed in.

Nate's mouth fell open. John couldn't help it—his face split into a grin, and he rolled around laughing. When he and everyone else had laughed it off, Nate asked, "So she's not pregnant?"

"Course not," snorted John. "But your face was worth more than your dad's newest car." He erupted into a fit of laughter once more.

The conversation turned to classes, but soon the other three noticed that Nate's eyes were fluttering, even though he insisted he wasn't at all tired. They stopped talking, and Nate lay back and breathed deeply. His eyes closed, and he drifted off to sleep almost immediately. Sofia, Baako, and John eased themselves quietly off the bed and joined Nate's parents by the door to get dinner. Sofia turned one last time to check the now steady and strong beat of Nate's heart before Emma ushered her out of the room and down the hallway.

Nate awoke several hours later. His room was bathed in moonlight, but shadows creased the corners and the furniture. The hallway outside was deserted, and his room was empty. He stood and grabbed hold of his IV stand before walking to the window of the hospital room. The clouds obscured most of the stars but seemed to have created a hole for the Moon to shine through.

The hospital was set on the outskirts of the city, looking out over a hill toward a forest. The trees looked forbidding in the darkness. The moonlight bathed the land around the hospital, giving eerie depth to trees and hills and casting long shadows on lampposts and cars. It reminded Nate of the night in which he had lost everything.

A ray of moonlight hit his torso and slowly spread up to his face. Nate ignored it until it hit his eyes. Pain shot through his body—pain like he had never experienced before. He dropped to the floor, and the IV yanked free. Blood and IV fluid splattered everywhere. He lost feeling to parts of his body as the pain seared through him. He writhed on the floor, his eyes screwed up in pain. The first shockwaves receded, and Nate painstakingly raised his hand and fell backward from his knees onto his back, in shock.

No longer was it a hand. No longer did it look anything like a hand. It was a paw—a huge paw with fur running swiftly up his arm toward his shoulder as he watched. With the change came more waves of pain. Nate got up and staggered to a mirror. His hair was shrinking back into his head, and his eyes were growing and turning yellow.

Another shot of pain shrieked through his body, and he fell thrashing once more onto the floor. The pain was becoming unbearable. Nate struggled to stand. When he finally made it to his feet, he stood upon four legs. His arms and legs felt strong and laced with muscle. His paws powerfully gripped the floor. The pain had receded more quickly than it had come. He felt stronger than he ever had in his life. His eyes barely reached the mirror, and he stood up briefly on two paws to see his face. His face was no longer his—it was an animal's. It was a wolf's. He was a wolf. His eyes were large and on two paws, his head almost reached the ceiling. He was bigger than any wolf he'd ever heard of in his life. His body came well above the bed that he had been sleeping on only several minutes before.

Thoughts and questions spun around Nate's head, each one chasing the other away. How on earth had this happened? The carousel in his mind turned once more, and he thought back to the previous week. He remembered a class, lingering in his distant memory, in the slot for Tuesday. He tried to focus more on the class, but it was hard. He remembered Mrs. Jones talking about werewolves. *Am I imaging this?* he wondered, staring at his transformed hands.

Another piece of Mrs. Jones's lesson floated around on the carousel. She'd said that a werewolf became a wolf when the Moon set its light upon the werewolf's eyes and that he could not become a human again until sunlight hit his eyes. Nate shook his head. He had to think through this somehow.

Another thought came: How was he supposed to get through the night when doctors and nurses would probably pass his room every couple of minutes? One of them was bound to notice that his bed was empty, and when they came in, they would find a wolf sitting on the floor, looking up at them. He couldn't help but grin wolfishly at the thought, but then he crawled under the bed, hoping that the moonlight cast enough shadows underneath that he could not be seen. *What if the Sun doesn't even come out? How would that work?* Nate shook his head. *I can't think like that.* He poked his head out from underneath the bed and looked over at the clock on the wall. Four-thirty—not bad. The Sun would rise in two hours, and then he could become normal again ... at least he hoped.

Nate noticed another thing: His nightshirt was lying in tatters on the floor beneath the large window. Of course, his nightshirt wouldn't have turned with him. Figuring he must have pulled it off in the midst of pain and confusion, he crawled out from beneath the bed and grabbed it in his mouth. He then walked over to the chairs by the window and dropped in behind one of them. He used his paw to push it under the chair then turned to his bed where his sheets were a tangled mess. That couldn't be helped, so he returned to the underside of the bed to think. As he crawled under it again, he realized his fur brushed the underside of the bed, even though his belly touched the floor. Confusing thoughts ran around his head as the carousel started up again, much faster this time, until he could not think straight anymore. He drifted off into a deep, but baffling, sleep.

His large eyes opened an hour and a half later. The first rays of sunlight were thankfully shining through his window. He felt strong; no pain. He crawled over to the window and stood up on his four paws. He felt a sunray on his face, his nose, and then his eyes. The pain returned, but it wasn't quite as bad as it had been when he had changed into a wolf. His fur shrank back into his skin, leaving it feeling considerably smoother, despite being covered with dark hairs. His fingers grew longer, and the claws became nails. Finally, he was standing in the window—naked. Still unable to believe what had happened, he ran over to the chair and pulled on his nightshirt. It was ripped at the back, but he couldn't do anything about that. He clambered into bed just as a nurse passed. His eyes fell onto his IV drip.

Liquid covered the floor to the left of his bed, and the catheter was hanging by the stand, which held the bags. Nothing he could do about it now. He'd just have to tell them it must have come out while he had slept. He knew it was a lame story, but nothing more brilliant came to mind.

Nate knew that it would be impossible to feign sleep so he sat wide-eyed, running things over in his head. *They would die and rise from the dead again with the ability to change into a wolf. Of course, back in the Stone Ages, a heart attack would have seemed like death, and a coma reduced the pulse to close to nothing so people would have no reason to think the person was alive. Many of these werewolves must have been buried alive. That definitely explained the scratches in coffins.* Nate shuddered at the thought and was quite glad he lived in the age of modern technology.

He came out of his revelry just in time to hear the young doctor enter the room. He stared at a clipboard as he spoke. "You're up early. Okay, your vitals look good. No reason to keep you here past ..."

His eyes darted up from the chart and spotted the dangling needle. "Nate, what happened to your IV?"

"No idea. Must have pulled out during the night. I only just noticed it myself." He tried to put on a convincing expression.

The doctor looked suspicious. "That is very rare. Well, I will call a nurse to give you the IV again. As I was saying, I see no reason to keep you here past tomorrow. I'll see if I can get you discharged tomorrow afternoon."

"Thank you." Nate tried to keep the innocent expression etched perfectly on his face.

The doctor smiled and left the room, still looking slightly suspicious, but obviously not enough to push the subject any further. Nate turned on the TV and began watching ESPN. When the SportsCenter jingle was starting for the third time, and Nate was getting rather sick of the same news, Desmond entered with Emma and Sofia. Nate turned off the TV and turned his attention to his family, but he didn't mention what had befallen him the previous night. He didn't know how it had happened or why, and no sane person talked about becoming a werewolf, especially after waking up from a coma. Nate didn't want to be committed anywhere and have doctors wondering if he was crazy. After careful consideration and examination, Nate locked the incident away in the far recesses of his mind to a place where it would still be available, but not as compulsively.

Chapter 3
The Match

NATE COULD ALMOST hear the silent expectation emanating from the crowd. He ran forward and kicked, feeling his foot connect perfectly with the soccer ball. It arched gracefully, and Charles Owens was ready. He chested the ball down to his feet and dribbled it straight through the line of defense. Everything seemed to slow as each person turned and watched the ball fly forward. It sailed just above the diving goalie's outstretched arms and hit the back of the net. The cheers that followed were some of the loudest yet. Nate ran up to Owens with the rest of the team, who engulfed him in a jumping team hug. The Watson Academy players, bolstered by the goal, now turned into an unbeatable force. Their passing was flawless, and they barely lost possession. By the end of the first half, Watson had a 3-0 lead. Nate had scored one of the three goals, and the entire team was in high spirits.

"Hey! I know we're doing well, and I give you full credit for that," Watson's Coach Ford said. "But there is still another half to go. Let's not forget that Bell isn't the number one team in the league because they forfeit at the half. Bell never goes down without a fight and it will be difficult to keep them back. I have a couple changes that should help us counter them, but it will be no walk in the park. Nate, you're a little fast for forward center. Switch with Owens in left forward. I think your speed will work better for us on the outside."

The two of them nodded.

The green mass that was Watson ran out onto the opposite side of the field. The red soon flowed through them with new looks of determination and focus on their faces. They were resolute not to lose this badly.

The game resumed and from the moment their feet touched the ball, it was clear that something had changed in the opposing team's play. They were now playing a flawless game, and it was Watson's defense that shattered against their oncoming attack. Bell didn't let anything get to them. It was impossible to tell whether their defense had improved because the forwards didn't give them a chance to throw that into question. It seemed they knew their weakness and had decided to avoid it rather than risk improving it. Watson was hard-pressed to keep them from the goal box, and soon Bell had scored.

"Come on! Don't let it unnerve you!" shouted Coach Ford.

It did unnerve them. Taken aback by the sudden comeback, Watson retreated, tripping over their own feet as they went. Their defense fell apart against the players in red. After that one goal, Bell was bolstered on to score two more. The tied game, however, seemed to jolt Watson back into the game, and they began beating back the oncoming team. The fight for the ball was becoming vicious, and foul after foul slowed the game. Nate got a free kick after being blatantly slide tackled just inside the eighteen, but he was so angry, he overshot. The score was tied at 3-3 and, there was a minute and a half left in the game.

Nate purged all other thoughts from his mind. He shook his

head violently for he knew what needed to be done, and all else was just unnecessary clutter in his mind. He nodded to Owens, who nodded back. Some unseen communication passed between them and Nate dashed off on the left, quickly passing Owens. He sprinted down the field, avoiding anyone who got in his way. He impeccably dodged his way to the eighteen and turned to look at the field.

Charles looked at him, passed, and Nate felt the ball hit his right foot. Time seemed to stop. Beads of sweat rolled down Nate's face as he turned toward the goal. Time slowed even more—the time it took him to turn and extend his foot back seemed like an eternity. Nate made sure that his foot was at the correct angle. He felt the ball make contact for a split second and then leave his foot on course to meet the back of the net. Nate had already turned triumphantly when he heard a moan from the crowd. His eyes searched for the ball in the back of the net when he noticed the rainbow shirt struggling to stand up. There was something black and white clutched tightly in his arms.

Nate thanked the limo driver and slid out of the seat after Sofia. He closed the door, and the limo eased down the driveway to the first gate. Sofia was already at the front door, but Nate stood in the middle of the driveway. It was the first time they'd lost a game in over a year. Nate had missed the goal, and Bell had come storming back to score. Nate was about to head for the house when he noticed a black Maserati parked in front of the nearest garage door. Desmond had a Maserati, but his was a four-door. This one had only two. It definitely wasn't their car, and it was rare for them to have visitors. Usually, when there was a party or get-together, Desmond rented a hotel or something of the sort.

Shrugging off the thought, Nate entered the house. He was not at all in a good mood and definitely not feeling up to entertaining visitors. Come to think of it, it was rather odd that Desmond had missed his soccer game—he never had before. Whoever owned the Maserati must have something to talk about that was more important than the game.

There was a man sitting at the dining room table with Desmond and Emma. Sofia was standing just inside the door, and Nate nearly walked into her. The man stood out like nothing else in the room. Nate dropped his bag as soon as he walked through the door and headed over to the table. He hugged his parents. The man was powerfully built and would have been intimidating if not for his broad smile. His hair was cut short, and every feature of his face was intense but at the same time oddly rounded at the edges. Nate cocked his head and squinted. The man reminded him of a bear, and there was something familiar about him.

"Nate, please take a seat." He gestured to a chair. "I am John Hurst."

Nate nodded in response.

When he didn't say anything, Hurst continued: "I run a little-known school in upstate New York. There are students at our school who may be considered a little unusual. I don't mean it as an insult; I simply mean that our students have qualities most would die for. We think that you, Nate, would be a perfect fit for our school."

"You're pretty sure of yourself," Nate said before he could stop himself. Despite the man's smile and air of kindness, Nate couldn't shake his angry mood. He had played the hardest in his life and scored one of their goals, and would have had the win if Bell's goalie hadn't been so damn good. Then he'd come home, and some man wanted him to change schools. Nate liked his school and his friends. Why change?

"I'm sorry, Nate. As far as first introductions go, I know that was a bit much, but please trust me. I know what you've been through, and I know what it is like."

"You know what I've been through?" Nate's voice rose. *This man has no idea what I've been through.* His parents had been murdered, and he'd barely escaped with his life at the age of six. To make matters worse, he'd had a heart attack and had slipped into a coma. And on top of all that, he'd changed into a wolf a week ago. Granted, this man might have been through a lot, but there was no way he could've turned into a wolf. He definitely didn't appear to have a constant dialogue of voices in his head telling him he was crazy.

At that moment, Gatsby walked in and nuzzled his head against Nate's leg. Nate pet his dog and immediately felt himself calm down.

"Nate, you have the qualities we look for. You're probably not aware of it, seeing as they only surfaced about a week ago." Hurst turned toward Emma and said, "I am sorry to sound as though I know more about your son than you do, but Nate will have to explain. Nate, you must know what I am talking about."

"A week ago," Emma said, her voice cool and measured, "Nate was in a coma."

"Certain things that can't easily be explained may occur while in a comatose state. The visual and physical body is unmoving and unchanging, but the mind can do extraordinary things, Emma. I'm sorry, but I believe Nate has an answer for you. If you would be so inclined, Nate?"

Nate stared at the man, wanting so badly to feel hatred toward him for professing to know about the inner workings of his life. He felt Hurst was the same as those kids in school who had looked at him and saw a popular, talented, and wealthy boy, and figured his life had been picture perfect. They just didn't understand. But as he looked at Hurst, his anger drained away. He felt calmer and soon, he began to speak, slowly at first, but then he gained speed as he got more excited and confident about what he was saying:

"Something has changed. It isn't the kind of thing you would likely tell anyone. It isn't exactly something that anyone would believe." Nate was quiet. He looked out the window. Finally he pressed on. "I felt different the night after I woke up. The hospital was quiet, and the place around me seemed empty. I got up and went to the window, and the tiniest sliver of moonlight fell upon my face and chest. Then, something unbelievable happened: I changed. I would never have believed it without seeing it in the mirror, let alone feeling it."

Hurst kept his gaze fixed on Nate.

"It's difficult to explain. My hands ... they weren't mine anymore. They weren't normal either. They became wolf's paws before my own eyes. The pain was unbearable, and I writhed upon the floor." He grimaced. "Suddenly, it was over and I stood. But the thing is, I did not rise upon two feet. I stood on four. I felt fur on my paws, and my vision had changed drastically. I stood up on my two legs and saw a wolf in the mirror, staring back at me. In the moonlight, I had become a wolf. Something must have happened to me during the coma, but I just don't understand it at all."

Nate stopped. His narrative had left him gasping, and he took several deep, calming breaths while he looked at his family. He suddenly realized he was standing by the window. He had a habit of pacing when he talked for long periods of time, but he didn't even remember getting up from the chair. Desmond's face was masked with disbelief. Emma looked shocked and Sofia downright terrified. Desmond leaned forward and looked at Hurst. They all needed an explanation and Hurst obliged.

"When an elite group of children reach the age of seventeen, something changes. It doesn't happen right away, but it usually does by their seventeenth birthday. These children have heart attacks. At least that is usually how it begins. Back in medieval times, the induced coma following the heart attack slowed down the pulse to a point where they were presumed dead and therefore, were buried alive. Some might have been actually dead, for the unlocking of the mind is a dangerous and precise procedure, and not all people are prepared for it. We know that for some inexplicable genetic reason, something changes in their brain chemistry during the coma. Have you ever heard of the scientific theory that claims we only use ten percent of our brains?"

Desmond and Emma nodded in unison, but they didn't interrupt. Nate took his seat and began petting Gatsby once more.

"Well, during this so-called transformation, more of the brain is unlocked. We still don't know exactly how it happens, but when it does, an uncontrollable and permanent change sets in. These young adults can, over time, consciously induce this transformation. When it happens this way, they use some of the unlocked ninety percent of their powers to subconsciously change—"

"Are you saying this is happening to Nate?"

"That is exactly what I am saying. Noble College monitors the news for these occurrences and focuses specifically on unusual cases. When I read that Nate had had a heart attack at the age of seventeen and slipped into a coma, I knew he would transform when he woke."

Emma opened her mouth once more, but Desmond laid a hand on her arm. "Continue, Hurst."

Hurst inclined his head.

"Everything about their human genetic makeup changes, becoming an entirely different life form, a hybrid of some kind, if you will. Every young adult this happens to is unique in his or her own way and therefore changes into something different with various triggers. The Moon has always had a powerful effect on wolves. Hence, when moonlight touches the eyes of a wolf-child, for lack of a better word, they become the wolf. There are other similarities. Those who have the gift may change into any life form that walks on land or flies above it. There have been documented accounts of changes into marine life, but these are extremely rare for reasons no more specific than the fact that most marine life cannot survive out of water and vice versa. If a child were to change into a shark on dry land or shape shift into a child in the water, either way he would surely die."

"How is this relevant?" Emma was impatient.

"It isn't really. I'm sorry. The subconscious part of the human mind somehow knows this and usually prepares for it. It always seems to have a plan, whether the rest of our body knows it or not."

John Hurst's words were intriguing. Nate had leaned forward on his chair, listening attentively, drawn to everything that Hurst was saying. It all made perfect sense to him. He wasn't crazy or confused. He was just different.

"I assume you are one of these, um … were-creatures, Hurst?" asked Emma, choking over her words.

"I'm a bear. Smelling smoke is what sets me off. It's a defense mechanism that kicks in when there is danger. However, water is not the only thing that can turn me back into human form. At Noble, we teach you how to correctly use parts of your brain you've never used before and to control these triggers when you turn. We can also artificially unlock the brain's hidden potential to expedite and manage the transformation. All of this happens in a controlled and secure environment, making it safer for the student. So, what do you think, Nate?"

"I'm not interested," said Nate tensely.

His family looked at him in disbelief.

"You're saying no? Just like that? But why?" Hurst was clearly perplexed.

"No matter how amazing an opportunity it might be, I have great friends here and my family, of course. I like what my life has become, and I'm not up for a radical change or completely having to reinvent myself. I'm not interested in meeting new people, no matter how extraordinary this school may be."

Hurst smiled broadly. Everyone stared at him. It was obvious that was the last thing they expected from him after what Nate had said.

"Nate, at Noble we offer students the option of bringing two friends along as companions. We believe it makes transitioning into the school much easier. These students will be taught our ways, and they will have the unused portions of their brains artificially unlocked so they too can experience transformation."

Nate perked up at that. He began listening more closely.

"Noble College is an unknown yet elite educational institution. You will earn a diploma, which will give you the ability to do whatever you desire in life. Noble is not known by many, but those who do know of it firsthand have the power and enough knowledge to ensure that a student will get any job he desires upon graduation, so long as the student is properly qualified."

Hurst stopped and took a much-needed breath then looked over at Nate to see if he was persuaded.

Nate said nothing. Everything Hurst had explained kept running through his mind so fast, he felt as though he was riding on a carousel at top speed.

"Nate?" Desmond asked.

"I guess this isn't the kind of opportunity you pass up. But why is it that no one knows about us, people like me?"

Hurst calmly explained. "We integrate our students into every part of normal life. In a way we are our own unknown race. We are not segregated or mistreated because we exist under the radar, and it's best to keep it that way."

"But why? Why not tell people about Nate and others like him?" Sofia interjected.

"How do you think the world would react if we revealed that some of the most prominent figures in history or present-day individuals that we rely on heavily to create and enact laws, or who manage our money, turn into savage beasts every now and then?" Hurst smiled. "Exactly. It would be a tough pill to swallow, that's for sure. There is only one school like ours in the country. There are other schools located in the most heavily populated and progressive countries."

"There can't be too many of you then." Desmond looked up at Hurst.

"No. According to the latest figures, there are approximately forty-five thousand people, out of seven billion, genetically predisposed to transformation or taught how to do so. That is less than a hundred thousandth of one percent of the world's population. As I mentioned before, we allow each and every potential student to choose two friends to accompany them to Noble, and this has been factored into the figures I just gave you."

"Were my parents like me?"

"Oh, yes. They were both like us. I had the privilege of knowing them very well," said Hurst kindly. "They were outstanding people, both in our community and the greater realm."

"So you knew them? They were murdered eleven years ago. Do you know who did it?"

"The murderer was one of us. Your parents spent years tracking him down. This man believed he was safeguarding the order and secrecy of our world with his actions. The way he chose to go about it was by killing one of us every now and then. These murders may seem random to us, but the murderer believed each murdered member of our world would have exposed us to the wider world and thus wreaked havoc on everything we know. The murderer's father before him was one of the greatest mass murderers of our people. Both wish to reach the same goal, but have very different means. His father has not been heard from in decades, however. His son, the man who murdered your parents was far more active in the years leading up to their death.

"Your parents caught him, and he was sentenced to life in prison. That same night, he escaped and the first people he sought were your parents. No one really knows why he decided to spare your life. I am so sorry, Nate."

"What was his name?" Nate demanded.

"Gray."

Nate finally brought an end to an uncomfortable silence by asking the one question that kept hammering in his head. "Where is Gray now?"

"I've heard he's in prison."

Nate smiled satisfactorily, then frowned. *If the man has broken out before, who's to say he wouldn't do it again?*

Desmond turned and looked at Hurst. A question formed on Desmond's lips: "May I see this?"

"Do you have a match?" Hurst asked nonchalantly.

Emma looked completely perplexed. A simple glance from Desmond was all it took for her to get up and fetch a box of matches from a kitchen drawer. With it in hand, she returned to the table. She pulled out a single match and lit it in one fluid move. Everyone watched in awe as the tiny flame burst into life and grew with intensity. In a matter of a few seconds, it ate away at the wood. Hurst stood up and gently plucked the match from Emma's outstretched hand. He watched the flame burn until half of the matchstick was black and charred, then he blew it out. A wisp of smoke rose up to his nostrils. As soon as he inhaled the smoke, the matchstick slipped to the floor.

Nate knew what it felt like. The memory of the pain he had experienced not long ago was still fresh in his mind, but nonetheless, it was amazing to watch Hurst transform from human form. He grew bigger and bigger by the second. His arms and legs became so large that his jacket and shirt ripped apart, as did his pants. He pounced onto the floor, supported by four gigantic paws. The human version of Hurst had morphed into a giant grizzly bear. The beast could almost look into his eyes, and Nate shivered when he imagined how large Hurst would be if he stood up on his two enormous hind legs.

Nate ran over to wrap a protective arm around his little

sister. Gatsby cowered and whimpered in the corner. Emma had practically fallen out of her chair, and Desmond was steadying her.

The bear pawed at its clothes. Desmond understood the animal's gesture at once and hurried up the stairs for pants and a shirt. While he was gone, the bear padded around the living room. Nate could hardly believe just how massive Hurst had become. He thought that the beast he had become in the hospital room was comparable in size to Hurst, but to see the out-of-body experience in living color was something entirely different. Desmond brought down his clothes and gave them to the bear. The bear grabbed them in its teeth and walked on all four paws into the living room and out of sight. Two minutes later, Hurst walked out, clothed in Desmond's shirt and pants. Hurst sat back down at the head of the table as if nothing had happened. The others stared in disbelief, saying nothing. The tall man with broad shoulders looked at Nate. "So, what do you think?"

Nate clenched his jaw for a minute to test his control. "I think it sounds great. What about my friends? Will you explain it to them just like you have to us?"

"Yes, or something of the sort. But you will have to come with me. What do you think of tomorrow?"

"Sounds great! But there is one small problem. Have you ever heard of Baako Clark?"

"In passing only."

"What about football?"

"He's going to have to let it go, at least while he is at Noble. We don't have a football program, and we can't support a student who leaves that often for athletics. We do offer a sport activity that may take his mind off football, if he's interested that is. I'm sure he'd be very good at it."

"Well, I hope it works." Nate wasn't at all convinced. He had known Baako for years now, and he knew perfectly well it would be highly uncharacteristic of his friend to pass up such an extraordinary opportunity. But football was Baako's life—it's what he lived and breathed for every day. "All right, then. Tomorrow we'll go talk to each of them separately?"

"Their parents will be given the same demonstration. If they refuse to allow either Baako or John to attend Noble College, I will very carefully enter their minds and erase the memory of our conversation."

"And you can assure us there will be no permanent damage from this?" asked Desmond.

Hurst nodded. "They'll be fine, but I'm sure it won't be necessary—it rarely is. It's September now. I'll be speaking to your headmaster, and everything should be taken care of within the week. As long as neither of you have any objections." Hurst looked at Desmond and Emma.

Emma seemed to have finally gained control of her senses and didn't make any objections. "Do you have a place to stay, Professor Hurst?"

"No. Actually, I was wondering ..." Hurst let the last word trail off into oblivion.

"Of course," said Emma, without the slightest hesitation. "We have a spacious apartment above the garage. Please take it for as long as you need."

"Thank you, Emma.

Desmond rose to his feet, and Hurst looked around at the family. He spotted Sofia and proffered his hand. "I am sorry. We were never really introduced."

Sofia still looked flabbergasted, but grasped Hurst's hand quickly.

"I'm Sofia," she said in a small voice.

"I'm very pleased to meet you. Nate, see you tomorrow. Emma, it was a pleasure meeting you as well."

"Thank you for everything," Nate said, hoping he had conveyed his heartfelt gratitude and apology for his earlier behavior.

"Of course," Hurst replied. Desmond escorted him out the door.

As they left, Nate could hear them talking amongst themselves in low voices. Curious as this was, Nate thought nothing of it and turned to his sister and mother. Emma stood and embraced her son for a very long time. When they finally broke apart, her face was streaked with tears.

"It must all be a dream—a crazy and confusing one. It might actually make a good movie." Nate could tell she was trying to poke fun at the serious situation at hand.

"It would make an excellent movie." He left his mother and walked over to the window where the moonlight spilled in. The pain began, and a satisfied grimace spread across his face as it intensified.

Chapter 4
Thumper

"LET ME GET something straight. This guy shows up at your house, tells you some crazy story for twenty minutes, changes into a bear, and that's it? You're sold?"

Nate laughed. "When you put it that way, it sounds foolish. But honestly, that's what happened. I don't know. There was something about him that inspired trust."

"Trust can be faked, you know." John looked at Nate critically.

"I don't think so. At least, not this kind of trust. I mean, honestly, you don't know what it's like to change into an animal and to see it happen to someone else. You automatically feel a special connection to that person. At least, that's what happened to me," said Nate, getting slightly defensive.

"So ... you're going?"

"Yeah, definitely. You in?"

"Are you kidding me? I would never ...," he said, pausing for a minute, then continued, "pass up something like that."

Nate cracked a wide smile. They were sitting in John's bedroom. He lived in a penthouse apartment in one of Desmond's buildings. The view actually looked out over Nate's house, slightly above them. They had chosen to go to John's house first for no reason in particular. Hurst was downstairs speaking with John's parents while the boys remained in John's bedroom.

"Did the Guard check him out?"

"As much as they could. I mean, his Social Security number, name, and address all check out, but how much can you really investigate someone like that? I mean, the other part of his story, the one that made sense to me, that's not something you can really ..." His voice trailed off as he completely lost his train of thought.

The Guard consisted of retired Navy Seals. They were scattered throughout the property. Three of them were always hovering over Desmond. Sometimes they were in the same car, while the others followed closely behind. They were experts at not being noticed and had gotten Desmond out of several sticky situations. The highly trained men were his very own secret service.

"Your father must trust this guy to let you go off to some strange school just like that too, though. I mean, he isn't the type to do something so drastic without completely trusting the guy."

"Yeah." Nate was barely paying attention. His mind had drifted off into a sea of fantasies about Noble. The possibilities were endless.

"Hey, Nate." John's voice was tentative.

"Yeah."

"You ever wonder about your biological parents?"

Nate could tell John had been working up the nerve to ask this. "They were like me. Other than that, I really don't know anything more."

"Do you remember them?"

"I do," said Nate slowly. "Sometimes I can almost picture their faces and distinguish their voices. I remember being with them, but for the life of me, I can't recall that night. I used to be able to. I used to know what happened. But now the memory seems to be gone forever."

"Do you miss them?"

"I don't remember them well enough to miss them. It's been so long. I mean, Desmond and Emma are better foster parents than I could have ever hoped for, and they helped me get over the loss of my parents. Of course, I still think about them, but Desmond and Emma are just as much as my parents."

John opened his mouth then closed it without saying a word. This was the most Nate had ever shared about his past. Normally, they just talked about everyday things that didn't matter much.

The week following the visits to the homes of John and Baako went by in a flash. Nate was even more zoned out than usual in his classes, but for once he had plenty of good reasons to be. Baako and John were also caught up in the moment. Even John wasn't paying much attention to the teachers. All their classes became one large haze, and they passed much more quickly than usual.

It had only taken Baako several hours to decide that he wanted to give up football. No matter how good he was, going to Noble was a once-in-a-lifetime opportunity that was sure to change his life, and he was not about to let it slip through his fingers.

Baako's parents took a lot more convincing, but agreed largely because they trusted Desmond. If he thought the school was good enough—and safe enough—for Nate, it must be good enough and safe enough for Baako too.

Nate had been surprised at how quickly Baako had made his decision, but he was glad he'd made the right choice. Without Baako, their group would feel incomplete. From this point on, they would be a trio that no one could break apart.

Nate, Baako, and John sat together at lunch every day, laughing and joking without a care in the world. They had never been more excited about anything, and the other students would surely understand if they knew where the most popular boys in school were heading. Granted, Watson Academy was a great place; but it just couldn't compete with the brand-new adventure they were about to embark upon—the kind that most kids their own age dreamt about. Baako and John, in their excitement, pestered Nate so much that he finally agreed to become a wolf right before their eyes. Nate did it within the Williams's estate.

He chose a spot near the wall, deep in the woods, far from the prying eyes of the Guard.

"Stand back near the trees," said Nate from the shadows. "You don't want to be caught in my way when I'm transforming."

Baako glanced at John uneasily. "But after you've transformed, you'll be your normal self, right?"

"Yes." He looked up through the canopy where he knew the Moon was. The Sun would rise in about an hour or so, so he wouldn't have to remain a wolf for too long. He looked at Baako and John, gave them a reassuring nod, then walked out into the moonlight.

The transformation was less painful this time, but still not exactly comfortable. Nate writhed about on the forest floor while hair sprouted up and down his body and his clothes ripped off. Finally, his four huge paws grasped the cool earth, and his eyes fell upon Baako and John. The two had backed away considerably, and each had a look of shock and awe on their faces. Baako was the first to step forward. He walked into the moonlight and held out a hand to grasp Nate's fur on his back.

"Nate?"

The huge wolf inclined its massive golden head. Something Nate had noticed after his transformation in the hospital was that in the shade he appeared black as coal, but in any light he shone like gold.

John came forward and put a hand on Nate's head. "Not sure if I like you this way, Nate. It's a little intimidating."

Baako chuckled. Nate looked up from one friend to the other then padded off into the forest. John and Baako followed.

Baako and John, still marveling over Nate's transformation, spent every waking hour of the day talking about what animal they would become. John thought it was very likely Baako would change into a lion. On the other hand, Baako believed John would become a rabbit. Naturally, he didn't take too kindly to this comment. Eventually, they all laughed it off, but the nickname, Thumper, stuck.

On Sunday morning, they would all board Desmond's private jet that would fly them across the country to Noble.

Students at Watson gossiped about the trio transferring and the real reason for their departure. The students assumed the three comrades were going off on some adventure funded by Nate's father; an adventure that, once over, would return them to the academy. At every lunch and break, Nate, Baako, and John sat together, cheerfully joking and sometimes being loud and obnoxious. During these times, Nate often caught Sofia looking at him. Every time this happened, he smiled at her apologetically. He knew she would give anything to be coming with them, but she hadn't reached the age yet. She always smiled back and did her best to hide the slight hint of jealousy lingering on her face. Nate understood exactly how she felt.

Sofia loved her big brother dearly and didn't like the idea of him being away from her for so long during the year. But then, she was also enamored with everything Hurst had told them that night and greatly wished there was a way she could join Nate. Unbeknownst to her, it wasn't as impossible as it sounded.

Chapter 5
The Forest Room

SUNDAY MORNING DAWNED bright and breezy. Nate's eyes fluttered open and he glanced around his room. The morning light had steadily crept over the city and from his vantage point, he could see the shadows being chased away. The Sun's beautiful rays were scattered to the far reaches of the sky. The bright light rose slowly until it blinded him, and Nate was hit with a touch of melancholy. He had no idea where Noble was, and it was possible he wouldn't watch the sunrise again until he was home for Christmas. He quickly shoved off the feeling, knowing it wouldn't improve his mood to dwell on it. He rolled out of bed and headed for the bathroom. He entered into an expanse of marble and glass. The magnificent bathroom almost rivaled his bedroom, and Nate loved every part of it, right down to the modern silver faucets sticking out from the floor-to-ceiling mirror. Nate turned the music up all the way and started the shower. Freezing cold water sprayed out of the powerful showerhead, and Nate walked straight into the torrent.

Emma was silently making breakfast with a script in one

hand. Sofia sat in Desmond's favorite chair, forlornly staring out over the city. Desmond came in just as Nate sat to join his family one last time for breakfast before heading off to his new life. Nate was gripped by a flurry of sadness at this thought.

Desmond grabbed Nate's last bag and headed out to throw it into the Rover. On occasion, he would let the nearly invisible servants or a member of the Guard do this for him, but today was different. His son was leaving home. Loading his bags in the car was both emotional and symbolic.

Sofia, who seemed to have been in some sort of trance, looked over at the sound of the front door closing, smiled, and ran over to hug Nate good morning. Her embrace was longer and more intense than usual.

The kitchen became a flurry of activity as their departure approached. Emma flipped pancakes, trying to remain reserved and controlled. Next to her on the counter was a movie script she had been highlighting with a yellow marker. Her movie was to start very soon and every now and then, she would repeat odd lines several times in a row. Her upcoming movie, *The White Night*, was to be the newest drama/romance film of the moment. It was set in Italy, where the citizens were threatened by a terrorist who planned to wreak havoc during one of Italy's holidays. Emma was cast as a star who stumbled upon the plot just hours before it was to unfold. She and Oscar-winner George Ray were then to set off to stop the catastrophe. Although she shared quite an intimate relationship with the famed George Ray in the movie, Desmond did not mind that they were working together. This movie could make her career. Unbeknownst to Sofia, who wanted to be an actress like her mother, her birthday present was to be a small role that entered the film mid-production. Emma was to fly back a day before Sofia's birthday and then whisk her out for two weeks of shooting. Sofia would be ecstatic, and now Nate stared at his sister, sorry that he wouldn't be there to witness the surprise. After all, it had been his idea to get Sofia in the movie.

Nate started to ponder lots of things he would miss while away at Noble. Just one week from today, while he and his friends were at Noble, Desmond was to open one of the tallest, most advanced buildings in the country. Emma interrupted Nate's thoughts by setting two plates in front of him, piled high with everything Nate loved for breakfast. The plates were full to the hilt with bacon, eggs, potatoes, ham, waffles drowned in maple syrup, pancakes with a small slab of butter, oatmeal with brown sugar, and toast spread with pounds of Nutella. Nate dug into the feast with gusto after thanking his mother profusely. She waved it off with an "Oh, it was nothing dear," when Nate knew she had been up for hours preparing it all. He finished one thing after another. Finally, he reached the toast, and he leaned back luxuriously in his chair to eat it. He hoped the food at Noble would be as good as Emma's cooking. Desmond entered the kitchen just as Nate had taken his last bite of Nutella-lathered toast.

"The flight leaves in an hour. We need to leave in five minutes. I just spoke with Mark and Andre. They are leaving now."

"Dad? Seeing as it is a private jet—as a matter of fact, *our* private jet—it wouldn't really leave without us, would it?"

Desmond laughed. "True. But I don't think Hurst would like it very much if we were late. I am sure you make a very intimidating wolf, Nate, but that bear is a force to be reckoned with."

Everyone laughed, and Nate conceded, "Good point." He finished his toast and brought the plates to the sink, where he rinsed and loaded them into the dishwasher. Emma and Sofia left to dress, taking their time as all girls do, while Desmond and Nate sat and waited for them in silence. Several minutes later, the pair came down the stairs, both looking beautiful. Emma wore slim, dark jeans that led up to a white designer jacket and light-blue shirt. Sofia just wore jeans and a white T-shirt. The v-neckline extended considerably farther down than most shirts. Nate disapproved, but chose not to comment. Gatsby ran up to him just as he reached the door. Nate ducked down to give his dog a huge hug. Gatsby wagged his tail and looked at Nate forlornly.

"Don't look at me like that. I'll see you soon, buddy. Love you."

Gatsby inclined his head and sat staring at the door as Nate got to his feet. Nate took one last look around the kitchen and across the city before closing the door gently behind him.

Desmond had decided he'd be the one to drive the Rover to the airport. He tried to be discreet, but was instantly recognizable. He was often on TV news shows or pictured in major newspapers and magazines.

When they arrived at the airport and drove through security, they found two other expensive SUVs parked by a large private jet. Baako's tall and intimidating father stood in an expensively cut, pristine black suit. Mrs. Clark, beautiful and elegant as always, stood talking to Baako. Three young sisters ran around their Escalade, playing and laughing. Nate's eyes fixed on one of them.

Imani was young and the sweetest girl he had ever met. Often, when Nate was over at Baako's, he would sit with her in their colonial living room and just talk. He never felt like he was talking to a twelve-year-old. He always considered her to be more mature than him. She was slim and tall, with long black hair and a beautiful auburn complexion.

Mr. Reynolds, John's dad, was a cheerful man, like his son and his wife. Mrs. Reynolds was short and blonde and was hugging her only child as if she'd never lay eyes on him again. John looked tired and out of breath, and Nate guessed this had been going on for some time now. John had no siblings and despite his attempts to hide it, he was a mama's boy.

Both Baako and John's fathers walked over to greet Desmond.

The three business titans immediately began an intriguing conversation about Noble, but soon it turned to the exceedingly less exciting topic of the stock market. Nate and Sofia rolled their eyes. The conversation continued as each of them grabbed the bags out of their cars and gave them to the couriers waiting by the door. Then each family broke off into their own group. Baako hugged all of his sisters and his mother. John hugged and kissed his mother. Nate hugged and kissed his mother as she began to cry, tears running down her face onto his shoulder. He held her close.

"We've never had you away for more than two nights. It's going to be so different."

"I know, Mom. But I will be back before you know it. You will be filming and then Christmas will be just around the corner."

He turned to his little sister, leaving his mother in Desmond's care. She smiled at Nate and hugged him for a long time. After a while, they broke apart. "I'll bring you back something interesting."

"You better." Sofia smiled. It was a smile that made Nate's heart feel ten times lighter. Emma and Desmond embraced while Nate said goodbye to John's mother and Baako's mother and sisters. He had spent many hours at their homes over the years and knew each family well. He reached Imani last. He hugged her for several seconds then released her.

"I'm going to miss our talks." Her voice was sweet and light.

"Are you kidding?" Nate smiled. "I don't know how I'll get through the year without your great advice."

"Call me anytime." She smiled and hugged him one more time before turning to her brother.

The three boys took off for the plane. Desmond kissed his wife goodbye then scooped up his daughter and pecked her on the cheek. He then followed the boys, glancing behind him as he walked. Mr. Clark and Mr. Reynolds followed shortly behind him. The door of the plane closed, and the families watched as the sleek jet rolled back and slowly turned toward the runway. The turbine engines roared to life, and the plane gathered speed.

Inside, Nate was smiling broadly. His face was glued to the window. He loved the feeling of takeoff. His eyes followed the landscape as it sped by at a dizzying pace. The city flew by on Nate's right, the mountainous landscape in the background. At the center of the city, proud and magnificent, stood Watson Academy, which had been his entire childhood. He saw the fields where his life had changed forever. After Watson, he spotted Desmond's newest building—it wasn't hard to miss.

The building towered over the surrounding city, reaching almost thirty stories over the other imposing structures. Its unusual design consisted of the building going up with walls that slanted slightly inward in a large circle, then went wide again and began slanting once more. There were about six of these, and they became smaller and smaller until they reached the clouds.

After they had been airborne for several minutes, Nate unstuck his face from the glass and looked around. John was getting out a brand new poker set from an embossed leather case. "What about a game or two?"

Nate turned from the window. "I'm in."

"Me too."

They sat in sets of two seats that faced each other over a wooden table, which was attached to the floor. Nate and Baako sat on one side, facing the back of the plane, with John across the table from them.

The buzz of business talk was like background music as hand after hand of Texas Hold 'Em was dealt. Piles of chips rose and fell like sand in front of each of them. After two hours, the game began to fizzle out. John opened a book about World War I and began to read. Baako put a pair of large headphones on and fell back asleep. Nate lay back in his leather chair and drifted off to sleep too. The conversation in the background didn't change in the slightest, and the plane continued on its way across the country.

Nate felt the very tips of his fingers and the steady beat of his heart pounding away in his chest. His eyes opened slowly as he awoke from the mysteries of sleep. He looked out the window and looked down on the expansive Lake Ontario. They had crossed into upstate New York and would soon land in Albany.

He reluctantly pulled his head away from the window—the beautiful scene beneath his eyes had left him enraptured—and found Desmond watching him. He was sitting on one side of the couch near the back of the plane, and when Nate caught his eye he beckoned to him. Nate walked over to his father and sat. He barely remembered his first father. Desmond had been there for the majority of his life. Nate was sure that his birth father must have been a great man and a great father, but Desmond had stepped in to fill his place admirably.

"Nate, I know everything is new and interesting, but do me a favor?"

"Of course, Dad."

Desmond considered him for a minute. "Be careful. As I said, this is a brand new experience, and it's easy to get caught up in something new. Just watch yourself, please. Don't do anything too stupid."

"I won't, Dad." Desmond pulled a thick envelope out of his leather jacket and handed it to Nate.

Desmond smiled. "It's a little above your normal allowance."

Nate squeezed the package. "Just a little."

"You should have it. Have fun, okay? I wasn't sure if they accepted credit cards where you're going."

Nate nodded and hugged his father then returned to his seat, holding the envelope tightly in his right hand. When he sat down, he tucked the envelope into his jeans pocket. He stopped a passing stewardess. "Could you bring me a water?"

She smiled brightly. "Of course."

The jet touched down in Albany forty-five minutes later. The difference in weather from the West Coast was shocking. Nate stared out the window as the plane slowed, landed, and finally slid into the terminal. It looked cold outside—very cold—and Nate could actually see the wind. It buffeted the plane from side-to-side as it taxied into an enclosed terminal. Each of them thanked the pilot and pretty flight attendants on their way out of the plane.

Unlike the weather outside, the terminal was warm and bright. Leather seats and mahogany tables filled a large room. There was a bar in the corner where a very pretty girl stood watching them. They exited through the terminal and down into a garage where a stretch limousine sat waiting. An old man stood by it in a dark suit and sunglasses, even though the sky outside was completely clouded over.

The man helped them load their many bags of luggage into the back, and then one by one, they slid in through the only door. The entire inside was black leather and very comfortable. It easily fitted six. There was a bar and a television displaying a football game. Nate grabbed the remote once he sat down and turned off the TV.

He watched through the tinted windows as they pulled out onto an empty highway, driving away from the small city of Albany and into rolling countryside. A beautiful skyline flew by him. There were many trees and mountains topped with snow. Streams raced down the mountains, sometimes becoming waterfalls in their haste to reach the bottom. The scenery became more beautiful the farther they went into the wilderness, and soon, they were winding their way through tall mountains. Nate could barely see the peaks. No one spoke; they were all glued to their windows.

They passed a large lake, and Nate found his face pressed against the window, leaving breathing marks on the cool glass. The landscape had been carved by time: the greatest sculptor of all. Trees rose as if from nowhere. They sprouted out of the vertical cliffs and clung to the edges with desperate fear. Their roots extended, much farther down, almost to the water below.

In calm parts of the lake, lifelike images were projected onto the water, as if the water was just a doorway into a similar world. The cliffs were painted onto the water, as was the cloudy sky, dotted with patches of blue. It seemed that one could tumble down into this alternate universe.

The clouds were the most extraordinary part of the landscape. They created shapes like no other, fighting for position in the constantly changing sky. They fought to be the one that got to have the Sun shine through them in the most beautiful array of colors. The blue around the clouds complemented the fluffy white perfectly.

An hour had passed before Nate could pull himself from this extravagant view. The limousine moved onto an exit ramp and slowly wound its way up a precarious mountain road. They climbed for fifteen minutes, and the landscape below gradually fell away. They passed cliffs that rose straight up out of the ground and shot toward the sky without fault. Finally, they reached level ground, which opened up into a valley nestled against one of the mountains. A large waterfall began high above and ended in a lake far below. By the lake was a large and very modern building, one of several spread along a narrow, winding road. The limousine kept going until it ended in a circle by the large building. A giant tree crested a small hill in the middle of the circle and rose several hundred feet into the air. Its branches spread out over the building and almost reached the lake by its side.

The grounds were deserted, as far as Nate could see. No students walked the paths by the buildings or lounged on the grass, working. Nate found this peculiar. In fact, he could see no one. The place looked abandoned. Then, as they came closer to the largest building and began rounding the large circle, several figures emerged from the shadows. John Hurst and several others stood waiting for them.

Nate now noticed many birds and animals around the main building. Many looked oddly out of place: a mountain lion, a bear, a deer, several eagles, a panther or two, a lonely leopard, many rabbits, and even a large rhinoceros, which stood apart from the rest. Everyone else in the limo was equally dumfounded as the car rolled up in front of Hurst and his entourage. Desmond exited first, followed by the rest with Nate taking up the rear.

"Welcome, my friends." Hurst smiled widely.

They all murmured, "Thank you."

Desmond strode forward and grasped Hurst's hand. "It's good to see you again."

"And you," replied Hurst. "Let me introduce you to some of my colleagues. This is our newest faculty member. Professor Smith teaches Weather." He motioned for a young man with wavy brown hair and a contagious smile to come forward. They all shook his hand.

"Next, let me introduce Professor Carter. He is our professor of Transformation. Behind him, Professor Bell, Professor Wilson, Professor Ward, Professor Mathews, and Professor King." As he said each name, he gestured to each professor—three men and two women—who all stepped forward, in turn, and shook hands with everyone. Nate thought it was a little odd that the entire staff had been gathered to greet them. Surely, the staff and the headmaster did not gather to greet every new student.

Hurst turned on his heel and led them through the huge glass doors that rose thirty feet into the wall. When Nate stepped through them, he stopped dead in his tracks. He stood in the entryway, gaping in awe. The floor around him was earthy and trees grew from it. Not just small saplings, but huge oaks towered to the ceiling, which seemed to be over two hundred feet above him. Nate noticed arches of live trees that formed several doorways. He could just barely see them through the trees. Huge stairs made of branches led out from the largest tree and wound their way up to three more levels.

Hurst looked back to see the newcomers tripping and stumbling blindly as they gazed around, completely unaware of the mass of roots and depressions in the ground that surrounded them. He smiled. "As you can see, our talents are not wasted upon the school environment."

They barely absorbed his words as they stepped onto a small bridge made of pine trees that spanned a stream and led to an earthy path. The path wound its way through the trees, eventually leading to a large tree archway. They crossed the bridge and walked the length of the path all the while gazing at the ceiling, where they could see small birds flying about and nesting in trees. When they entered the archway, they looked on in amazement, for this hallway was filled with stars. As Nate walked through, he could not tell what was up or down—it almost seemed like he was walking through space. There were large galaxies of all kinds as well as supernovas, stars, and planets. Dark spaces where there were no stars marked barely visible doorways, presumably into classrooms. Nate looked back. It was very hard to tell, but he thought that all the teachers besides Hurst had exited through those doors or had left during their walk through the forest.

"It goes without saying, but this," said Hurst, gesturing to all that surrounded them, "is the Astronomy corridor. It is the main corridor of the building and leads to the dining hall."

When they stepped out of the corridor, everyone stopped once more. They had arrived at the top of a fifty-foot cliff that looked out over the dining hall. To their left, a winding path curved down the cliff and made its way to the floor. The tables were carved completely of stone and were as elegant as the cliff they stood before. The chairs, made of petrified wood, stood tall and proud around the tables. The tables were round and there were about fifty of them spread out across the stone floor.

"Come, let us eat." Hurst led the still awestruck group down the cliff path to the dining hall. They sat at the closest table. At each spot was a napkin with the menu of the day stitched into it with gold thread.

Intricate glass shapes fit together to create the huge windows that spanned both sides of the hall and traversed the ceiling, creating a large pyramid of glass. The pyramid's height diminished gradually until they reached a wall, about ten feet high on the other side of the hall.

"Place your orders." Hurst's voice startled Nate out of his contemplation of how the glass shapes seemed to fit together without anything holding them in place.

"With whom?" Mr. Clark asked.

"Look around."

They turned, but it took several seconds for them to notice the children, no higher than the table itself, standing beside each of their chairs.

"What are they?" asked John, rather impolitely. No one could blame him; it was a question that would come to most mouths if they gazed upon these little people.

"You mean, who are they?" corrected Hurst. "They are fairies. However, they may not be exactly the kind of fairies you read about in bedtime stories."

Nate agreed; they certainly bore no resemblance to any fairies he had seen portrayed in fairy tales. They were exactly the same as humans, except half the height. They also all looked to be about five years old. Nate turned with difficulty from the fairies and looked down at his napkin.

"Fried calamari," he said. The fairy beside him bowed and hurried off. Everyone else followed Nate's example and soon the table was free of fairies.

"Why do they serve us?" Baako asked, watching his server wind his way through the tables until he was out of sight.

"They are paid handsomely for their service. They make the best cooks. We pay a great deal to have them serve us, but in my opinion, it is worth every ounce."

"What do you pay them?" asked Mr. Clark. "Surely they do not accept dollars?"

"Perhaps euros?" Nate joked. To his surprise, everyone laughed.

"No, they do not take dollars or euros, Nate," Hurst said quite seriously. "They are paid in gold."

Each guest looked at Hurst in wonder. Most of them were still too flabbergasted by the unusual building to ask any further questions, so Hurst turned the conversation to the school.

"There are seven corridors, one for each subject. As you saw, each corridor is unique to that subject. There are two corridors per floor. The Astronomy corridor is the only one on this floor because the library and assembly hall are also here. There are five dormitories spaced throughout the campus and each is themed to a corridor. There is also a building for guests. I will give you a complete tour after we eat." He stopped because the fairies had returned with steaming plates of delicious-looking food.

No one talked as they ate. It took a long time for the plates to be pushed back and their satisfied owners to sit back in their chairs.

After the meal, Hurst stood and laid his napkin on his chair. Everyone else followed his example, and he led them back up the ascending path into the Astronomy hall. When Nate looked back, he could see the small figures zigzagging their way through the tables to pick up the plates that they had left behind.

The Astronomy hallway was just as impressive as it had been the first time. Nate felt as though he was walking in space as he tread upon the disguised floor. Everything moved around them, so it was hard to get any sense of direction or balance. Every now and then, a hard wall would notify Nate he was going in the wrong direction. He heard thuds and cursing. Everyone else must be experiencing the same difficulties. When they reached the end of the hallway, they stepped onto the earthy floor.

Hurst set off through the trees without looking back. The others stepped quickly to keep up. He led them to a large tree with stairs wrapping its exterior. They climbed to the second floor, taking great care not to trip and fall to the forest floor.

When they were about fifty feet up, Hurst stepped out onto what seemed to be water. They were standing at the edge of a small pond. Hurst walked out toward the middle, heading to one of the massive doorways against the far wall. Nate looked back out across the jungle stretching behind him and then at everyone else, who stared back, just as confused.

"Professor Hurst?" asked Nate, unsure of himself.

The professor turned and smiled. "If you walk straight toward a door, you will walk on a pathway concealed a quarter of an inch below the water. It's four feet wide all the way to the doors, but off the path, the water is fifteen feet deep. Pay attention and tread carefully."

Nate hesitated, then stepped out to follow Hurst, waiting for the water to soak his feet. It didn't come. His foot landed on something quite solid, and he swayed unsteadily. Catching his balance, he put the other foot on the water and then, feeling more confident, he headed out in a straight line for Hurst, who was watching by the doorway. Nate looked back as he reached Hurst and saw a very odd sight: three grown men, one of whom was in a clean cut business suit, walking on water toward him. He was followed by Baako and John, who had boyish grins on their faces. Nate shook his head, knowing he would never see a sight quite like this one ever again. Mr. Clark, who was gazing side-to-side and looking behind him, almost stepped off the path, wobbling forward before regaining his balance. Everyone laughed.

When they reached the other side, Hurst showed them through the doorway to the hallway beyond. Nate followed and once again, he stopped. It was snowing very hard in this hallway. The cold air brushed his face, and his feet were covered with snow within seconds. He struggled through the blizzard, barely noticing where he was going. He heard yelps of astonishment behind him. Suddenly he no longer saw Hurst in front of him, but he did see a glow ahead. He headed for it and stepped through a doorway and into a warm classroom. It was bright and sunny and as he entered, Nate felt softness beneath his feet. He glanced down to find that he was standing on a vibrant green field. Desks stood on the grass, as though this was a normal classroom.

Hurst beckoned them farther inside. "This, as you might have guessed, is the Weather hallway. We teach students how to manipulate and understand weather. It is one of our more enjoyable and accident-prone classes." He smiled at the astonished faces. He jumped off the desk he was sitting on and said, "Come. I must show you languages."

When they had all just about adjusted to the warmth of the classroom, they were off once more. Hurst led them into hallways of screeching and growling animals; hallways filled with the sounds and sights of major battles being fought; a long forest-clad hallway with ferns and wild flowers; a long cave with diamonds glistening from gaps in the wall; and the weirdest hallway of all, which contained a swirl of colors and designs that made everyone feel woozy. They crossed a large field and a deep ravine to get to these various hallways, but in no time, they were back on the stairs of the great tree.

As they descended, Nate thought of something that he had noticed when they first arrived and called down to Hurst, who was several people in front of him.

"Where is everyone else?"

"Assembly," Hurst answered simply. "That's our next stop."

They found themselves on the forest floor once more, and Hurst led them to another doorway hidden behind a grove of aspens. They emerged to find a truly astonishing sight. They were standing at the top of a stone amphitheater that reminded Nate of his trip to Rome the previous summer. Steps flowed down many feet to a wooden stage at the bottom. Just as Nate was trying to comprehend the size of the theater, the sound hit him.

Students were talking, joking, laughing, and in the case of two monkeys, hanging from the lights, chattering. There were animals everywhere—almost as many as there were students—animals Nate had never even known existed. He stepped forward and immediately jumped back, cursing. He had barely set his foot down when a huge boa constrictor hissed at him then turned and slithered down the stone steps.

"That's Alejandro, an exchange student from Brazil." Hurst laughed good-naturedly.

"I see," said Nate, for it was all he could muster.

Hurst turned back to the doorway. "You don't need to attend Assembly today. I will show you to your dormitory. And you," he gestured to the adults, "to the guest apartments. Then Baako and John must have their unlocking. It must be done as soon as possible."

Baako and John exchanged excited glances as they all followed Hurst enthusiastically.

The cold air hit them like a wall, knocking all of their breath from them. They had gotten too used to the warmth and humidity of the main building to remember that it was freezing and windy outside. The limo was gone and so was their luggage. Nate assumed it was already in their rooms. Hurst led them through the cold to a dormitory several hundred yards from the main building.

"The Transformation dormitory," he announced as he grandly opened the door for them.

They stepped into a room that could hardly be considered a room. It had the exact shape and feeling of a hollow tree, stretching over fifty feet across and filled with leather armchairs and bookshelves. It was empty, no doubt due to Assembly, but it was not difficult to picture people lounging around and reading.

Stairs that seemed cut into the wood wound up around the side of the round hollow to three more floors. On the first floor, a door led off to what was presumably a hallway. Doors made of nothing more than wooden blocks led off from small platforms that interrupted the flow of the stairs.

"Every floor is either boys or girls. The first floor is girls, as is the second. The boys inhabit the top two floors. Each room sleeps three, and your room is on the third floor." Hurst started up the stairs and everyone followed, still listening. "Although your beds, couches, and other furniture will remain the same all year long, your surroundings will change daily."

He led them to the third door up the wall, which sat on a widened step. They stepped through the doorway into a hallway that curved out of sight on both sides.

"This is your floor." Hurst led them around the hallway, which seemed to be a complete circle, and then to their room. Number 5 was carved into the wooden door, and Hurst pushed it open and gestured for everyone to enter.

The room was very spacious. The far wall, which curved, was made of glass and looked out on a stream that led from the lake. There were three levels in the room. The first was several steps up, leading to a wooden platform. It was pushed into the wall like an alcove while the stairs continued in front of it. The alcove contained a double bed with a night table and dresser. Up more stairs were two similar platforms. Nate looked up and could just see a little into the top one, which was just above the door. He noticed that several leather suitcases sat at the foot of each of the beds. In one section of the room sat a couch and bookshelf. On the other side of the room, there were three desks that formed a triangle. The room, like every other in the dormitory, was completely made of wood, though that was not likely to be the case tomorrow, according to what Hurst had said.

"There is one bathroom per room." He gestured to a door on the right. "You will meet the rest of the boys on your floor tonight.

You are freshman; there are also sophomores on this floor. Never be surprised if you see a lion prowling the hallway. Well, that's pretty much it," he said as though he'd just shown them some boring office space. "I will show your fathers to their guesthouse while you unpack and get settled in. Then I will send someone to come fetch Baako and John to get unlocked." He left the room.

Desmond, Mr. Clark, and Mr. Reynolds would be leaving early in the morning, and they would not see them again. Each boy said goodbye to his father, then the three followed Hurst out the door.

"How cool is this?" John looked around in wonder—an expression that had been etched on each of their faces ever since they had entered the forest.

"It's amazing."

"I wonder what it will all look like tomorrow," said Baako.

Baako found his bags on the first loft, John on the second, and Nate on the third. Nate was happy with this arrangement—he liked being up high. They unpacked their things and made their lofts as much theirs as they could. John put up several posters of his soccer, football, and baseball teams. Baako put up some inspirational posters with big impressive words scrawled beneath beautiful pictures. Nate put a picture of his family on the bedside table. He then put up a poster of an Audi R8, an unknown bikini-clad model, and his soccer team. They had barely finished putting their socks in the top drawer of their dressers when someone knocked at the door.

"Come in," said Nate, poking his head over the landing by his loft. The door opened, and Nate almost fell. Jenna White stood looking up at him. Nate could hear Baako and John jump back in disbelief.

"You're … you're, Jenna?" asked Nate.

The girl laughed sweetly and looked up at Nate's head ten feet above her. "I'm guessing she never told you she had a twin."

"Uh, yeah. Must have slipped her mind." Nate stared at the

girl. He came to his senses and jumped the ten feet down from his loft right in front of her and held out his hand. "I'm Nate."

The girl looked slightly taken aback, but shook his hand nevertheless. "Rebecca."

John and Baako jumped down from their lofts and greeted the girl as well.

"Why didn't Jenna tell me she had a twin?" Nate asked.

"I don't know," Rebecca answered, catching Nate's eye. "Maybe she likes that people at her school think there's no one quite like her."

"I used to think that was true," John whispered to Baako, and the two chuckled quietly.

"So, where did you go to school? Clearly not Watson. This must be your first year."

"No, not Watson. I went to Bell."

Nate, John, and Baako passed a look between themselves, and Rebecca giggled. "You are clearly Watson boys, born and bred. Nate?"

"Yes," said Nate so quickly that John snickered behind his back.

"Are you Nate Williams?"

"Yes. Why?"

"Well, I've heard my sister talk about you. Plus forgive me for saying, but who hasn't heard of the Williams family?"

"They are well known in the city," said Baako.

"In the world," corrected Rebecca.

"The world?" Nate had always known his foster family was powerful and wealthy, but he thought their name was only known to people in their city.

"Everyone here knows of the Williams, and I have been to other parts of the world where your name is known as well. Anyway," she said, turning to Baako and John, who were standing slightly off to the side, irritated they'd been excluded from the conversation, "Hurst told me to fetch you two for the unlocking."

John and Baako were out the door and waiting for her before she could utter another word. She smiled at Nate. "I'll see you later." With that, she turned and left the room.

"Sounds good. Good luck!" Nate shouted after them and closed the door on their retreating backs. He looked around at his room and smiled. *This place is ten times better than Watson.* He headed up to his loft and lay down to rest. He did not expect Baako and John to be back for a while, so he fell asleep right when his head hit his pillows. He awoke several hours later to the sound of Baako and John entering the room and the animated conversation that preceded them. Nate jumped out of bed and looked over his loft.

"So?"

"Jaguar!" shouted Baako.

"Lynx!" shouted John.

"And what's the trigger?" Nate jumped down from his loft.

"Professor Mathews told us we don't have triggers. Triggers only occur when it happens naturally," Baako explained.

"So, how do they do it?"

"We were told not to say," John said smugly.

Baako laughed. "Shut up, Thumper. He did say that, but we were never not going to tell Nate."

"Thumper doesn't make sense anymore." John looked annoyed.

Nate laughed. "All right, Baako. Fire away." He flung himself onto the couch.

Baako walked forward and sat on the windowsill. He was quiet for a minute, and then he began slowly at first then picked up speed. "Rebecca led us into the main building and up the stairs to the fourth floor. She didn't say much. She led us across the field on the fourth floor to the hallway with all the colors, all the way to the end where there was a small office. We met Professor Mathews. He told us each to sit and then he sat across from us.

"He looked me in the eyes, and I felt everything leave me. I felt blank, actually." Baako looked thoughtful. "I don't think I felt anything. It was like I was dead. Then I was back, and it was amazing! Things flooded into my brain that I had never, ever considered before. I had memories I didn't even know I'd kept. It really was like something had been unlocked—like a whole new chamber of my brain had finally been opened. I saw a jaguar in my mind and Professor Mathews smiled and said that was what I was. He said he would teach us in our first class to become our animals whenever we wished."

John described much the same experience in his session with the professor. He had slipped into a trancelike state, felt as if he was floating, and had lost sense of time and of place. "I couldn't have really described it better than Baako did. It's really difficult to even pin down in my head. Everything left and then came back, and I saw the lynx in my mind. I will never forget it." He looked wistfully off into the distance.

They were all silent for a minute. John came back to reality first. "What time is it?"

"Eight ... I think. It was around then when you guys came back."

Nate stopped talking at that moment because he heard something. It sounded like an avalanche was coming. They heard voices—many of them. When they opened the door, boys their age or a little older were heading to their rooms, joking, laughing, and throwing things. The boys stopped and fell silent when they saw Nate and his friends. Then a boy, who looked about Nate's age, stepped forward. He had crazy dirty-blond hair and a tan.

"I'm Sam. Freshman."

They all shook hands and introduced themselves. Another boy came up to them. He had dark hair in waves that reached about his eyes. He pushed his hair from his eyes with one hand and held the other forward. "I'm Curt. Freshman, as well."

Five or so more boys introduced themselves. They seemed

friendly enough.

"Come down to the common room. It's way more interesting than sitting around up here," Curt said cheerfully as he led them out onto the staircase.

The common room was packed with students their age. There were also several birds near the ceiling and an assorted group of animals by one of the fires. The monkeys from Assembly were there, and they chattered and pointed at the newcomers.

Nate and his friends were immediately bombarded with wave upon wave of students, all yammering to be heard. A group of pretty girls by the fire spoke in excited whispers as the three newest members of their dormitory cast looks in their direction. Most boys saw new role models instead of competition, and they clamored to be the first to shake their hands. There were, however, several boys who hung back.

Everyone wanted to show their animal to the newcomers, and Nate marveled at the mammals, birds, and reptiles that had only moments ago been boys or girls. The night passed with laughter and jokes, and each of them felt quite content as they walked up the stairs surrounded by eagles, foxes, bears, deer, lions, antelopes, owls, alligators, and even a flamingo.

Nate and his friends undressed and readied themselves for bed, still talking about the night. It was only once the lights were off and each of them were settled into their own loft that Nate heard two whispered "Thank yous" that he rightly assumed were meant for him.

Chapter 6
The Fields

NATE HAD WOKEN to find the walls and floor made of granite, which made him feel cold just looking at it. They dressed and joined Curt, Sam, and two other boys heading for breakfast.

They all had tousled hair, and their eyes were half-open. No one talked until they reached the main building. It was just as cold outside as it had been the day before, and they held their coats tight until they reached the doors. The warm air of the forest was comforting, and they walked through the trees and listened as Nate asked questions at top speed.

"So what exactly is Mind? What do you really learn in it? I mean, isn't every class about the mind? What other classes are there? I mean, besides Weather, Mind, and Transformation?"

Sam and Curt looked at each other to see who should field the litany of questions. Sam went first.

"In Mind, you'll learn to control when you turn, and that's about it," he said. "Then it becomes all this practice of reading thoughts and stuff, and it gets ridiculously hard. Mathews is fine, but he has mood swings, so watch yourself."

"Then there's Horticulture," Curt interjected "It's all right. We haven't really reached the fun stuff yet, but I hear that's coming soon. Right now, we're just learning the history of certain plants. Soon we'll begin learning how to manipulate how plants grow—that's where it starts getting fun. Professor King is always nice and understanding. She gets a little overenthusiastic when teaching us about some of the most boring plants you can think of, but we learn a lot."

"Combat, as you might guess, is fun," Sam said, as if on cue. "There's no real classroom—just a huge gym. We are almost always our animals, and it's kind of like wrestling. Ward is intense, but you get used to him and honestly, it'd be weird if we had a Combat professor who wasn't."

"Wait," John interrupted mid-flow. "There's an actual class where we just hang out as our animals?"

"Well, yeah. Pretty much," Curt said. At that very moment, he tripped over a large tree root and fell, sprawling into the damp dirt. Nate laughed, but no one else did. Curt looked reproachfully up at him and then took Sam's proffered hand. He swatted his clothes violently, but when he began speaking once more, there was still mulch covering the back of his jacket.

"Transformation is really difficult, but very cool. It's what makes our dorm change walls and stuff. We learn how to change substances into something else—like wood to gold—but to do that, we need to know almost everything there is about what we have and what we intend to change it into. You need to know everything about the material so you change its structure. Professor Carter is good-natured, but demanding. You gotta work hard to keep up, and if you don't, he won't allow you to transform things. Astronomy is good, and there's some really awesome stuff that you learn, but I'm gonna let you hear it from Professor Wilson 'cause it's not as exciting if you're expecting it. She is really nice and very pretty. A lot of us get distracted,"

Sam said.

Baako and Nate shot John knowing looks.

"Weather has to be the best class. You learn about all kinds of weather and weather patterns, and you can make storms come and go and warm yourself if you get cold, or vice-versa," Curt said. "Well, you don't really warm yourself so much as the air around you, but it does the trick. That's pretty much all that we've covered so far. We haven't gotten too far. Smith is kind of a joke. I mean he is strict and he teaches us, but sometimes he gets a little carried away and ends up having more fun than we do."

"Lastly, there's Animal Language, which is good, but isn't really what it sounds like for the first half of the year," Curt said. "You learn about all kinds of animals and, most importantly, you learn everything about your animal. At the end of the first year, you have to write a fifteen-page paper on it. Professor Bell doesn't really say much and isn't that helpful, so you sort of have to make your own way." Curt sighed, then cleared his voice several times for it had become somewhat hoarse.

By the time Curt and Sam had finished explaining, they were walking down the path from the cliff to the breakfast tables. They picked one in the center of the dining hall and ordered a feast. The food was even better than Nate had expected, especially after yesterday's dinner, and they ate their way through everything that came in front of them.

The talk of the table gradually turned to their backgrounds. Nate was surprised to hear that it was rare for a natural like himself to have parents that were both naturals as well. Usually, parents were unaware of their child's supernatural abilities until they somehow stumbled upon a child's transformation. In Nate's case, his parents knew at his birth that Nate had inherited their abilities.

They finished breakfast about twenty-five minutes before class was to start, and Curt suggested he show them some of the things they hadn't seen on the tour. He led them back up the cliff and through the Astronomy hallway, but instead of turning left for the stairs, he turned right and led them through the forest to a network of wooden slots in the wall. These looked like they belonged in a wine cellar. Some of them had letters in them, others had magazines, and there were some that had nothing. Each of them had a glass door with their name embossed in gold lettering on a wooden plank secured with tiny golden screws. Nate found his near the bottom right-hand corner. He hadn't expected anything to be in there and was disappointed to find he'd been right.

After each of them had checked out their unusual mailboxes, they went to the library, the door of which was situated just slightly to the left of the mailboxes. It was a large arched room. There was no plant growth or anything too unusual in this room due to the fragility of some of the books. There were corners with leather chairs for working and reading. Shelves towered high to the ceiling, very far above them. Long wooden ladders that looked like they might slide led up to the highest of shelves.

"Well, that's pretty much it," Curt said as they left the library. "Class starts in seven minutes, and we have Double Mind class on the fourth level."

They walked back through the forest and up the mammoth tree to the fourth level where they crossed a wide field to the corridor with the colors and shapes. They walked into a dull classroom, by Noble standards anyway, with grass beneath and the Sun shining down from above. Professor Mathews was sitting at his desk, impatiently waiting for them.

"Everything is organized by floor," Sam explained. "All of our classes this semester will be with our floor and the first floor. Then we'll alternate by year. By then, you will be in different dorms with different people." Sam had been whispering, warily glancing at Professor Mathews as they slid into chairs at a round table close to the desk. The class filled quickly and quietly and soon, every chair was occupied.

Nate noticed Rebecca White and her two friends sitting at a small table behind them. He caught Rebecca's eye as he always had with her sister, and then turned away. Curt and Sam caught the look and shook their heads before turning their attention to Professor Mathews. Curt seemed a little put off, but appeared to get over himself quickly enough. He tossed Nate a look that could be taken many ways and then pulled out a textbook and notebook.

The stern professor read out the attendance in a bored tone. What little hair he had was graying, although he didn't look a day over fifty. He looked at each student as they answered him to make sure that everyone was who they said they were. His dark, intense eyes focused on each face as it answered and didn't leave it for several seconds. When it was Nate's turn near the end of the list, Mathews caught his gaze for a particularly long moment. The look was curious not stern, but Nate held it anyway. After what seemed like minutes, Mathews glanced back down at his attendance sheet, defeated. He finished by checking off Nate's name and then turned to the Smart Board. "Please forgive me while I give a short recap of last month, for we have new students with us today. Nate Williams, you are a natural, are you not?"

"Yes, Professor."

"Did you ever find that, as a child and throughout your teen years, you were able to get away with things? Find that you could always make people see your side no matter how twisted?"

Baako and John grinned, but Nate ignored them.

"Yes, I always got away with things."

"Well, you won't here! Naturals are born with the ability to use their words and looks to their advantage against normal people, but it doesn't work against your own kind. You could say it is a form of hypnosis that works only on weaker minds. Do you understand?"

"Yes, sir," said Nate, grudgingly. *Isn't he a natural?* Thought Nate. *Why is he railing on us?*

"Good. Now," Mathews said as he turned in his seat to look at Baako and John, "you two have not become your animals, am I correct?"

They nodded.

"You have third period free, am I correct?"

John checked his schedule. "Yes. That's right, Professor."

"Come back to this classroom then, and I will teach you." He turned back to the rest of the class. "The mind is a complex and dangerous thing. Average people do not know the mind's full capability. Everything in these buildings and everything you can do on your own is done through the power of the mind. Every class in this school uses the mind. This class will teach you how it works.

"I know you must have many questions, especially those who just joined us," continued Mathews, gazing at Nate. "Why are you able to do these transformative and seemingly supernatural things? And why, if the powers of us naturals are so special, is it possible for regular people, artificials like some of you," he said, flashing a look at John and Baako, "to also learn transformation skills?

"The answers will come to you in time, I promise. You will learn the techniques to transform, but you will never be taught how to unlock. That responsibility is only held by Mind professors. It can happen, very rarely, by accident. Those incidents are extremely few and far apart. It is also dangerous, and mistakes can be made with one careless move or thought. The most dangerous thing about unlocking is you must be able to tell whether the person you are turning into an artificial is not a natural already, just waiting for his or her transformation."

Professor Mathews droned on about the mind for the next hour and a half. Finally, a bell sounded, and the students packed up their things for the next class. Professor Mathews left his desk for the first time and descended upon Nate and his friends with three copies of their textbook. They were labeled *The Mind: A*

Complex Phenomenon.

"You will read through chapter three and take notes for a quiz next lesson. Dismissed."

When they reached the field, they found students sprawled on the grass, reading and relaxing in groups. Nate and his friends found a spot and flopped down, throwing their bags down next to them.

"You're right—he has mood swings." Nate leaned on his elbows.

"That's nothing." Sam laughed. "You should hear him when he gets on a rant about artificials." He looked at John and Baako.

"I take it he doesn't like our kind," Baako said.

"Sometimes it feels that way," Sam responded.

Break passed very quickly. Nate noticed that most students didn't bother going back to their room, preferring instead to stretch out on the grass. When the bell rang for third period, Baako and John got up, excited.

"Good luck! Have fun!" Nate called from the ground. Then, without missing a beat, he turned to ask Sam about Rebecca White.

"You and everyone else," said Sam exasperatedly. "She hasn't shown interest in anyone yet."

"Very different from her sister."

"She has a sister?" Curt looked surprised.

"Yeah. Seems like they keep each other pretty quiet. What is she?"

"An Arctic fox," Jake chimed in. "She and her group are one of the most sought after girls in the school. Or, at least, in our grade."

Nate was caught off-guard. Jake had pretty much ignored him last night and when they saw each other at breakfast. In fact, Nate was surprised Jake even hung around while they were on break in the field. He didn't really seem to fit in with Curt and Sam.

"So, what's your animal," Jake asked Nate.

"Wolf. What about you guys?" Nate asked.

"Golden eagle," Curt said proudly.

Nate looked at him in awe.

"Red-tailed hawk," said Sam.

"Weasel," said Jake rather quietly. Nate looked at him for several seconds until he realized the boy was actually serious.

"Your animal's the most popular," Sam said. "No one's ever heard of any of us. I always wondered why the term was werewolf. We have all been around for thousands of years, but you never hear of animals besides wolves. Maybe wolves are just reckless and tend to get noticed most?"

"Maybe. Or they are the most exaggerated and the ones that are best fit for the stories," said Nate. "No one really wants to hear about the boy who turns into a tree frog when he feels the bark of a tree."

Everyone laughed. Even Jake smiled.

"What's it like to fly?" asked Nate, once he had recovered.

"Like your best dreams. If it weren't for school, I'd spend every hour of the day flying. It's such an adrenaline rush—like you are free, freer than any other meaning of the word. On land, you can go forward, backward, and side-to-side. Above, you can soar in a thousand different directions—up, down right, down left. And it's such a feeling to have the wind go through your feathers. It is like you are in control. After flying, walking just doesn't have the same appeal."

Both he and Sam looked wistfully out the windows toward the sky.

The bell rang a little while later, and Baako and John caught up with Nate and his new friends as the group descended a level to the Transformation hallway. Nate caught looks of utter delight on John and Baako's faces as they joined them, slightly out of breath, on the edge of the ravine.

"So how was it?" asked Nate, knowing the answer.

"Unbelievable," said John. "It's so boring to walk on two legs."

Baako nodded in agreement.

Together, they walked through an ice tunnel to a classroom made of granite. Carter, the Transformation professor, was in a much better mood than Mathews had been in the last class, and they had fun watching him turn their chairs into a hundred different substances. There was one particularly memorable moment that occurred while they had been studying the composition of granite. Professor Carter had been staring at Sam's chair for a minute when Sam fell to the ground with a slight thump. A mess of grass lay beneath Sam, and the entire class burst into laughter. After everyone had calmed down, Carter apologized, saying that he couldn't resist. Sam just laughed and smiled. Carter gave them very little homework, and they left his classroom for lunch in good spirits.

After lunch, they headed back along the Astronomy corridor and into a room by the doorway. The floor was basic, but the walls were part of the large dome that also made up the ceiling. All over the dome there were galaxies just like in the hallway outside. Astronomy was the most interesting class of the day. Professor Wilson was as pretty as they'd been told, and she spoke in a quiet, but clear, voice.

"Do you think there is life beyond our planet, John?"

"Yes, Professor," John answered confidently. Nate could tell John struggled to focus on the female professor's question—not her beauty. Professor Wilson was French with long blond hair and quite a figure.

"Well, you are quite right. But contrary to public belief, extraterrestrial life has been here, and we have met with it." She then started a slide show. There was a black-and-white picture of a large oval-shaped ship landing and then others of creatures unlike anything Nate had ever seen or imagined. The entire class sat entranced by her words and the images that flipped across the screen. There were pictures of humans meeting with many different forms of extraterrestrial life, some of which were completely unrecognizable. The last few photos in the slide show showed foreign planets with red skies and purple greenery or three suns and pink oceans.

John, Baako, and Nate left Astronomy in a daze. They climbed back to the gorge for Horticulture. Horticulture was nowhere near as interesting as Astronomy. After being given definite proof that life existed outside their planet, let alone their solar system, no one was really interested in plants. Professor King spent most of the lesson enthusiastically teaching them all about some rare grass that grew in South America. Unfortunately, the class didn't share her enthusiasm and their eyes soon glazed over as she droned on.

"Hey! Sports!" Curt had leaned over and was shouting in their ears. They rose and staggered down the stairs.

"It's cold outside," John pointed out indignantly. He tried to catch a glimpse of the weather through the tangle of branches, but it was impossible.

"Ha! Outside!" Curt gave a hoot of laughter and Sam and Jake joined in, leaving Nate, Baako, and John feeling as though they were missing something.

"It's not outside?" asked Nate.

"Of course not. Follow me." Curt turned and led the way.

"Of course not. Why on earth would it be outside?" John muttered under his breath just so Baako and Nate could hear him. They shot him approving smiles and followed Curt down the stairs and then off through the forest. Soon, they came to a hole in the forest floor where stairs wound down into the earth. Around the edge, roots held back the earth around them. Curt descended with the others following close behind. When the stairs ended, they came out into a rather earthy tunnel that they followed for about a minute until they saw light. When Nate exited through the opening at the other end, he gasped and stopped dead in his tracks. A field with rolling hills and lush grasses greeted him. Sunlight seemed to come from every part of the ceiling, yet when Nate strained his eyes, he saw that the ceiling was a beautiful sky-blue and there was no sun. The trees looked as though they had been transplanted from the African savanna. As Nate watched, he noticed a small pride of lions resting in the large tree's shade. He observed in astonishment as a huge elephant ambled grandly across the fields. Large spotted cats chased other animals playfully. They sometimes caught their targets and let them go, and other times, they just gave up and wandered over to one of the trees. As the boys watched, they saw animals race out of tunnels similar to the one they had entered through. They saw every animal imaginable, including a golden eagle and red-tailed hawk. They flew up into the—for want of a better word—sky. It must have been one hundred yards to the top of the ceiling. Nate watched a jaguar bound off through the grass and a lynx follow it.

Jake broke the silence: "Just picture yourself as a wolf." Then a weasel slunk off into the grass toward the pond.

Nate shivered as he focused on the image of a wolf locked in his mind. He felt the strength and strain in his limbs as the pain came, just like that day in the hospital, just like that day he transformed for his friends. He then bounded off into the grass.

Chapter 7
An Unpleasant Addition

THERE WAS A new boy in the Transformation dormitory. He had short, black hair and a slender frame, but had a look about him that seemed to appeal to most girls. Nate couldn't see it, though; he had an abrasive and jealous attitude and, although he hadn't yet been introduced, he didn't like the feeling he got from Ryan Daniels. He had arrived late, as they had, and had brought along two friends as well. Nate might have some unfounded animosity toward Ryan, but soon he had plenty of reasons to hate the new boy.

Nate caught up with Rebecca just as she was zipping her bag shut. The classroom was still covered in several inches of snow and it dusted her beautiful brown hair. They had been working on snow the whole lesson and several students, including Nate, had really nailed it.

"Rebecca." He had finally caught up and stood just behind her.

She turned, looking a bit frazzled, but the look fell away as she caught sight of Nate's face. "Nate. Nice job." She gestured to the blanket of snow on the grass.

"I'm sure some of yours is in there too."

The rest of the class had already left. John gave him the thumbs-up before being dragged through the door into the hallway by a powerful black arm.

"Thanks, but it was you who started the blizzard." Rebecca smiled.

"True, true." He had been staring at Rebecca and kept repeating the word. "True, true, true, true, true ..."

"Nate." She grabbed his arm and shook him gently. "Don't be so modest," she said sarcastically.

"Right. Sorry. So did you grow up in the city?" He tried hard to regain his composure. Rebecca smiled broadly and Nate immediately knew that he had failed, but she'd decided to humor him.

"Yes." They headed through the rain toward the open air of the pond. "I grew up with my sister and older brothers on Twenty-Eighth Street," she said, still grinning.

"Classy place," said Nate, who knew the area well.

"Yeah, well, I'm sure your dad owns it, along with everything else there."

Nate flushed with embarrassment, remembering that his dad had mentioned that he'd bought all the apartment buildings up to Seventh Avenue. "I don't really have much to do with my dad's business decisions," he said sheepishly.

They left the hallway and began their way across the pond. They didn't speak much for the next minute as each was trying desperately to concentrate on the large tree to make sure they didn't go off the path. When they reached the large branches of the tree, Nate sighed and they descended the steps together.

"All right. My turn." Nate had just opened his mouth to ask another question, but he clamped it tight and listened instead.

"Did you ever hook up with my sister?" asked Rebecca.

"What? No! Of course not ... I wouldn't ..." He stopped as he realized what he was saying. His impulsiveness seemed to be causing a lot of problems lately. "Well ... I mean, I would ... but—"

"Nate."

"We talked a couple of times and everything, and she's a good friend to my sister, Sofia." Nate knew he was just digging himself deeper. "No, but nothing happened between us."

"I'll take your word for it." She searched for something to change the subject. "You're quite the talk of this place."

"Why?"

"Your father."

"Right, of course."

A sleek, unnatural voice interrupted the awkward moment. "Are you Williams?"

Nate turned to see a slim boy with dark hair about four stairs behind him. It was Ryan Daniels.

"Ya, I am."

"Williams," he said, spitting out the name like it was a curse. "Your parents die and you get scooped up by a Forbes Top Fifty and live the dream?"

"Don't talk about what you don't understand." Nate's tone was heavy with the warning. He had stopped on the stairs, now two steps below the boy, and Rebecca stood next to him, looking slightly nervous.

"I understand more than you know, Nate. Did it occur to you that Desmond only adopted you for the publicity?" Ryan accused. "He was getting a lot of criticism about a recent shady company acquisition, so he adopted an adorable lost boy to take the heat off."

"You don't know what you're talking about. Barely anyone knew he had adopted me." Nate could feel his invisible hackles rise.

"Only the ones who mattered knew. The heat lifted right

away. Of course, you were too young to know. My father was one of the ones on the board of directors for the company that was taken over. Your foster father forced him out for bringing up the issue." The boy's face was now red with anger.

"Is that what he told you?" *What if this was true?* Nate wondered. Desmond had never mentioned why he'd taken Nate in, and Nate had never questioned the things he had received and all that had been done for him.

"Yeah, that's what he told me. He also told me about the time he met your foster mother at a company party."

Nate's fists clenched, and Rebecca grasped his left arm tightly. "Don't say another word." Nate's anger resonated in every syllable.

The boy smirked. "Your mother. Back then, she was still whoring herself out to anyone who would get her a toothpaste commerc—"

Nate jumped the two stairs between them and slammed his fist into Ryan's face. The boy stumbled back, blood dripping from his nose. Nate punched him again, and he staggered back, stepping off the branch and falling eight feet to the forest floor.

Nate turned and looked up at Rebecca. She looked startled, and as he ascended, she stepped back. He stopped and looked at her. "Would you have taken that?"

"No, but—"

"But what?"

She stopped short, watching instead the figure that descended the steps toward them—a tall, imposing, bearlike figure. Nate swore under his breath then raised his eyes to the headmaster.

"I had hoped this wouldn't be a problem," he said sternly. "I heard from your previous headmaster that you couldn't keep your temper in check. Is this going to be a problem, Nate?"

"No, sir." Nate held his gaze.

"You may have gotten away with it at your old school, but as Professor Mathews informed you, it is not so easy to talk yourself out of things when you are face-to-face with another natural."

"He informed me. But, sir, did you hear what he was saying?" How did he know what Mathews had told them in class?

"I heard, Nate, but that doesn't change anything."

"Wouldn't you have done the same thing?"

"It doesn't matter if I would or wouldn't have. I would still deserve punishment."

A thought popped into Nate's head, and he glanced down upon the forest floor. It had seemed weird that Hurst was so calmly talking to him when a student of his lay unconscious, several feet below him. But he now saw that several teachers were gathered around the figure, tending to his injuries.

"I will be phoning your parents tonight."

"That's fine," said Nate, and it was. Once his parents heard his side of the story, they might be a little angry, but they would understand the motive.

"Now, if you'll excuse me, I need to check on Mr. Daniels." He moved past Nate and Rebecca and down onto the forest floor.

"Nate, honestly, I probably would have reacted the same way, but you really need to start looking around for teachers before you do anything like that," Rebecca admonished.

Nate hung his head. He and Rebecca continued the rest of the way through main building and back to the dorm in an awkward silence. When they reached the common room, Nate said goodbye to Rebecca and hurried upstairs to tell his friends what had just happened. John was the first to weigh in on the situation.

"The little bastard deserved it, but I agree with Rebecca, you should've looked."

"I know, but when you're in the moment, you don't think—"

"That's clear." Baako was trying hard not to laugh.

Nate shot him a stern look, and John changed the subject. "Hey, how about we get Curt and Sam in here and start a game of poker?"

Nate nodded and headed to his loft to change into sweats.

Ryan Daniels was in the infirmary. His tibia had been shattered when he'd hit the ground, but apparently, this was no big deal. Those who could handily turn diamonds into grass had no problem with his injuries. He returned to classes just two days later. Nate passed him in the hallways, but the most they'd exchanged were a few dirty looks.

They had their first Combat class, which Nate found exhilarating. There were only three rooms off the Combat hallway, and they were huge and lined with mirrors and windows. The mirrors gave the impression that the rooms were ten times bigger than they actually were. Combat was also the only class that they never had homework.

Animal Language was very interesting. Despite what Curt had said about them not learning any languages until second semester, Nate could now have a formal conversation with Baako as a jaguar.

Weather was definitely the best class, as Curt had told them. Storm clouds now frequented the dining hall and the downpours routinely soaked him and his friends. Most of the time, the storm cloud was created by Nate or Baako, who despite average grades in most subjects, seemed to excel in Weather. This was probably because they liked showing off. One day, Nate woke from a nap in the common room to find snow dusting the couch he was lying on.

"Baako!" Nate laughed.

Nate, Baako, and John's group had expanded to include Curt's, and they spent most of their free time in each other's rooms. Nate went out of his way to seek out Rebecca White, who, despite their eventful first conversation, had agreed to have lunch with him. The two were sometimes found sitting in the fields talking or walking back from the main building to the dormitory. It was also not uncommon for them to take a long detour and walk for almost an hour around the campus.

It was on one of these excursions that Nate found himself walking with Rebecca down by the lake. It was nearing sunset, and it was getting quite cold. The lapse in their conversation had gone on too long. "Are you cold?"

"I'm fine." Rebecca shivered.

Nate wrapped his arm around her and pulled her to him. She looked up at him and smiled, then kissed him on the cheek. "Thank you."

"My pleasure."

Rebecca laughed coyly.

"What?" asked Nate playfully.

"How long were you waiting to ask me if I was cold so you could pull that?"

"Um ..."

Rebecca silenced him with another kiss.

Curt and his friends were astounded that Rebecca had chosen Nate so quickly after his arrival at the school. Just about every other boy had failed miserably to garner her attention. In addition, Curt became increasingly jealous of their relationship, and Jake was tiring of Nate's popularity.

Baako laughed when Jake and Curt complained about Nate's luck with girls and his charm.

"We don't get it," Curt said. "I mean, we like Nate, he's friendly and chill, but why does everyone faun all over him?"

"You got me," Baako said. "When you hang out with Nate, you just get used to it. It's just the way it is."

Rebecca and her friends Olivia and Jasmine became part of Nate's clique of friends almost overnight. Olivia had light-brown hair and when one compared her and Rebecca in looks, it always ended in an argument. She had a prominent upper lip and was sweet and rather quiet. Jasmine had brown hair and was arguably prettier than her two friends. She was a little shorter and a bit louder than the others. Her comments always came at the wrong time, but Nate eventually found Jasmine funny and childishly innocent.

Nate had liked school before Noble, but he had never had fun in it. Now, he was doing just that. Apart from having much more interesting and hands-on classes at Noble, Nate and his friends had quickly resumed their positions as the most admired boys in the grade. The downside was that the group that resented Nate had grown larger and even more vindictive, due mostly to the instigation of its leader, Ryan Daniels.

Friday morning dawned cold and rainy. Nate propped himself up among a sea of pillows and blankets and looked around at what seemed to be dirt walls and an earthy floor. When his feet hit the ground of his small loft, he recoiled slightly. It was like wet mulch. A little repulsed, he stood, feeling the ground squelch beneath his bare feet, and he walked over to his dresser. As he put on his clothes back in the safety of his bed, he heard two yells of disgust as John and Baako closely examined the day's surroundings.

"It's kind of like carpet," Baako declared.

"Are you kidding?" Nate asked incredulously. "Wet, soggy carpet, maybe. It's revolting. I have to pick little bits off my feet to put on my socks."

Nate jumped down from his loft. He landed unsteadily on the uneven floor and summersaulted to land with his face in the mulch. John and Baako laughed, and each of them grabbed one of Nate's arms and pulled him up. Nate shrugged, trying to get the mulch off as he simultaneously dusted off his clothes.

"Smooth," said John, still laughing. "Next time, I'd try the stairs."

Nate shot him a dark look then began to laugh in spite of himself. Soon, they were all laughing. They were still chuckling as they picked up their bags and exited out into the hallway. Despite their mirth, they were still slow moving and dazed.

"What did I miss?" asked a bleary-eyed Curt as he closed and locked his door.

"Nate was under the impression he was a gymnast, but I think his dreams of the Rio Olympics might be dashed now." Baako chuckled again.

Nate laughed and appeared to shake off the joke as easily as if it were water, but as with water, some of the mulch had plastered itself to his hair and clothes.

"So what do you think of today's surroundings?" asked John, jumping the first two steps to the common room.

"Disgusting. We've had it once before. You just wait until diamond. That's what happened there." Sam pointed to two chunks torn from the wall by the second landing. "Some kids thought they would be clever and get some diamond out of the wall, but the next day, they had lumps of wood instead. Even when it's disconnected from the source, the material still changes along with it."

"I don't understand how it changes like that without someone thinking about it." Nate ran his hand along the wall.

Curt only said, "Carter will explain someday. I don't really understand either."

They ran through the rain to the safety of the indoor forest. They each shook the water out of their hair before walking through the trees to the Astronomy hallway. When they had descended the cliff, they noticed a fully awake looking Sam chatting animatedly with Olivia and Jasmine at one of the largest tables in the dining hall. Nate and his friends joined them. Rebecca arrived several minutes later and singled out a seat next to Nate.

"Good morning." Nate gave her a hug.

"Nate, you have dirt in your hair." Rebecca leaned over and ruffled his hair. John mimed puking into his napkin for the rest of the table while her back was turned. Everyone laughed.

"You'd better get it all out," said Curt. "Tomorrow, it may

turn to limestone. That might be unpleasant."

The rest of the table roared with laughter. Nate got over himself and laughed along with everyone else. Rebecca smiled and turned to the fairy standing expectantly beside her.

"Pancakes with strawberries, please," she said to the little boyish man with a mop of blond hair. He smiled and bustled off through the tables where he joined tens of his fellows in a flood streaming toward the kitchen.

Nate had gotten used to good food at Noble and to the fairies who waited on them. His bacon and eggs were delivered to him ten minutes later, and as he ate, he vowed to never tell Emma they were even better than hers. Soon after, he swore to himself to never think that again.

"What is there to do on the weekends?" asked John as he shoveled down waffles topped with a mountain of whip cream.

"Oh, we find things to do," Sam said vaguely. Nate could tell he wasn't going to spoil anything without being prodded.

Baako rolled his eyes. "Find things to do," he snorted. "There's probably an underground city just a couple of minutes away."

Nate, John, and Baako laughed until they noticed Curt and Sam exchange looks.

"Wait a minute," said Nate. "Is there?"

"Well, it's not quite a city," said Curt slowly. "It's more of a small town."

The trio's forks clattered to their plates.

"Let me get something straight." Nate finally found his voice. "You're telling me there is a town—an entire town—underground?"

"Yeah, Nate. There's a country down there too, and a dragon. It lives in a cave and guards a treasure," said Ryan, passing the table.

Curt ignored Ryan. "Well, yeah. Where else would it be? I mean, honestly. You've seen the fields. Is it really that much of a stretch?"

Ryan looked annoyed at not being noticed and slouched off.

"Plus, do you think it would be good if normals found a village of half-humans?" added Sam.

Nate turned to Curt. "There isn't really a country or a dragon in there is there?" he whispered. In Nate's defense, it wasn't much of a stretch after everything he had seen, but he did tend to be rather gullible.

"Of course not."

"Oh." Nate was slightly abashed, but he rallied quickly. "But what is it like?"

"It's somewhat like the fields downstairs. There's fake sunlight and weather, and yes, it's a full-sized town." Curt grinned.

"What do you do there?" asked John.

"Well, there's a bar and a post office," chimed in Jasmine. "There's also a grocery store for personal food, a bookstore, and others."

"A bar?" asked Nate skeptically.

"How do we get there?" Baako was sold.

"There's a tunnel leading from the fields. It's about a ten-minute walk," said Olivia, "and yes, Nate, a bar. We aren't allowed to order alcohol, obviously. There are other places leading off those fields as well, like the Jeka fields."

"The what fields?" Nate asked, ignoring Olivia's snide remark.

"It's like football," Jasmine remarked.

"It's more like soccer," countered Olivia. They both exploded into fits of giggles.

"Football?" Baako's face lit up.

"Well, more like rugby," Olivia clarified.

"There are no pads and the formation is like soccer," Curt explained. "Put it this way, it's football, soccer, and rugby because there's only one school per country and it doesn't work to have more than one sport for so few people.

"Yeah," Sam agreed. "We'll bring you down there after class."

They finished eating five minutes later and headed up to the cliff to Transformation on the third level. Nate noticed there were shooting stars zooming past him when he walked through the Astronomy corridor, and when they entered the forest, it seemed somewhat wetter than it had been earlier in the week. A drizzle gently soaked their clothes as they headed up the stairs and crossed the bridge spanning the gorge until they reached a hallway that seemed more like a tunnel. It was filled with the same earthy muck as the dormitory.

"Professor Carter? What is this stuff?" Nate asked when he entered the classroom and after he shook his head violently to get rid of the mulch that was dusting it.

"Decomposing wood," Carter answered cheerfully. "I know it's not the most pleasurable or interesting thing in the cycle, but relax, tomorrow is gold."

Carter was a tall, dark-skinned man in his mid-forties. He had a kind face and was built like Baako. He could almost have been his father.

"Gold?" Nate looked up as he got his books out. "Like real gold?"

"Yes, like real gold."

"I already told him not to take any," Curt said as he sat down next to Nate.

"Come on, Curt." Carter looked crestfallen. "Why do you have to ruin it? Whatever. Anyway, today also happens to be the day that I teach you how to transform things into gold."

"Really?" John's interest piqued as he entered with the rest of the class.

"Yes, really, Mr. Reynolds."

The rest of the class took their seats, removed their books, and looked up expectantly at Carter. Their textbook had over one hundred chapters, all on different substances, from gold to diamonds, to grass, to concrete.

"Well, as I told several of you already, today we make gold." Excited murmurs rippled through the class.

"Yes, gold." Carter smiled. "You will never find a poor one of our kind, because they can turn anything into gold or diamond. Gold, no matter what you may think, is one of the easiest substances to turn. Unlike other rocks, which are composed of many different materials, gold is fairly straightforward. It's pure and hasn't been tampered with."

He stopped and looked at his desk for several seconds, and they watched as the light-colored wood turned into pure gold. It glimmered like a thousand suns, and the light coming from the ceiling bounced off it and blinded them. Everyone shielded their eyes and looked astonished at the priceless desk standing at the front of the room.

"Think of gold. Think of its properties and what it means. You should be well versed in this because we have been studying it for the past week. Think of its weight in your hand. Think of its substance." He passed out fist-sized rocks from a large wicker basket to the entire class.

The room was soon full of students staring very hard at their small rocks. Nothing happened for twenty minutes. Their concentration was intense, and no one noticed Professor Carter walking through the tables, continually watching their progress. Finally, Nate heard a triumphant whoop and looked up from his rock to see John holding a gold stone in his hands.

"Well done, John. Tonight's homework is an essay on gold. You may start it."

"Thank you, sir." He put his gold rock gently into his bag and pulled out his laptop. Soon, the sound of rapid typing filled the previously silent space. The rest of the class looked on jealously, then returned with renewed vigor to their rocks.

By the end of the lesson, most of the class had succeeded in changing their stones into gold and left very pleased with themselves. Nate and his friends headed down to the second floor and across the pond to the Weather corridor.

"Dammit." Nate did not look back, but he had heard the small splash and knew that Baako's foot had gone off the path and into the water. If he looked, it would probably happen to him. Nate kept his eyes fixed on the archway leading to the Weather hallway.

"I understand everything else, but has anyone considered this is a little dangerous," Baako grumbled under his breath.

"Come on, Baako." Curt slapped him playfully on the back. "Where's the fun without a little risk. Plus, most people know how to swim, and they'd be right next to the path. You can just clamber up."

"Yeah, well. I don't like it."

Once they crossed the pond, they encountered a storm. Gail-force winds buffeted them as they fought to reach their classroom, inconveniently located behind the last door of the hallway. Nate was the first to stagger into the calm classroom. Professor Smith nodded and smiled at Nate as he sat down, breathing heavily. Baako was next; the rest of the class followed. Once they had all taken their seats and gotten their breath back, Professor Smith began the lesson.

"Today ends our two-week lesson on snow. By now, you should all be able to produce a perfectly good snow shower." He stopped for a moment at a sound coming from the hallway. A minute later, a hand grasped the doorframe and Sam pulled himself into the room. His hair was windswept, and he looked out of breath. Everyone laughed and congratulated him. Smith allowed himself a smile.

"You all can produce a snow shower. Am I correct?"

They all nodded.

"Good. For homework, you will each write a paper on snow. It will be no shorter than five pages, and I expect it on Monday. Every day it is late, I subtract a letter grade. Understood?"

Everyone nodded once more. Smith was strict. Five pages on top of everything else seemed excessive. And then subtracting a whole letter grade for each day it was late—that was terrible.

"Well, then. Snow," the professor began in a voice that clearly suggested a long lecture. They each pulled out their notebooks and listened as he recapped what they should've learned over the course of the previous two weeks.

"That wasn't the best of lessons," Nate grumbled after they had surfaced from the wind storm that was still raging as strong as ever. Its howling winds faded to a low moan once they left the hallway.

"Ah, well." Sam had taken a while to get himself settled in class, but he had finally begun to dry and relax. "The last lesson of the week is usually a recap, so don't be discouraged. The next three lessons should be good."

"Yeah, but a five-page minimum essay?" John groaned. "That makes two essays for the weekend, and it's only break."

"Don't worry. Wilson never gives us much, and then there's only Animal Language and Combat, and there's no homework for Combat. So cheer up, Nate. It's not all depressing."

"Yeah, I guess so." Nate was unconvinced. "Let's go to the gorge for break. It's always so much less crowded than up at the field."

They all agreed without much debate and found themselves a nice spot in the tall grass, several feet from the gorge. When their break was over, they got up reluctantly and proceeded to Astronomy. It wasn't Astronomy they were reluctant about, it was leaving the nice breeze and comfortable atmosphere of the gorge. After the first five minutes of Professor Wilson's class, they all perked up considerably, and Nate's thoughts about what else he could be doing at the moment vanished.

She taught them about black holes, and it was a very interesting lesson. Curt had been right because at the end of the lesson, they were assigned a worksheet. When the class heard this, there was a collective sigh of relief, and they left for Animal Language.

"Don't get too relaxed!" Wilson called after them. Her cheerful French accent put everyone at ease, despite her ominous words.

After Combat, they went down to the fields as usual, but they didn't change quite yet. Curt led them across the left side of the field toward an area where Nate could see an opening in the wall. It was the wall of mirrors that gave off the illusion that the room was several times bigger. There was a black hole in the wall, and Curt led them through it. Nate and his friends walked along it for several minutes until they arrived at a much smaller version of the fields. There were no ponds or trees, and these fields were perfectly round and mowed.

"So, instead of having seating on the sidelines, it's above," said Curt. "It's like a one-way mirror, and you lie down and look through. You get three points when you get the ball past those lines." He pointed to lines that cut across the last bits of the circle on either side. "The ball is round, and you can hold it or kick it. You can pass it with your feet or hands. When you score a goal, you must have it in your hands. You can pretty much do whatever you want to get the ball out of the other player's hands. There are half-hour halves. The ball starts in the middle. The offense stands around where the ball lands and when the whistle blows, the game starts."

"So how many teams are there?" asked Baako.

"There are varsity and JV teams for both boys and girls. There's a playing field for each. It's a bit difficult to get onto. There are nine people on the field and each team has about twenty-five players. You can sub in whenever you want."

"How do you really play?" Nate was examining the white line beneath his feet.

"Well ..." Curt thought a moment then elaborated. "It's best to use your feet till you get to the goal line. To score you have to have the ball in your hands before crossing the line."

"You can't pass to someone behind the goal line?" Baako asked.

"No. If you are in an opposing team's goal area without the ball, it's a penalty."

"We should try out." Baako's eyes sparkled.

"Yeah, sounds good," said Nate. "When are tryouts?"

"Next week," Sam spoke up. "You got here just in time."

As Nate walked back through the tunnel, he felt like life was built around those "just in time" moments. Sam was the first to reach the edge of the fields, where it had started to snow. A red-tailed hawk soared up into the sky and a golden eagle soon followed. Nate closed his eyes and imagined. He felt the pain and the odd sensation, and then he landed on the grass with four powerful legs. He bounded out onto the field into a blizzard, his sleek black fur cutting a stark contrast with the white as the snow began to fall in earnest.

Chapter 8
The Town

NATE AWOKE WELL rested on Saturday morning. He rolled over and looked out the window. It was bright out, but the rays of light were going by his window, not into it.

The homework had not been that bad, as Curt had said. Nate and his friends had finished the long Weather essay and the Astronomy worksheet. Nobody had been too rowdy the night before. Sam had told them people saved their energy for Saturday.

The others had listened as the three naturals—Nate, Curt, and Rebecca—talked about their first transformation. In Rebecca's case, she had made the transformation five times before Hurst had visited to explain everything. Her stimulant had been the smell of fir trees, and she lived in a forest of them. They had all had heart attacks and slipped into comas. Nate's had lasted the shortest, while Curt's had lingered on for two weeks and Rebecca's an entire month.

They split at twelve-thirty. While John and Baako raised their hands as the others left, Nate walked Rebecca out. He turned to face her in the hallway, about to hug her good night, when she smiled and stopped his progress with her lips. Nate came back in, looking like he had just conquered the world. John and Baako exchanged looks and didn't ask Nate what had happened.

Nate heard someone rising from the loft below him and looked over at his clock: 9:45. He decided it was time to get up and rolled out of bed onto a golden floor. He looked around and noticed that the walls were also solid gold. Much happier with today's choice of surroundings, he walked over to his dresser and pulled on jeans and a sweatshirt.

He chose to walk down the stairs this time. John was still sleeping, and Nate didn't disturb him. Instead, he continued down to Baako's loft and sat on his bed. When he sat, he noticed a small bit of gold lying on the ground. He picked it up.

"The town should be good today," said Baako as he pulled on his socks by his dresser. He watched Nate weighing the piece of gold in his hand. "Come on, Nate. You heard. Don't bother. It won't be the same tomorrow."

"Yeah, I know. I'm just appreciating the surroundings a little more than I did yesterday." Nate slid the gold into his pocket anyway.

"I noticed you walked today." Baako smirked. He had pulled on his socks and was now focusing on pulling on jeans, but was having a little trouble.

"Yeah, I find it works better."

"Someone should wake up Sleeping Beauty over there," Baako suggested, pointing to the loft above him.

"I'll do it." Nate bounded up the stairs to a point several feet higher than John's loft. He waited a minute then leapt onto John's bed. John sat up when he felt the pressure just below his feet, and rubbed the sleep from his eyes.

"Gold," he muttered, still half-asleep. He swung his feet over to the golden floor and sat there for a minute, looking groggy.

Nate left him to change and headed down the stairs to Baako, who was sitting on his bed with his laptop. Nate was about to say something when he heard a slam. The door had banged open, and Sam stood there with a lopsided grin on his face.

"What happened to you?" asked Baako, looking up from his computer.

"So it's official." Sam walked into the room with a triumphant look.

"What's official?" Nate demanded, even though he had a pretty good idea what Sam was talking about.

"You and Rebecca." Sam looked pleased with himself. "I've just been talking with Olivia."

"Yeah, I guess so." Nate tried to look nonchalant. He decided to leave out the fact that it head been "official" since he'd kissed Rebecca by the lake the other day.

"You guess so?" Sam snorted. "People are already jealous of you. Now it's going to be worse than ever. I also doubt Jake will ever talk to you again. He has a huge crush on her ... and he's not the only one."

Curt came in wearing the same look on his face as Sam had just a moment ago, though with a slightly more severe and jealous edge.

"Ready for breakfast?" he asked the room at large.

"Yeah, just about." John got out of bed.

They headed downstairs and joined up with Rebecca, Olivia, and Jasmine in the common room. Today, the Sun was showing, and although everything glistened with rain, the air was rather dry. Nate saw something in the light that he'd never noticed before. Although the walls, ceiling, and floors of the dorm changed daily, the outside seemed to stay the same. It was a twist of steel and glass and gave no hint that the floors inside might be made of diamond.

They entered the Astronomy hallway and walked through a supernova explosion. Bright purples and yellows almost blinded them, and they walked faster than usual to the cliff. Nate had to close his eyes for a minute once he entered into the natural light, and he still felt a little nauseous as his eyes adjusted to the dining hall. It was extremely loud this morning, as most people had finished eating and were talking about weekend plans. Nate and his friends headed down the path and sat at the same large table as yesterday. They ordered more food than usual. Soon, they were contributing to the uproar and several minutes later, their food arrived. That quieted them for a while until they pushed their plates back once more.

Students at several tables shot Nate reproachful looks, including Ryan's. Half an hour later, Nate and his friends joined the large crowd, winding through the forest and down the stairs to the fields. The crowd flowed out of the tunnel and off to the right once it reached the fields. The tunnel led to a rather large archway in the mirrors and into a larger tunnel with bright lights. This tunnel was somewhat longer and after fifteen minutes, they were still walking with no end in sight.

"How far is this place?" asked Nate.

"About another ten minutes," said Curt. "It's worth the walk to get away from the school and mix with some other people. Hey, Nate, have you ever heard of Gray?"

Nate froze in his tracks. Jasmine, who was walking behind him, bumped into him.

Nate stared at Curt. "You have?"

"Of course. Are you all right?"

Nate knew that the blood had completely drained from his face. He was sure he looked almost ghostlike in the dim light. "He murdered my parents, and I just escaped with my life. There was nothing I could do."

John grasped his arm and nudged him to begin walking once more.

"I'm sorry to have brought it up," said Curt, truly looking it.

"Nate, aren't your parents alive?" Rebecca asked.

Baako shot her a look that shut her up immediately.

"No, no. It's fine. He murdered my real parents. Desmond found me two days after I escaped." He turned back to Curt. "I don't know much about him. Hurst was the one who mentioned the name to me. What do you know?"

"Well ... he is the most well-known killer of our kind in history. What he has done could be considered genocide in our population. I don't know his reasoning exactly, but it's something about keeping the balance and making sure the normals don't find us."

"It's an extreme view," said Baako, looking at Nate.

"Where is he now?" asked Nate.

"He's in jail. They caught him eleven years ago, probably right after ..."

Nothing more was said on the subject, or any subject, until they reached the town.

They arrived at a version of the fields. The forest in the distance was conifer instead of tropical, and the grass was much shorter. Behind the forest, Nate could just make out the shapes of mountains.

"How big is this place?" asked Nate.

"Miles and miles," said Curt unhelpfully.

"Are there places like this all over the world where our kind live?" asked Baako.

"I know there are more, but I never really thought about it. I guess it's quite possible."

"So where's the town?" asked John. He, like Nate and Baako, had been searching the landscape for a cluster of buildings.

"You're looking in the wrong direction." Sam glanced at Curt, then up at the wall behind them.

"I've looked in every direction," said Nate. He spun around and found that the wall was not made of mirrors, but stone. It was a giant cliff, rising up into the sky. He was about to reprimand Sam and Curt for spinning them this tale about a town when Baako nudged him.

"Those look like windows up there." He pointed up about two hundred feet.

Nate backtracked out into the field until he could see the cliff better. Sure enough he saw windows, balconies, and railings cut into the cliff wall above them. There were five levels from what he could see.

"How do we get up there?" asked Nate, still aghast.

"Climb," said Sam.

"Bullshit," said John.

Everyone laughed. Curt came to their rescue. "Follow me." He walked up to the cliff, and right into it.

Nate and Baako followed and found that the wall was not solid. There was an opening which opened onto a stone staircase that trailed back and forth on itself to their right. There were gaps in the cliff above their waists, serving as windows, and these seemed to continue all the way up the cliff wall. They watched as students pushed past them and mounted the steps.

"Jesus, how many steps are there?" John furrowed his brow.

"Three hundred and eighteen. Better get climbing." Rebecca gave Nate a playful look and bounded up the stairs two at a time.

John and Nate were the last to reach the top. Nate grabbed Rebecca and proceeded to gasp exaggeratedly.

"So the bar?" asked Rebecca.

"We're seventeen," Nate reminded her, still huffing.

Curt grinned. "We don't get beer. It's just a bar environment. You know—pool, darts, that sort of thing."

"Oh." Nate looked slightly abashed.

"Don't worry," said Sam. "Only another year. Lets go to the store first."

They walked along the solid stone street to the grocery store. Like the stairs, the street was open to the landscape from the waist up to a few feet above their heads. The view was spectacular. The girls went ahead to a clothing store, while Curt and Sam stayed with Nate, John, and Baako.

The grocery store was small, but well stocked. Several aisles were packed with things that kids would want at boarding school. After Nate took in the store, he noticed an old man. Although he looked old, Nate couldn't help but notice he was strong. Cords of muscle showed through the sleeves of his simple purple T-shirt.

"That's Old Sam," whispered Sam.

"So you in sixty years?" asked Nate.

He, Baako, and John grabbed a cart while Curt and Sam did the same. They loaded everything from fizzy drinks to chips to cakes and cereal. The cart was almost overflowing when they wheeled it up to the checkout counter. Old Sam ran everything through and they paid. He didn't say a word. Curt and Sam unloaded their cart and paid as well. They left with three bags of groceries each.

"Why doesn't he talk?" Nate couldn't help but be curious.

"Talk?" Sam asked, half-laughing, half-serious, for the effect was quite unsettling. "Because he can't. Old Sam used to live in a normal town. It was a small town with many suspicions, and this was back about seventy years ago. Someone saw him change. They thought he had been possessed by the Devil. So, the town cut out his tongue so he couldn't spread Satan's word. They wanted to burn him too."

"Jesus!" Nate looked away. "I'm glad I live in a big town."

"Slash, own it," John corrected.

"You should be more watchful," Curt admonished. "There are more people who are poorly educated in this world—especially this country—than you'd care to believe. It happens and Old Sam's lucky to have his life. He was tired of not fitting in, so he came here and asked the then headmaster if he could build a town for us. He cut the main buildings into the rock, and over the years, people have come and it has expanded."

"So he's kind of like the mayor?" asked Baako.

"Yeah, I guess that you could say that," Curt agreed.

"So why does he work at a grocery store?" John asked.

"Cause he likes it," Curt said simply. "Not everyone needs a Bentley and a Rolex to be happy. You'd better be careful what you say around him. He's a wild wolf."

Nate looked up from the street. "Do you mean what I think you mean?"

"Yup. You've got yourself a new brother."

"I'm thrilled. Really looking forward to it."

"Pretty orphan boy! Where's your Rolls Royce?" An unpleasant voice filled the air.

"Haven't you learned your lesson?" Curt turned to find Ryan and his two friends right behind them.

"Apparently not," said John. "Come on, Nate."

He and Baako grabbed Nate by the arm and hurried him away before he could get into any more trouble.

Nate and his friends wandered in and out of stores at their leisure. Several times, Nate had to be restrained as Ryan passed by, but soon he disappeared, and they were left in peace. They saw Rebecca, Olivia, and Jasmine sitting among the large bookshelves, but did not disturb them. They also noticed Jake wandering around by himself. "He's the one avoiding us," Curt whispered. It was true. Jake completely avoided them, and when they bumped into him and greeted him, he turned his back on them.

"You know, it's not our fault." Sam watched Jake walking slowly down the street by himself.

"I know it, but I still feel bad," said Curt.

"We always knew you had a ten times better chance with Rebecca," Baako blurted. "I know it's not nice to say, but he must've seen it coming."

"You can see something coming, but it doesn't make it easier to deal with when it actually happens. I'm sure he saw it coming," insisted Sam.

"How philosophical!" Baako ran his hand along the cool stone railing.

Sam scowled and continued, "It was coming like a freight train, and there wasn't anything he could do about it. That probably made it worse. He saw it coming, so he grew distant until he finally—"

"Snapped," finished Nate.

"Exactly," said Curt. He had grown silent since the topic had changed. "And now I don't know what else we can do. He never talks to us in the dorm anymore."

"Well, there really is nothing you can do about it," said John.

Baako spoke up: "So the bar is actually worth it? I think I'm gonna feel pretty stupid sitting at a bar drinking a Sprite."

Curt and Sam laughed. "It's worth it. Half the people in there are going to be our age. It's pretty much built for students. Besides, we'll probably run into Rebecca's crowd there." Sam winked at Nate.

"Stop with all the hints, Sam!" Curt shouted unexpectedly. Everyone looked at him, and he glanced at his shoes.

"Talk about snapping," whispered John, just so that Nate could hear him.

Curt acted like nothing had happened and began talking about the weather.

The bar didn't look too bad. It was situated at the end, right after a small inn. The bar, like most of the other buildings, was set back fifteen feet from the railing and had windows and a door all cut into the stone. Through the windows, they could see many students playing pool, darts, or sitting at the bar, talking. Nate saw a cascade of wavy brown hair contrasted against a white blouse sitting at the bar. He went up and put his arms around her waist.

She turned. "Can I help you?" A pretty upper senior eyed him calmly.

"Oh, no. Sorry." Nate's cheeks blushed red. He turned and headed over to join his friends at a booth. All of them were roaring with laughter, and he couldn't help smiling as he sat down. "All right, all right. I hope you didn't see that coming!"

"Actually, I did," Curt admitted while fighting to keep a straight face. "Rebecca's a little shorter than the adult over there. Did you even notice she was drinking a beer?"

"Uh, no. At least it's a good story."

"Ha!" exclaimed John, who had finally sat up straight with a serious face. "A story? There are a lot of stories that put you in a better light than that one."

"Oh, right. Because you never embarrass yourself."

"Of course not. I make mistakes like the next person, but I don't embarrass myself that badly. At least not most of the time."

"Most of the time?" Curt cocked a brow at him.

"I'd rather not get into it."

"All right, but I'm not gonna let it pass completely," Curt persisted. "So, Nate, I think that's Rebecca."

"Very funny."

"No, Nate." John laughed. "It really is. At least I hope it is, for your sake."

Sure enough, Rebecca and her friends had just entered the bar. He held up his hand and gestured for them to come and sit. Rebecca saw Nate and smiled, and they headed for the booth.

"So, Nate, I heard you met Zoe," said Rebecca when she reached Nate's side.

"What are you talking about?"

"Well, I ran into Zoe, who told me a good-looking freshman guy put his arms around her," she said, trying not to laugh.

"Oh, that. Whatever."

"It's so funny how you pretend nothing matters to you." Jasmine drew up a chair from a nearby table.

"Things matter to me. Things like Rebecca, my friends, family."

"Really?"

"Yes, really." Nate tried to keep his cool facade, but he wasn't sure everyone bought it. Jasmine, who always seemed to catch him, was gazing at him oddly.

"Ah, well." Jasmine looked amused but a bit disappointed. "So, Baako, are you trying out for Jeka this Wednesday?"

"I plan to, and I'm expecting Nate to join me. He's kind of good at things like that."

"You are?" Olivia feigned. "I would never have guessed."

"Why don't you pick on John instead?"

"Ha!" said Jasmine. "We would pick on John if there was anything to pick on him about. John's perfect."

All eyes shot to her, and she blushed. "Well, you know what I mean. Don't you?"

"No," they echoed in unison.

"Fine. I guess I will have to come right out with it." Jasmine smiled. "You can tell that Nate's good at things, and he's lived well all his life. It's the way he talks and walks. It's quite obvious, and there's nothing wrong with it."

"Obvious?" asked Nate, but Jasmine held up her hand.

"John knows he's perfect and just accepts it. But he doesn't let it affect anything he does."

All of them stared at Jasmine.

"John, do you want to take a walk?" she asked boldly.

"Yes." He got up, and they left together, chatting animatedly.

"Wow," said Curt.

"Well, we all know Jasmine says what's on her mind and doesn't care what others think." Olivia tried not to laugh, but failed.

"Ha," said Sam. "Well, if we didn't know then, we know now."

Nate stared at the table. He, John, and Baako had always joked about how he was arrogant, but no one else had ever said it to him. He had grown up in a way that had made it impossible for him not to be arrogant.

"Nate, snap out of it." Baako punched him playfully on the arm. "Jasmine was just trying to play up John. We don't care how you walk."

"I guess so," Nate said, trying to laugh it off. Even so, he spent the rest of the afternoon in silence while the others talked about Jeka and the coming week. He only came back to life when they asked him if he wanted to get a coffee. Nate loved coffee and found it always boosted his spirits, yet he couldn't shake off Jasmine's words. He wasn't really arrogant or insufferable, was he? He spent most of the afternoon trying to find a rational explanation for his arrogance, but in the end, the only thing he could come up with was that it had protected him from remembering his previous life and the night when it had been torn away from him.

"Can I have a large mocha?" asked Nate at the counter.

"That will be four fifty." Nate proffered the cash, and when he received his mocha, he instantly cheered up, even enough to laugh when Olivia pointed to John and Jasmine walking hand in hand down the street outside their window.

"That was quick." Sam huffed.

Olivia and Rebecca giggled. "I wouldn't expect anything less of Jasmine.

"I guess so," said Curt. "So, Nate, what position are you trying out for?"

"Forward or wherever they need me. Maybe center left."

"You better watch it; an upper senior plays that," Curt warned. "He won't be happy if you take his spot."

"I can't play better than an upper senior," Nate acknowledged indignantly.

"That's what he says," said Baako. "Just wait for it."

"If you've finished your work, we can go down there tonight," Sam offered. "It should be open 'til check-in at midnight. I'm sure I can dig around and find a ball."

"I'm up for that."

An hour or so later, the virtual sunset found Nate strolling down the streets with Rebecca. Everyone else had headed back a little earlier, so the couple strolled nonchalantly. The streets were deserted and quiet even though it was only six o'clock.

"You don't think I'm arrogant and self-centered, do you?"

"No, of course not. Jasmine didn't mean it."

"But I kind of think I am."

"Well, then that's who you are, and no one would like you any different than who you are."

"I guess so." He walked silently for a moment then leaned in to kiss her. It was at that precise moment he realized Rebecca was exactly like him. Of course she defended him tooth and nail. She was the spitting image of himself. He had yet to find a single thing wrong with her. Most guys wanted a perfect girl, and Nate was no exception, but he now looked at her, confused. For the first time in his life, he felt like a dog chasing cars.

After several more minutes, Nate broached the subject that he knew they were both thinking about. "Did you know this thing with Jasmine was going to happen?"

"Of course I did. She's been talking to Olivia and me about it all week long. I'm glad she finally did it, because she certainly talked about it enough."

"John never mentioned anything," Nate muttered, more to himself than her.

"Would you expect him to?"

"Well, no, I guess not."

Rebecca laughed and the sound echoed down the street, pleasantly bouncing off the cliff walls and lining the stairway down to the fields. "We might miss dinner." They left the town and headed for the glowing doorway to their right.

"Doesn't really matter." Nate kissed her again.

Two hours later, they arrived at the dorm. Rebecca left

Nate and headed to her room on the first floor where Olivia and Jasmine were sure to be gossiping about John. Nate headed up the stairs to his room where he was sure the same thing was happening, but with a slightly larger crowd.

"That took a while," Curt smirked when Nate walked in.

"We may have made several stops along the way." Nate walked over and sat down on the couch next to Baako. John was lying on the floor, staring at the ceiling, looking like a king.

"You happy?"

"Yeah, I am."

"So, who's next?" asked Nate, looking around at Baako, Sam, and Curt.

"Me," all of them replied in unison.

"And who are all of you planning on hooking up with?"

"Olivia," they all said seriously. They looked around at each other and laughed.

"That's going to be quite a contest," John and Nate said in unison.

Chapter 9
Jeka Tryouts

THE NEXT COUPLE of days raced by uneventfully. Nate noticed their lunch and dinner tables now looked more like a mandatory third-grade play because with him dating Rebecca and John dating Jasmine, the formation was boy then girl and so forth. The talk leading up to the Jeka tryouts inspired a good amount of bragging, although Nate doubted that half the kids who claimed they would make the team would even tryout. Curt had pointed out some of the existing team members in the hallway, and they were an intimidating group. Most of them weighed at least thirty pounds more than Nate and were at least three inches taller. Most of that weight advantage was muscle. Nate was still thinking about what Jasmine had said about his arrogance. It bothered him, but he was watching himself more carefully now.

Sam and Curt taught Nate and his friends the basic rules of Jeka, and they played two on two. While it couldn't simulate actual game play, it would help them learn how to handle the ball.

"Unless you are sure you can get the ball, don't dive for it when it drops," Sam advised.

"Penalties are a free run at the defensive line." Curt passed Nate the ball.

"What qualifies for a penalty?" Nate kicked it to Baako.

"Slide tackles, straight-on punching or kicking. Being behind your opponents goal line without the ball." Curt watched as Baako repeatedly flipped the ball between his feet and his hands.

"What happens if there is a tie?" Baako chested the ball and kicked it to Nate.

Curt caught Nate's kick with his hands then said, "I'm not sure. You'll have to ask the captains about that."

"Who are the captains?" Nate was barely paying attention to the ball's location.

"The main one is Johnson. You'll like him, trust me. He's a good guy. Don't let the fact that he dresses like a jock put you off."

Mid-game, Professor Mathews stormed at them for being on the Jeka field without a teacher. However, they got away with a warning. Baako joked that Mathews would fail all of them on the next day's quiz, but nothing of the sort happened.

Nate was now looking forward to the tryouts. He held several championships for soccer, and he didn't see how Jeka could be that much different. To him, team sports were all the same: fool the minds, beat the defense, and score—simple, easy, and very effective. He never let things distract him when he was playing soccer—he always focused on the ball and the players around him. Jeka was slightly different, but it had the same general idea because it was formed from three of the most popular sports in the world. No pads and a small rule book suggested rugby, and a round ball that they had to pass around with their feet fit in to the soccer category. Lastly, a ball that could be picked up, thrown, and run past a certain point to score suggested football.

As they practiced, Nate realized that Jeka was easily becoming much more fun than either soccer or football. Baako clearly felt the same way. He had even replaced the football on his bedside table with a decorated Jeka ball. He and Nate got up early and practiced before their first class until the tryouts. They had the basic rules down and had a handle on the game strategy, so they entered the field with a good amount of confidence.

Nate couldn't help but notice John shooting them jealous looks as they left practice each morning or when they were talking about moves over dinner. It was clear John felt left out, and he missed playing his sport—baseball. John had given up baseball to come to Noble, and although he held no state records, he had been the best pitcher on the team, and Nate knew he loved it.

One night while Baako was showering, Nate brought it up. "John, I'm really sorry I convinced you to leave baseball behind."

"Don't sweat it, Nate." John was lying on the couch tossing a championship ball in the air. "I easily chose Noble over baseball."

"But you were so good."

"I never would have played professionally. Anyway, maybe I'll start a baseball club here."

"What are you talking about?" Baako came out with a towel wrapped around his waist.

"Baseball." Nate caught the ball John threw to him and tossed it back.

"Oh yeah. I'm sorry, John."

"Guys, it's fine." John got up and tossed the ball to his loft. "I'm going to go see Jasmine."

Baako and Nate arrived for the tryout fifteen minutes early. John, Curt, and Sam came along for moral support. The original Jeka team looked even more imposing on the field. They were doing running drills, and they seemed about twice Nate's size. Baako and Nate ignored this and put on their cleats. They then grabbed a bright-yellow round ball a little smaller than a basketball.

Baako passed to Nate with his feet, and Nate kicked it up and threw it back for several minutes and then they switched. They had hit an extremely fast pace by the time the rest of the hopefuls had arrived. Several upper-senior players looked at them with approval and then called the hopefuls into the middle of the field.

The current team captains introduced the team and the rules to the group. The current team—with the exception of the captains—could be ousted by a better player. There were twenty-five spots available on the varsity team and nine players on the field at a time. There were also JV teams and a girl's varsity team, but they practiced and played on separate fields.

Nate joined the group of forward hopefuls, and the captains ran them through a series of drills. They did time trials, running, passing and footwork. In all of these, Nate excelled. The captains watched his progress, clearly pleased. Only one member of the team looked on with disapproval: the current upper-senior forward left was also watching Nate's performance.

It was rare for freshmen to make the varsity team, and the few who did usually didn't get much playing time. Nate figured he and Baako would at least make JV, although he never expressed this to anyone, not even Baako. He was learning that being humble and understated was an asset, that people who are the best at things need not constantly remind others of the fact.

Nate also noticed that the coach, who he recognized as their silent limo driver, was sitting on the bench, watching them. Unlike other sports, the coach just observed and let the captains run the practices. This was an interesting way of doing things, and Nate was unsure how he felt about it. On one hand, his old coach had been nasty at times, but he also had pushed them to the point where they were better than anyone else. With students running practices and games, there was a silent suggestion of less discipline and more fooling around. Not that Nate was against fooling around, he just liked someone making him and his friends toe the line. In the end, it made them better people and better players. However, the team captains could do all of that by themselves, if they were so inclined.

After two hours of intense tryouts, the captains called the hopefuls back to the center. Baako had been chosen for right defense, and Nate was chosen for left forward. Both had made varsity.

Players whose names had not been called out stood with their heads hung. There was still hope, however. Each position had a backup who would be assigned the junior varsity squad. And, finally, there were a few alternates who would be permitted to practice with the squads, but not play in games unless they were called to fill in for someone injured or absent.

"You two," the captain called to Baako and Nate. Chris Johnson was a tall upper senior with short, jelled hair and blue eyes. He had the general build of a jock and was reportedly the best forward center left in the school's history. "Congratulations. You made varsity. Practice is every weekday during sports time. You will receive your uniforms by the end of next week. Our first game is two and a half weeks from now against Germany. They won the championship last year, so let's hit them hard!"

Chapter 10
Changes in the Weather

NATE AND HIS friends decided to stay on campus for the Thanksgiving weekend, as did most students. Christmas break was only a month away, so they'd be home soon enough.

It was a busy time for the students, who maintained a rigid and fast-paced class schedule. They had already learned four animal languages and could create short bursts of snow and rain or even part the clouds for a time to let the Sun through. Nate and Baako were also busy with Jeka, trying to keep pace with the upper classmen on the team. They had been throttled in the match against Germany and were putting in extra time to prepare for the match against England.

There was a lot of excitement about Thanksgiving week— Nate and his classmates would meet their first extraterrestrials. A group of ambassadors from some far away moon would be landing at midnight, and the entire freshmen and sophomore classes would be there to meet and speak with the aliens. Professor Wilson was trying vainly to teach the much-anticipated visitors' language to the students, but it was extremely difficult. They were easily frustrated by the completely unfamiliar sounds, and she eventually gave up with the line: "It's a good thing they find English easy."

Tables in the dining hall were no longer limestone; some had been turned to wood or gold, or the most complex and beautiful of all—diamond. Most students were still struggling with diamond, and John had been the only person in their class who had successfully changed his gold ring into solid diamond. He wore it proudly on his right hand.

Mind was practiced often. Students would sometimes walk to places they didn't mean to or throw things at teachers whom they wouldn't have dared touch during normal consciousness. Mathews had warned that anyone who used Mind to make someone else do something unacceptable would be severely punished, but so far no one had been caught. It was very difficult to tell which of the hundreds of students made the girl in the corner throw her food at a passing Professor Hurst.

Nate couldn't describe the feeling of having someone else controlling his mind, but he had felt like he was a puppet. He had been walking through the forest talking to John about learning how to make rain when he had gone rigid. Professor Mathews was walking several feet in front of them, and Nate went up alongside him and stuck out his foot. Mathews, in his pristine white shirt and black suit pants, fell sprawling into the dirt, his face just missing a large rock. It was at that moment that Nate regained control and looked down, horrified at what he had done. He furiously looked around for the one who had made him do it; he didn't have to look far. Ryan and a couple of his friends had been walking some twenty feet behind them, and they were now doubled over, laughing.

Mathews, on the other hand, was far from laughing. He

stood and dusted himself off, staring at Nate intently. Then he noticed that Nate was not looking at him, but at Ryan, who was stupidly still laughing.

"Mr. Williams, be on your way," he said coolly, and he pushed past Nate and John and headed for Ryan. Nate and John exchanged looks of glee and walked with exaggerated slowness, turning back as often as they lost control to see Ryan being reprimanded. From this moment on, Mathews spent a considerable amount of time teaching them how to block these mental attacks.

Rebecca and Nate were still going strong along with the slightly more enthusiastic pair of Jasmine and John. Olivia had sweetly rejected Sam and Baako, and now everyone was waiting for Curt to make a move.

As Thanksgiving drew near, Nate noticed that most teachers laughed less and seemed concerned. On the rare occasion when a student asked them what was bothering them, they simply answered that they were tired.

Snow fell often, which was why Nate and Baako were found struggling through a foot of it, five minutes late to first period on a Wednesday morning. It was hard to know if the weather was natural or fabricated by one or more students. Either way, it had grown progressively more depressing.

John had gone ahead with Jasmine, and the others were scattered about. When they were finally free from the snow, they raced up the stairs and across the field to Animal Language. Nate and Baako dodged a very lifelike lion and dove into the classroom.

It was empty. Everything was still and quiet.

"Where is everyone?" Nate was the first to break the silence.

"Not here, apparently." They looked around the clearly abandoned classroom, where the same class had been held for the past month.

"We should check the other classrooms," Nate suggested. They went out into the hallway and passed by several animals. They opened door after door; every classroom was deserted.

After checking the final classroom in the hallway, they left and headed downstairs to Assembly.

The room was packed with silent students looking down upon Professor Hurst, who was speaking. Nate had never seen such rapt attention being given to the speaker. The teachers stood solemnly to the right of the stage, straight-backed and in a single line. The looks on their faces showed no emotion. They usually sat in the front row. Nate glanced around and noticed several black-suited figures standing in the shadows. The students' faces were more telling. Some of them looked terrified, others so fascinated that they were leaning far out of their seats.

Nate noticed John gesturing to him from the back row. He sat between Jasmine and two empty seats. Nate and Baako edged on by as quietly as they possibly could along the row until they reached the empty seats. They then turned their full attention to Professor Hurst.

"Many of you have heard of Senator Davidson. He often graced nightly news channels. He was a distinguished senator who had held his seat for more than twenty years. He was murdered late last night in an Albany hotel. Several members of his entourage were also found dead in their beds, but no murder is as curious as Davidson's. There were no stab wounds or bullets. No sign of any human damage. However, two teeth marks were discovered on his right shoulder. He was found stark white and completely devoid of blood. If you have grown up knowing our ways, you may have heard rumors of vampires."

The entire assembly erupted into whispers. Hurst held up his hand for silence. "Our community has tried to hush up other rare and confusing murders such as these, but none of them have been this public. Therefore, I must tell you that the rumors are true. I didn't believe them myself, but there are no plausible explanations for this death. Albany is closer than the faculty and I would like, and therefore I would like to impose several new rules that will not be lifted until this is resolved.

"All students must be in their dormitory by no later than eight o'clock. Visits to the town are henceforth banned. You may not visit the fields, except during sports hours. You may not stray out of school boundaries at any time. Am I clear?"

There was a general murmuring of obedience.

"Very well. There is one last thing." The entire assembly of students grew deathly silent. "There are very few of us, so few that we must not be careless with our lives. We are one of the smallest known races, and I implore you to obey these rules. Members of the Special Police have been dispatched for your safety." He gestured to the men in black lurking in the shadows. "They will be stationed throughout the school, at your dormitories, and near the school boundaries. If there is something to report and there is not a teacher around, tell one of them. They are here for your protection." He glanced up at the back row and looked directly into Nate's eyes. This unsettled Nate, but Hurst looked away almost instantly, and Nate convinced himself that he had imagined it.

"Very well. Follow the rules and do not attract trouble. Return to your classes."

A rumble began as students burst into conversation about the new revelation, and they stampeded through their rows and up the stairs. This was not the normal chatter after an assembly. There were no bursts of laughter, but the noise swelled to a roar as the crowd broke out into the forest.

"What did he say before we came in?" asked Nate, leaning around Baako to catch John's arm.

"It only started a minute ago. Jasmine and I ran into someone who was late, which is why we didn't make the same mistake you must have," said John.

"Jesus, though." Baako pulled his arm away as they freed themselves from the still-packed assembly hall and ventured out into the glistening forest. "Vampires."

"Well, would you have believed in werewolves before I showed you?" Nate grinned.

"I guess not," John said.

Rebecca and Olivia caught up with them as they set off across the field to Animal Language. Rebecca kissed Nate on the cheek and greeted Baako.

Nate almost stopped in his tracks. He had a chilling thought. Nate turned to look at Curt, who had been walking several feet behind. "Curt, how were the Gray murders committed?"

"I don't remember, Nate. Sorry."

"What, you think that ...?" John looked perplexed.

"Makes some sense. The senator was a natural."

"I don't know, Nate. Our prisons are pretty well guarded, and I think we would have heard if he had broken out."

"He broke out the night he killed my parents. If it had been broadcasted, my parents would have known and they might be alive. He may have never gone to prison."

The rest of the day passed with the students paying very little attention in class. Most people were still thinking and talking about the murders and nothing much else was mentioned. Most teachers gave up trying to teach them, and even Mathews postponed their test to their next class and let them sit around the tables, talking about vampires. He even chipped in what he had heard about it from Hurst himself that morning, though Nate doubted he told them the whole story, for there were some very clear holes. *What if they know nothing and they're clueless? What if they're powerless? What if there is something major that they aren't telling us?*

At lunch, it was the single topic of conversation and most unusually, the fairies chipped in their opinion. Nate soon got bored of the topic, despite the fact it would probably take a long time for the vampire thing to calm down.

The new curfew didn't bother Nate much. The only times that he ever really stayed out past eight were the nights he spent with Rebecca when they didn't get back to the room, but they could easily find a way around that. However, Jasmine and John beat them to it. When Nate and Rebecca entered Nate's room, they heard someone swear and a thud resound as a body fell from John's loft. John got up shirtless and looked around at Nate, smiling.

"Sorry, Nate. This room's taken."

"I can see that. Hey, Jasmine." He waved when she poked her head over the loft.

"We'll leave you two to it." Rebecca pulled Nate out of the room.

"Do you think you could finish up by nine, cuz I have a paper to write for Wilson," said Nate casually, poking his head around the door before Rebecca had a chance to close it.

"We'll try," John chuckled.

Nate just shook his head incredulously as he and Rebecca closed the door and headed for the common room. There, they found Baako, Sam, Curt, and Olivia killing time.

"Thanks for letting me walk into that," said Nate, punching Baako on the arm as he sat in an armchair next to him. Rebecca squeezed in beside him and glared at Baako.

"Honestly," she said, trying to keep her face as serious as possible, "you could have saved us some embarrassment."

"Where's the fun in that?" Baako laughed.

Rebecca looked as though she was about to retort, but Curt cut her off. "Forget it, Becca. There are more serious and interesting things to talk about than where John and Jasmine decided to hook up."

"That's definitely true," agreed Sam.

"Did we hear about something serious?" Nate asked in a tone of mock surprise. "I thought everyone was talking about the latest addition to the dining hall menu."

"Well, actually, there's a filet mignon on there, and it wasn't there yesterday." John licked his lips.

"Cut the crap," said Sam. "See that girl over there?" He pointed to a small girl sitting alone in a corner, looking absolutely distraught.

"Yeah, I see her." Nate didn't appreciate Sam barking at him, particularly when none of them had made a personal jibe to the girl, whoever she may be.

"The senator was her grandfather."

"Oh." It was all Nate could say. He looked guiltily at John.

"Shouldn't someone go over there and comfort her?" asked Rebecca.

Nate wasn't in a hurry to get involved. "I am sure she has friends to speak to." It wasn't that he didn't care, it was that he just wouldn't know what to say.

"I don't see any friends." Rebecca held his look.

"I don't know. It would feel weird," said Nate.

"Nonsense, Nate." Olivia stood and walked over to the girl. She sat beside her on the couch and put her arm around her. She was clearly speaking words of comfort, and they looked like they were working for the girl, who looked up and answered something back through several tears.

"She is an incredibly decent girl," Nate said about Olivia, looking knowingly at Curt.

Curt nodded. "Her heart is in the right place, that's for sure."

"She likes you, Curt." Nate was still looking at him.

Curt said nothing.

An hour later, they parted company to finish the night's work. Nate kissed Rebecca good night, and they left Curt and Olivia sitting by the fire. The two had struck up a conversation since the senator's granddaughter had gone up to bed. Their room was made out of diamond today and everything sparkled.

Nate needed to focus, so he pulled a blanket over his head

and his computer and began writing his essay, with only his keys and screen breaking the darkness. The paper on the visiting alien's homeland was relatively easy. Professor Wilson had provided several sheets on the Moon and had highlighted the most important points. They breathed much more oxygen than available on Earth. The animals were bigger, the planet was bigger, and the gravity was double. There was no doubt about it, she was definitely their best teacher. She gave them what they needed, but it wasn't as if they didn't learn.

Nate had just put the finishing touches on his conclusion when Curt burst in, looking jubilant.

"That went well," was all he could say.

"How well?" Nate was the only person brave enough to surface from their blankets.

"We said good night very personally." Curt wagged his eyebrows.

"That's great!" Nate jumped down and patted him on the back. "Sam can't be too happy, though."

"He might not be happy, but it's hard to tell. He's good at keeping his feelings and opinions to himself. Besides, I think he had his eye on the girl who lost her grandfather, and I am sure he's going to start working his magic tomorrow."

"That's a little soon, don't you think?"

"He'll just talk to her. Sam would never be that disrespectful. He knows what to say and when to say it and vice versa. Trust me."

"I trust you."

"What's this about Sam?" asked Baako. He had also surfaced and was rubbing his eyes, trying to get used to the room's brightness. "And I definitely don't trust you."

"Oh, come on," said Curt.

"Well?" asked Baako.

"Curt and Olivia." Nate couldn't believe he actually had to spell it out.

"Really?" Baako was never one to be jealous. He respected when a cause was lost and easily moved on to someone or something else to keep his attention and his time, but there was something a little off about his response.

"Yes, really." Curt grinned.

John surfaced from his blanket. "You and Olivia, for real?"

"So you're really over Rebecca? Finally? No hard feelings, okay, Curt?" Nate said. "Olivia is a great girl."

"So, what are saying? I got the runner-up prize, you narcissistic son of a bitch! You think everything and everyone revolves around you."

Nate was stunned. "I didn't mean anything by it. I'm happy for you, and I don't want hard feelings."

"Don't try the 'shy little orphan boy' routine with me. You're a selfish prick," Curt barked. "The Moon, as you might have noticed since you look at it far too often, doesn't revolve around you! And spare me the sob story of orphan boy." His face flushed red.

Nate's fist clenched.

Baako gave Curt a dark look.

"Yeah, yeah. I got it." Curt stormed out, slamming the door behind him. As it smashed closed, it shattered. The door had been turned to glass the second before it had made contact with the frame.

Nate was almost through the doorway when John reached him. "Nate, give him the night to cool off. It was over the line, I know."

Everything became quiet. Baako went to his loft and called home. John went up to his and began reading a book. Nate headed slowly up to his own loft and opened his computer. Rebecca was online, and he immediately engaged her in conversation. He didn't mention Curt's hurt feelings; he was still thinking about what Curt had called him.

Nate had trouble sleeping, as did several others in his group.

No doubt they were all up late talking about Curt and Olivia, the murdered senator, his granddaughter, and vampires. They were all bleary-eyed and didn't talk much at breakfast until they had ordered and eaten their food. As a group, they dragged up the cliff for their first-period class.

Nate and Curt wouldn't even look at each other. They talked to everyone else, but it was clear neither of them was ready for a rematch. Jasmine was naturally the first to notice, or more realistically, the first to say anything. Everyone had noticed.

"Hey, what's you guys' problem?"

Before either could answer, John pulled her away. "Leave it for now, Jasmine."

Nate tried to pay attention in class, but his mind wandered, preventing him from considering such mundane things as how sparrows communicated. He looked forward to Combat, a place where he could blow off steam.

Professor Ward set up a tournament where Nate found himself paired against Ryan. He relished the idea of forcing the coyote up against the wall and showing him he wasn't all talk. It was always about ground given up and the first to force the opponent against the opposite wall won. To make it simple, Ward turned one wall black and the other white and assigned each opponent a wall. The idea was simple. Keep your opponent from reaching your wall. Whoever reached the opposing wall first would win. It was a test of agility, speed, and strength.

After several minutes, the jaguar managed to force his opponent, a mountain lion, up against the black wall. Next up, Ryan and Nate, who walked to the center. The two stared each other down like boxers going nose-to-nose. Nate's eyes morphed to yellow and fur was creeping up arms toward his bare chest. He was growing bigger, his arms growing stronger and more equal to his legs. His nails elongated into sharp points, and his feet shrank while hair encompassed his remaining bare skin. His gym shorts split as he fell to the ground on all fours. A gigantic wolf with sleek gold fur stood ten feet away, staring at Ryan with huge yellow eyes.

Ryan's transformation was also complete, but the smaller gray form was nowhere near as majestic as the golden wolf. They began to circle one another. The wolf lunged and the coyote cowered, but Nate had underestimated him. Ryan had done the classic move, and Nate had fallen for it. The more agile coyote dodged every single move and struck back with lightning speed and agility. The wolf backed up and lost ground quickly as the coyote kept up its onslaught of attacks. Then the coyote lunged, and Nate leapt aside. Before Ryan could turn, Nate hit him full force. The coyote went sprawling, and Nate slowly advanced. The coyote stood. Its legs wobbled for a minute then it became more steadfast. Ryan stared at Nate, and he could see the hatred even in those greenish-yellow eyes.

Nate thought back to what Ryan had said about his mother, back to what Curt had said about him and his family, and his determination resolved. He lunged forward and collided with Ryan once more. The wall was only a few feet away, and Ryan was pushed up against it. Nate held him there, long after he heard Ward call an end to the match. Their eyes met, and Nate refused to release him until the message had been received loud and clear. His grip relaxed, and Ryan slipped to the ground, cowering. Nate turned on his heel and headed for the locker room, never looking back.

At the end of class, Curt and Sam were paired against each other. It was a pretty unfair fight, but the only other bird in their class was a small sparrow, so it was the only feasible pairing. The golden eagle was able to get the red-tailed hawk to the ground in a matter of seconds, and Ward let them out early.

As with any transformation, the students would not return to their human form until they were back in their dorm rooms, a locker room, or someplace they had set aside a change of clothes. On occasion, a student would be seen streaking naked in human form. The school kept plenty of towels and robes in storage areas or closets just for this reason.

Nate joined the group once again, and then he and Baako headed down to practice with the rest of the team while the others went out onto the sports fields.

John frequently kept his camera in his locker. During some sports, he would sit out and photograph some of the students as their animals, but today he was going to photograph Nate and Baako's practice. He grabbed the camera as they changed and then joined them heading out onto the fields. When they reached the fields, they turned left, dodged a cheetah, and walked until they reached the dark space in the wall. They walked through it and in several minutes reached the Jeka fields. There was a huge archway that opened up onto the watching area. John took this door while Baako and Nate headed out to practice.

Practice went better than it usually did. Team co-captain Chris Johnson was with his girlfriend and was joking and laughing with her, disinterested in running practice. The guy who had just gotten with the best-looking girl in the lower-senior class told the rest of the team they could do whatever they wanted. Baako and Nate broke off with two seniors and passed the ball around.

"Hey, Nate," called one of them, who had just passed the ball to Baako. "I heard you put Ryan in his place."

"I heard you pushed him off the tree," said the other one, laughing as he caught the ball Baako had just kicked. He threw it to Nate.

Nate didn't say anything. It was a bittersweet victory, even if Ryan was a rival and instigator. "You should've seen the beating he gave him in Combat today," said Baako, obviously proud of his best friend. "Nate left the room before the kid even stood up on his four spindly legs."

"Really," said the taller of the two seniors. "I get the feeling no one likes Ryan. I don't, and I haven't even spoken to him."

"I don't like him either. He's a sarcastic twit," interjected the other boy.

Practice had only lasted an hour, and before Nate knew it, he and Baako were walking down the tunnel with John, who was showing them his pictures. Unbeknownst to them, he had actually spent most of his time with Jasmine, but she'd left ten minutes before and John, talented as he was, had snapped some good ones in his limited free time. The best were of Nate running for the score zone and one of Baako performing an impressive leaping catch.

They met Curt and Sam on the cliff, and they all headed down to dinner.

"Good practice?" asked Sam.

They both grinned.

"In a sense."

"Not too bad. Johnson got with Abby, so he was in a good mood for a change," said Baako. "I think I played my best without his voice in my ear."

The group walked in silence. Curt dropped back a few steps and, as he did, tugged on Nate's arm. Nate tensed instinctively, but relaxed when he saw Curt's face.

"Nate, I'm sorry about last night," Curt said, extending his hand to shake. "You didn't deserve that. I'm with Olivia now, and all that stuff is behind us."

Nate grasped Curt's hand. "Thanks."

Chapter 11
Lost in the Snow

"PROFESSOR, I HAVE a question." John fidgeted in his seat.

"Then ask it." Professor Mathews didn't seem to be in the best mood. They were sitting in first-period Mind and were in the middle of outlining a paper. Most of the class had already looked up in anticipation of anything that could give them even a second of respite.

"Why are we all beautiful?"

Everyone burst out laughing. Mathews stared at John, stunned, almost amused. "Excuse me, Mr. Reynolds?"

"Well, you know? I mean, look around. There isn't anyone in the classroom or even at this school really who isn't good-looking and in good shape. I mean, what is the likelihood of that?"

"Well—"

John boldly interrupted him: "I mean, there is probably some reason that all naturals are beautiful, like something to do with surviving and all that, but I mean as far as artificials, no one knows what we will become until it's done. It isn't in our gene structure. So why?"

The class looked expectantly at Professor Mathews. Some of them were glancing around and nodding to themselves. Nate had never really noticed this himself, but now that John mentioned it, it stood out more clearly than ever.

"I guess ... well ... you see ..." Mathews floundered, trying to find the right way to begin. "I don't think I've ever been told, but I have a pretty good idea. First of all, naturals are descended from other naturals. The process may skip many, many generations, but every natural has a relative like them somewhere along their family tree. They are genetically predisposed to being strong and healthy as a survival mechanism. They are attracted to and pair with other naturals like themselves so the species can survive. So, as you said, John, naturals need to survive and it is what Professor Hurst touched on in the meeting a week ago. The body is extremely smart. It knows how to heal itself. It knows how to balance out your blood even when gravity tries to pull it down. All of this is subconscious. The makeup of a natural—and of any animal—is entirely bent on survival and procreation. All animals have attributes that help attract a mate. This trait exists in most humans, but it's very powerful in naturals."

There was some immature snickering at this. Nate rolled his eyes, and Mathews actually smiled at him.

"Since there are so very few of us, we are born, genetically, almost perfect. It's not harmful to the survival of regulars if one, or even a hundred thousand of them don't pass on to the next generation; but with us, with naturals, we can't afford to dilute our gene pool. So, naturals are, in a sense, hard-wired to be attracted to other naturals."

"So what about artificials? Does it mean we just randomly reproduce? I mean, we aren't naturals, and our bodies don't know how they will change until it happens." John leaned forward across the table. "Can anyone be an artificial?"

"Well, you're here, aren't you? Doesn't that tell you enough?

Unlocking is dangerous. Not everyone is cut out for it, and some can't go through it and live to tell about it. Your bodies are built in such a way that perhaps you will become an artificial. It's the charge of this school to help you make the transition, to make you a natural. You are predisposed to be an artificial. Some people aren't at all, and those people could never be an artificial. There are three tiers. The first is the average human who has no ability to unlock more potential. The second is an artificial to whom that extra brainpower is available but just beyond reach. These people—you—are prepared to become an artificial, and therefore you are able to make the transition. We make sure that all friends of naturals who come to Noble are already predisposed to be an artificial. The third stage, as you might've guessed, is a natural."

The class sat mesmerized. No one had really wanted to ask the question they'd all been thinking about, perhaps thinking that asking might somehow shatter the unbelievable world they had been exposed to.

"Each of you are here because you have the potential to learn and master the skills and knowledge of your natural student colleagues. No one is invited to this school unless they have exhibited rare intelligence, physical strength or both. You need both to become a natural.

"Baako and John are here—not just because they're Nate's friends—but because each of them—of you—were exceptional at your previous schools. When Nate was recruited by Noble, it was anticipated that Baako and John would join him. We knew both boys were strong enough to face the challenge. The same is true of all of you. Each of you were the best and brightest," Professor Mathews explained. "It is a good hunch that the subconscious part of your brain knew that you would become an artificial. It may be what motivated you to excel in the first place. The subconscious is wonderful and mysterious, and part of our job at Noble is to unlock it."

"Come on, Professor," said John. "That's impossible."

"Many things in life are impossible, John." He looked straight at him. "Yet they happen, don't they? A human turning into an animal is impossible. A person making it rain is impossible. Our job is to remove the letters 'i' and 'm' from the word impossible."

This left John and the entire class sitting there dumbstruck.

"I know this is an intriguing subject, but please return to your outlines."

"How does he expect us to write about the part of our brain that learns other languages when he just said that? My head is still spinning like a top, and it's showing no signs of ever stopping," whispered Nate to Baako.

"No idea," Baako tossed back.

"Williams. Shut up and work on your outline!"

"Well, guess show-and-tell is over," John whispered.

"Reynolds!"

"Yes, sir. Sorry, sir." John focused on his outline.

By the end of the class, the only one who had finished his outline, and even started his essay, was John. Everyone else was lucky if they had added a single point to their outlines after John had asked his questions.

"Come on, John," said Sam, catching up with them as they left the nauseating tunnel that was the Mind hallway and entered out onto the field. "Couldn't you have waited until, I don't know, the end?"

"Sorry, Sam. I honestly thought it would stump him and he'd use the rest of the time to try and explain."

"And of course you're the only one who listens, and it all automatically registers so you can keep on working," hissed Curt. "My mind is still spinning with the hundred thousand things that need to happen for one thing to transpire in a certain way."

"Shut up, Curt. It was an awesome question, John. How did you think of that?"

Curt glared at Nate but didn't retort.

"I don't know. I mean, didn't you guys ever notice that every single girl in this school is at least pretty, and most of them are beautiful. I mean, it's so unlikely."

"Yeah, I guess so," Nate admitted. "But I still don't understand how you have time to formulate stuff like that, what with work, practice, and everything else in between."

Nate stopped and looked at John. "Sorry. I meant Jasmine and work."

"I know what you meant, Nate, don't worry about it." John never got angry. He might become quiet for a bit, which was what he did then, but he never retorted. He thought things through too much to be a hothead, whereas Nate was the complete opposite.

"Hey," said Baako, who had been walking along in silence. "The snow hasn't stopped."

"Wow!" They all ran to the floor-to-ceiling windows that curved along one side of the fields facing the dorms.

It had been snowing for three days. Anything from flurries to full-blown blizzards that lasted for hours had hit Noble, but it had never actually stopped. There was only really a three-hour window when everyone was asleep for some reason or another that it could have stopped, but Nate doubted it. He had asked Smith in yesterday's lesson, ironically on certain types of blizzards, why it hadn't stopped.

"I mean, I watch the Weather Channel at home sometimes. I have never seen any place on the East Coast get more than like three feet at a time. I mean, with the wind, it's impossible to tell, but that's definitely more than three feet. It's got to be at least five, and in some places, the drifts are up to like twelve feet," said Nate after trying—and failing—to make a snowflake the size of a quarter with Rebecca's name on it.

"Well, no one really understands the weather," said Professor Smith as he showed Nate his fist-sized snowflake bearing his name. "But I can tell you this: There isn't this much anywhere else in New England right now. For maybe fifty miles around us, it's been snowing. But nothing like this. We've had at least three more feet than anyone else."

"Really?" John's curiosity was piqued.

"Yes." Professor Smith concentrated on making a blizzard hit directly above Baako's head.

"So ... why?" asked Nate, who'd completely given up on making named snowflakes and was contributing to the considerable snowfall over on the other side of the table. Baako's head now looked like it had a white Santa Claus hat on it.

"Well, if I had to guess, I'd say it has something to do with you."

"Me?" Nate almost choked.

"Not you particularly. I mean all of you. It's one aspect of our kind that I never understand. When something is happening— something big that everyone is focused on—you all contribute in some way. I probably contribute too."

"What do you mean 'contribute'? You mean this snowstorm is us? I couldn't make this storm. I don't know anyone who can," said Nate.

"All of us together," Smith interjected. "It's already snowing, that's for sure. But we all contribute. We make it stronger and make it last longer. We are all thinking about the snow so much that we sort of make it happen."

"That's so cool," said Baako, shaking like a dog to rid himself of the snow that hadn't already melted off his head and shoulders.

The next morning, the walls were made of ice. *Fitting*, Nate thought as he sat up in bed and looked out the window. It was still snowing violently. He blinked and then looked closer.

He leapt out of bed, pausing only to pull sweatpants over his boxers before making the mistake of once more taking the quick way down to the ground. He hit the ice with all his weight and lost his footing, His feet slid out from under him, and he landed on his backside.

"Ow!" Nate struggled to stand, but it was quite difficult on the smooth floor. He kept slipping and landing on the ground. Every time, his tailbone throbbed. He finally crawled over to the couch and pulled himself up onto it. He then used it as a support as he edged much more carefully toward the floor-to-ceiling windows, and yes, there was snow piled up against the first six inches or so of the window. A huge drift ran down from the window like a small mountain and dissipated almost fifty feet away on the edge of a small stream.

Nate ran and slid out the door, almost bumping into Curt. He used his socks to slide rather than walk over to the stairs. He grabbed the railing and headed down to the first floor. He finally arrived at the hallway to Rebecca's room. He reached it in a matter of seconds; the room was directly below his. He knocked furiously and almost lost his footing again as the door opened almost immediately. Rebecca grabbed his arm and steadied him. She was wearing pajama pants and a T-shirt, but looked like she'd been up for quite a while.

"Nate, what's wrong?" she asked, looking concerned.

"Nothing. I just ..." He couldn't help himself. He slid into the room and smiled. The only light in the room was the light in Rebecca's loft. The window was completely black, and it was slightly lighter at the top.

"It reaches up to my window." Nate pointed at the black wall.

"Really?" Rebecca was stunned.

"What's the height of the snow outside the door in the common room?" asked Jasmine, groggily poking her head out of her second-floor loft.

"No idea, I didn't even look. I just wanted to see your room. I didn't believe it. We never had more than a couple of inches at home."

"Yeah, I know. It's great." Rebecca's enthusiasm was contagious.

"Yeah. Just lovely." Jasmine looked beautiful, even though

it was obvious she'd just woken up. Her blond hair was tousled, and her face was completely devoid of makeup. "So why did you have to wake us up, exactly?"

"I just wanted to see the drift. Sorry."

"It's fine. I was about to wake her up, anyway. And you didn't wake me up," said Rebecca.

"You were?" asked Nate and Jasmine at the same time. She laughed, and her angry mood vanished immediately.

"Nate, what do you say you go get dressed, and we can head down for breakfast?"

"Yeah, yeah. Sounds good. I'll go get dressed, and we'll go to breakfast. If we can get out the door, that is."

He left them to change and with one last giddy look at the black window, he began his arduous journey back up to his room.

"Wow," said Nate.

"Yeah," Baako agreed. He was directly behind them. He, Baako, and John had headed down to the common room about five minutes earlier and had been stopped in their tracks by what they saw. The common room was somewhat like a much larger version of the rooms at Noble. It looked like the hollow of a tree except the entrance was an arch, not a hole, and it was glass, not open air. The archway was almost as tall as the entire building, so it stretched nearly a hundred feet. There was snow halfway up it. They were still in pause mode, dumbfounded on the platform just outside their hallway. People bottlenecked the hall behind them and crowded the common room.

"What do we do?" Nate heard one of the girls down below ask.

"I don't know," said another.

"They can't expect us to get to class in this."

"Oh, come on," John shouted over the hubbub. "It's just a bit of snow."

"A bit of snow? That's taller than my house!" retorted one kid.

"Well, someone's got to try," Nate said.

"How about you?" Ryan suggested from the platform above and to their right.

"Yeah, yeah. All right," Nate pushed past everyone else on the platform and made his way down the stairs. They watched as he made his way through the crowd. Most of the people he passed helped him along the ice, and he soon stood before the large glass door, which thankfully opened inward.

"Well!" shouted Ryan.

"I'd stand back," Nate said to the people around him. They took his advice and backed up about ten feet. Nate grabbed hold of the door handle and after several seconds, he pulled. The door sprang open, but nothing happened. Nate stared. There was a wall of tightly compacted snow in front of him. It was so tightly packed that none of it had fallen in when he had relieved the pressure of the door.

"Wow."

The whole crowd laughed.

"So now what?" asked the senator's granddaughter. She was standing several feet back from Nate.

Nate stood there for a minute and then knew what to do. He concentrated on the snow directly in front of him—only the patch that was in the doorway. In a second, it was gone. In its place, water rushed into the common room and lapped around the feet of those immediately behind him. It ran all the way through and hit the walls. When everyone looked up, there was a block gone from the snow wall exactly the size and shape of the glass door. It extended about ten feet into the drift. Everyone cheered except for Ryan. Nate led the way with Baako and John following close behind, clearing a path through the snow. He wasn't quite sure exactly where the main building was, but he just followed his instincts. After around fifty feet, they cleared the roof, and the tunnel through the snow became a huge trench with ten-foot-high walls. They were so focused on what they were doing, they didn't look behind them, and when they finally did, there was nothing.

"Weren't the others following us?" asked Nate.

"Yeah. There should be like seventy plus kids following," John agreed.

"They probably diverted from our path for some reason," Baako guessed.

"To what path? It's not like we met a road sign," John said incredulously.

"Some sophomore who probably had a better idea of where the school was in relation to the dorm must have realized we were going the wrong way," Nate explained.

"Yeah, we are, aren't we? We should definitely have been there by now."

They all stopped after moving away another ten-foot-deep block of snow.

"So, now what?" asked Baako.

"Well, um …" Nate realized they were both looking at him because he was the reason they'd been able to get out of the dorm in the first place. "This stuff is pretty damn compacted, right?"

"Like dry concrete," John blurted.

"Right. So let's make a ramp up to the top and see where we are," Nate suggested.

"Ingenious." John rolled his eyes

"Well, I thought it was a pretty good idea," said Nate, deflating slightly.

"How about we just follow the path back to where they diverted and follow their trail?" Baako seemed to have become the voice of reason.

"Good idea." John glanced at Nate. "A ramp? Honestly, Nate?"

"Yeah, yeah. Let's go," said Nate.

They turned and followed the trench back. It felt like they'd gone nearly a mile when they reached the place in the tunnel where it turned to the trench.

"Wow. We were oblivious for *that* long?" Nate stared down the new, much-larger and more-used trench.

"Someone must have turned into a bird when they were unsure," said Baako.

"Yeah, probably."

"Well, come on," said John.

They turned down the new trench and followed it. After a much shorter amount of time, they reached the main doors.

"And to think we could've been here already," said John.

"Yeah. And be in Language," Nate added.

"And have eaten." Baako grinned.

"Right. Well, then. Thanks, Nate," said John.

They opened the door and entered the forest. It was much warmer and less windy in the forest, and they all relaxed a couple of notches.

"We might even be in our free," said John.

"Nonsense!" Nate said. "It's deserted."

"Do you think there's another all-school meeting?" asked Baako.

"Nah. Probably just everyone's in class. If anyone has first period free, they're still asleep."

Nate headed into the forest toward the stairs. They went up the stairs, passing the pond and the gorge until they reached the very top of the stairs where the tree stretched up above them, and the branches became mismatched and thin. The field stretched out before them, empty like everything else.

John was about to venture forward when Nate held out an arm. "Look."

The other two looked and saw a figure walking away from them toward a seemingly blank wall. Nate and Baako waited until the figure had disappeared then crept forward.

"Nate," hissed John, "we're missing class."

"Oh, come on. There's only like ten minutes left. Plus, aren't you interested in where he just disappeared to?" asked Nate.

"I am, but I'm not going to creep after Mathews, especially when we have class."

Nate looked exasperatedly at Baako, then at John. "Well then, see you at break," Nate said as the two crept off into the grass.

John shook his head at their retreating backs then turned and headed for the Animal Language hallway. He was going to have to think of a pretty good story to explain his two best friends' absence.

Nate and Baako crept across the field to the seemingly blank wall. Once there, they pressed their hands up against it.

"Nothing," said Baako. "It's like he just walked through it."

"Wait." Nate inched along the wall until Baako heard a whisper of triumph. "Come here."

Baako crept over to Nate and looked at him blankly. "Nate what the—"

"Put your hand against the wall right here." Nate pointed to a gray spot on the wall. Baako placed his hand on the wall, but there wasn't a wall—his hand went into open air.

"It's a passageway made to look exactly like the walls around it. It's genius!"

"How come we never saw this before?"

"I don't know. Come on." Nate stepped into the passageway. Several concealed hallways branched off it until they reached one that was lit. They followed it to the end, where they came upon a huge mahogany door. There was a very thin bar of light creeping from under the door, only visible because the last light on the ceiling was ten feet behind them. The two bent down to the crack between the door and floor and listened. At first, all was silent. Then they heard Professor Mathews's voice emanating clearly from inside the room.

"Do you think he's close?" the voice asked.

Surprisingly, Carter's voice answered: "I think he's got a

ways to go. You know what he wants?"

"I know what he wants, of course."

"Why is John insisting we wait to tell him?"

"I don't know, maybe ..." Mathews's voice trailed off.

"Do you suspect him?"

"Hurst?" Mathews sounded incredulous. "No, of course not. Why, do you?"

"I don't know. I asked him about it the other day and—"

"And what?"

"I think someone's outside the door."

Nate swore under his breath. He and Baako turned and sprinted back up the hallway. They ran until they passed several corridors and darted down the last one before the door even opened. They reached the end of the new hallway and slammed into a door. The two waited for several minutes then crept back down the hallway and out the secret entrance. They ran as hard as they could into the Animal Language hallway. When they entered, they collided with John and tumbled to the floor.

"Nate. What the hell?"

Nate was about to reply when he noticed Professor Bell standing at the entrance to the classroom, looking curiously at them.

Chapter 12
A Deathly Truth

"DOES CARTER THINK Hurst has something to do with all this?" Sam asked in disbelief.

"Yes," Nate said. He had answered this five times already. "That's what it sounded like, but Mathews disagrees."

"Who do you think knows Hurst better?" Curt stared at Nate with rapt attention.

"Seems like Mathews does," Baako chimed in. "Plus they were both Mind professors. Hurst probably trained Mathews for the job. He may have even been his assistant for a while."

"Wait a minute! So who is *he* and what does *he* want?" John chose this moment to jump in.

Baako and Nate had waited until after classes to tell the others what they had overheard. They were in a secluded spot on the fields outside their class hallway; the girls were preoccupied with some new gossip and were barely paying attention.

"I think the 'he' they were talking about is the murderer, but both Mathews and Carter seem to know what he wants." Nate shook his head.

"Do you think they were referring to a student?" asked Curt.

Nate glared at him and didn't answer, so Baako did. "I doubt it. It sounded like they were talking about something or someone who can move around. Most students are stuck on this campus."

Buzzing filled Nate's head. He shook it to clear his mind, but he was unsuccessful. Next came a dull throbbing in the front of his head that escalated into a full-blown stabbing pain. Every word was like a knife.

"Nate, are you all right?" Rebecca was the only girl who had begun to pay attention. Nate winced.

"Yeah, fine. Just tired, and I've got a bit of a headache."

"Let's pick it up after homework," Sam suggested.

Nate woke up very early Saturday morning. He groggily turned to his clock and tried to make sense of the red blur on the screen. The numbers finally focused, and Nate noticed a little number six on the far left of the display. He looked out the window, but all he could see was the blackness of the night. Their room was also black, and Nate was unable to discern what the walls were made of today. He rolled out of bed and dressed quietly. He then tiptoed down the stairs and out the door into the hallway beyond.

Within another two minutes, he was outside walking in the crisp air. There was a small sliver of light on the horizon reflecting on the icy frost that covered the ground.

As Nate walked, he watched as the small light on the horizon began to glow and spread across the sky, lighting the landscape. He walked between a trench of snow, much smaller than the one several days ago. The temperature had reached fifty the day before, and the snow had melted to around two feet or so of compacted ice.

The first weak rays of sunlight hit his face. They became

warmer, while every other exposed part of his body remained cold. Nate felt the solid frozen earth beneath his feet and looked ahead; he was only about one hundred yards from the edge of the cliff. The late fall air was cool and pleasant. It smelled like spring due to the melting snow. He felt rejuvenated.

As he reached the cliff and saw the Sun make its first full effort to rise above the horizon, he sighed. It had been several months since the last sunrise he'd watched. The cool air rushed up from the valley far below and pushed Nate backward, filling his nostrils with the sweet smell of crisp mountain air. He felt calm, almost peaceful.

He felt the air push away all his worries and problems. He stood there for twenty minutes, until the Sun had found its place low in the sky.

On the way back to the dorm, he noticed a doe walking on slender legs upon the frozen ground. Something about the way she walked made him realize that this was the first real animal he'd seen in quite a while. He stopped for a moment in the full shadow of the building and watched it silently. It nosed its way across a tiny patch of grass, looking for bits that were still green. Obviously finding none, it bounded off into the woods.

"Where did you go?" asked John the second Nate opened the door.

"I just went for a walk."

"Alone?" John asked in disbelief.

"Yeah, alone. I didn't go too far. It's Saturday. Why are you awake?"

"Dunno," John answered, reclining back upon the couch. "I woke up and couldn't go back to sleep so I went up to see if you were awake, and your bed was deserted. Leave a note maybe? And the rules, Nate. I know you're used to getting out of stuff, but in the present circumstances, that's dangerous in more ways than one."

"Yeah, I know. I just needed it, and I wasn't really thinking.

Next time, I'll leave a note. I thought you'd be asleep long after I got back."

"Do you know what tomorrow is?" asked John with his eyes half-closed.

"No. My head has been spinning nonstop for days, and I have this constant damn headache."

"The E.T.s are coming tonight at midnight. I guess you can call that tomorrow."

"Really?" Nate perked up.

"Yes, really."

Nate's mind was filled with the images Professor Wilson had showed them. He flipped through everything from the old black and white images of meetings with ambassadors to the more modern hi definition photos actually taken by naturals on far distant planets.

"Hey!" shouted John, startling Nate. Baako fell out of bed and hit the floor with a loud crash. "You've been sitting there staring into space for the last minute. Are you all right?"

"Yeah," said Nate unsteadily. "Yes, I'm fine."

In the background, Baako cursed and muttered something about "pillow floors the next time John shouted." He got back into bed and pretended to sleep. John and Nate looked at each other and began to laugh at the same moment. "Hey, Nate. What's your problem with Curt?" asked John.

"Not really a problem," corrected Nate. "You heard what he said."

"Yeah, but Nate, everyone says stuff like that, even you, and they usually don't mean it. Plus, he apologized. I think he really meant it."

"I know; we shook hands. I'm just getting tired of all the jealousy. It's not like Rebecca dumped Curt to be with me. She wasn't dating anyone. And Ryan! I didn't do a damn thing to him. And all of this stuff about my parents! I never even tell anyone about, about Dad or Mom."

"I know, Nate." The conversation trailed off from there and they both dropped off to sleep—Nate with a pillow on the floor and John lounging across the couch.

The door crashed open, and Nate turned lazily on the floor. He opened his eyes in time to see Curt stride through the doorway.

"What's going on? Why you busting in here?" asked Nate groggily.

"Guess what Sam did last night?" Curt blurted.

"Didn't I tell you to stop slamming the damn door?" Baako was now fully awake and began pulling his socks on with exaggerated slowness.

"Right." Curt smiled contritely. "I'll try to cut down on that."

At this, Baako snorted loudly, but no one else laughed.

"Let me try," said Nate. "How about he went to sleep because you guys must have left here at around two? I was asleep two hours before that, I'll have you know."

Curt shook his head, but decided not to answer.

"So?" prompted Nate. He was now fully awake and tired of guessing and screwing around. He wanted to hear the news without further delay.

"Remember the girl Olivia was comforting the night after we found out about the vampire?"

They all nodded—even Baako, who wasn't interested in the least bit.

"Well, they took a walk last night," said Curt, putting heavy emphasis on the words, "and now they're inseparable. I woke up to a pretty, quiet girl sitting on my couch. Either she's joining our group, or Sam's taking a leave of absence 'cause I don't see that ending any time soon."

"Sam won't leave us," Nate said dismissively. "The girls will make her feel welcome."

Curt waited in their room while Baako and John got dressed. Baako took longer than usual to get ready.

Baako was unusually subdued when the group gathered in the common area to go and have breakfast together. Nate knew his friend was troubled and had a pretty good notion why. Everyone in their group now had a partner—except Baako.

When the group left, all holding hands or displaying some sort of affection, Baako stormed off, running hard down a trail leading into the woods.

"What's up with him?" Sam asked.

"Just leave him alone. He'll be fine." That's what Nate said, but not what be believed. He had never seen his usually effusive, positive friend act like this.

After breakfast, John and Nate found Baako underneath a tree on the fields where they had sometimes gathered to relax and gossip. "Baako! How about we go find you someone to go with you to the landing tonight?" Nate said as they approached.

Baako didn't answer for several minutes. "I need a little more time alone," Baako said as he stood and walked off quietly toward the pond.

"Come on, Baako! I've never seen you beat yourself up so much over not having a girlfriend!" John shouted after him.

"And I never would you idiot!"

Nate sprung to go after Baako, but John held him back.

"Let him alone, for now," John said. "He'll talk to us when he is ready."

About an hour later, Baako stepped into the locker room. He began to speak in a voice so soft, Nate could hardly hear him. "My sister, Imani. She's dying."

John and Nate didn't know what to say.

"Brain cancer. She started having headaches. The MRI results came back yesterday. Dad called me this morning. She has five years, at the most. Chemo won't buy her any time. It's very early on, but it's in a completely inaccessible area. I can't …

I just can't ..."

Nate saw two glistening drops slide down Baako's cheeks. He'd always been such a strong person; bad news didn't ever visibly hurt him. Looking back, Nate remembered Baako's reluctance to get ready this morning. He must have been talking to his father. Nate now felt horrible. He stood and put a hand on Baako's shoulder. Baako grabbed it with both of his and began to cry in earnest.

With the strongest person he knew crying against his arm, Nate began to think. He had never quite grasped what life was— how it could be taken and destroyed by simple words. A death sentence could break the strongest person, and Nate felt utterly lost. He could always count on Baako to be the strong one. Nothing ever got him down and he lifted up their group when it was needed most. Now, it seemed the roles had been reversed, and Nate was not prepared to take his place.

"Please," pleaded Baako. "Please just keep this between us three. I can't stand too many people knowing."

Nate and John nodded dumbly as their friend stood and wiped his eyes on a nearby towel. He shrugged out of Nate's grasp and headed outside. John and Nate followed silently. They stumbled upstairs behind him and out into the fresh air. The bright sunlight blinded them as they headed out to the dorm.

Chapter 13
E. T.

ALL OF THE petty problems that had plagued Nate over the last couple of weeks seemed to vanish that moment in the locker room. Homework and the last Jeka game, anger toward Curt, and even Ryan, all seemed insignificant now. Nate knew Imani well, and he couldn't imagine a world without her. She was so young and vibrant, and when Nate pictured her, he saw a bright light that was slowly growing dimmer. This image disturbed him to no end.

The day had passed well under the gloomy circumstances. Baako was understandably quiet and didn't seek company. Even Nate sometimes found himself silent. He was usually impulsive and talkative, but he had become much more withdrawn. They were expected out by the lake at 11:30 pm.

Nate and John waited in their room. Baako had left for a walk around the dorm and told the guys he would catch up with them later.

"It's crazy," said John, breaching the silence. "I never think about death. It just never crosses my mind. To tell the truth, the first and only time I thought about it was when you were in a coma, Nate. It's mind-blowing to think that something could be eating away at our lives without us even knowing it. It scares me." John paused. "You almost died. What was it like being in a coma?"

"Waking from a coma is like waking from a nap. You're not sure what time it is, but you have a sense of restfulness and energy. You think that less time has passed than what the clock says. The change came so soon after that I just never had time to think about it. I mean, from what Hurst said, it was possible that everything could have just ended there."

"I think we need to live every day like it's our last," John said.

"It's also mind-blowing that we're going to meet beings from light-years away in just a couple of hours," said Nate, trying to lighten the mood.

"Yeah, that's for sure. When I was much younger, I would sit outside for hours, staring out at the night sky and wondering if I would ever meet E.T.s. Now it's really going to happen. It's absolutely crazy, but it's also a really weird feeling."

"Yeah ... I hope Baako comes back soon. He loves that stuff."

"He will. I never thought I'd see Baako Clark break down like that. I'm sure he'll be able to push it to the back of his mind for tonight at least."

The dorm door opened without a knock.

"Um, yeah ... what?" Nate was staring open-mouthed at the doorway where a stunningly beautiful girl in a short blue dress stood. She had a dark complexion, dazzling hazel eyes, and a wide, but shy smile. Baako stepped in behind her.

"By the way, I found someone to go to the landing with me tonight. Nate, John, Erica," he said, gesturing to the beautiful girl.

Nate and John gawked at the girl.

Nate was the first to break out of his stupor. He got up and crossed the room to shake her hand.

"Hi." Erica's voice was clear and sweet.

"What year are you?" Nate asked, sounding like an excited boy.

"I'm a junior."

At this, John and Nate gave Baako approving and admiring looks then they all began to laugh.

"Did I miss something?" asked Erica sweetly.

"Oh, yes. Everything," said John.

"No, nothing," said Baako, violently shaking his head at John. "We should head down to the common room and get ready to leave."

"Yeah, sure." Nate and John put on their shoes and each grabbed a coat on their way out. They tripped over their own feet as they watched Erica with Baako.

"Can juniors come?" John asked. "I thought it was just for sophomores and freshmen."

"Anyone can come. It is required for underclassmen," said Erica, simply.

Nate watched the spring in Baako's step as he walked beside Erica. When they reached the common room, Sam and Curt joined them, each with a girl clinging to them—Curt with Olivia, and Sam with the nameless pretty girl. Nate and John looked at her, waiting for an introduction.

"Isabella," said Sam, winking at Nate. Nate and John greeted her.

Soon their excited group grew to include Rebecca and Jasmine. Rebecca joined Nate and cocked a brow at Isabella and Erica. Nate whispered something into her ear and she nodded, smiling. She moved forward to engage the two of them in conversation.

John sidled over to Nate, while Jasmine joined Rebecca in greeting the others. "So that was quick."

"Tell me about it," said Nate, softly. "I hope he's all right. It seemed a little too quick."

They looked like a group of kids going to their prom in very cold weather. They all dressed warmly. Nate and his friends were rather carelessly dressed, however Rebecca wore tight jeans and high-heeled boots. She had on a white double-breasted coat that flowed to her hips and wore her hair glossy and curly. Jasmine and Olivia were similarly dressed and Erica, eccentrically. The only girl among them who looked casual was Isabella. She had a simple beauty and didn't need ornate or high-fashion clothes to look her best. Nate had to slap himself several times to pay attention to Rebecca instead.

Nate and his friends were leading the cluster of freshmen and sophomores from their dormitory, and as Nate looked around, he noticed similar groups. Something made the pathway that stretched around the main building glow.

Rebecca was saying something about Horticulture, but Nate was only pretending to listen. His head was already filled with images of the coming night. Professor Wilson had said that she would not show them pictures of the ambassadors because it was better for them to be surprised. For this reason, Nate's imagination ranged from little green men to blobs that were unrecognizable as life.

The main building of Noble was gigantic. They walked around the great modern structure for almost ten minutes. Their feet tread upon the same faintly glowing path. It had been forbidden for anyone to transform on the way to or at the landing. Several owls hooted mournfully as they fanned out and sat upon the grass where the teachers checked them all in.

Someone pushed into Nate; he didn't have to wonder at who it was. He watched the unmistakable back of Ryan gradually growing smaller ahead of them. He was holding on to a very pretty girl who Nate had spoken to only once. It blew his mind that this beautiful girl had ended up with Ryan. He had probably gotten inside her head.

Nate and his friends were some of the first to arrive and chose the prime location—directly in the middle of the sitting area that looked toward the landing spot. The area was framed by hundreds of tiny blue lights that formed a large rectangle. More students flooded in until two-fifths of the school's student body sat grouped on the grass. Professor Wilson addressed them.

"They are due to arrive in twenty minutes," she announced in a loud, resounding voice. "No pictures, please." Several disappointed girls pocketed their cameras. "Ten of them will be coming. When they land, they will address you, then you will stand and form an orderly line. You will then filter through the ten of them, shaking ... well, hands and then you will be given a tour of their ship. As ambassadors to our planet, they speak English as well as can be expected."

A girl, who was much smaller than the rest, raised her hand timidly. "What will they look like?"

"You will see soon enough." Professor Wilson walked around to the back and quietly spoke to the rest of the teachers, who had gathered slightly apart from the students. Excited talk roared up around them; students speculated wildly on everything from the size of the ship to whether the aliens had hair. Sam and Curt jumped into a nearby debate about what Professor Wilson had meant by the pause before she said hands.

Despite the excitement floating around, the minutes passed by slowly. Every time Nate checked his watch, it seemed it had broken. Had it only been four minutes? Seven? Eleven? He finally gave up on his watch as a bad job and looked around.

A whisper spread through them. It was almost silent, but everyone seemed to hear it. They all stopped talking and looked up. One by one, the entire assembly of students looked up to a sight they would never forget. Thoughts of typical flying saucers each and every one of them had thought of growing up, were wiped from their minds forever.

The ship was enormous and every inch of it glowed iridescently. Through the blinding light, it was hard to get more than a rough idea of what the ship was shaped like. It was not circular. A rounded point at one end expanded until it reached its full breadth at the middle of the ship then doubled in on itself slightly to end in a flat stern where blue light could be seen. It was shaped like a fish more than anything else. The ship descended slowly and pushed the air beneath it aside to flower up into all of their faces.

The massive vessel remained suspended above the ground with seemingly nothing holding it up. The teachers had edged around to the front of the group and now led them, one by one, toward the front of the ship. As they reached the vessel, it stopped glowing and the entire front folded back on itself, exposing an opening. A platform led down from the front of the ship to the ground, and it was at this point the teachers stopped.

The beings that descended on the platform were nothing like Nate could've ever imagined. The entire student body watched as five limbed beings descended. They walked on three legs and stood upright. Their faces were flat, like cardboard masks. Nate could see no visible ears. The creatures seemed to have a mouth; it was separated from the bottom part of the face. Diamond-shaped bright-green eyes peered from both cheeks. Two narrow tubes extended halfway down their face up their cheeks and into their heads. The ends opened and moved in and out, as if they were breathing. Their bodies were covered with a bluish material that hid all but their hands, feet, and face. Each limb had two long fingers that looked brittle. Their skin reflected all shades of the rainbow. When they reached the ground, seven of them spread out in a line. Nate guessed that they were all about eight feet tall. Professor Hurst was the first to step forward and shake the hand of an older-looking being that had some sort of patch on its breast. "Welcome," he said with his arms out wide.

The alien responded with a click then spoke in English. Its voice was strongly accented in a way Nate had never heard before.

"Hello, I am __," he uttered an odd sound that Nate could not discern as any language. "Professor Hurst invited us here today as he does every other year to widen your horizons and open your minds. We are the ambassadors to Earth, but we spend most of our time on our home planet. Your race has not evolved enough to interact with visitors from other planets. Your people are driven by fear, which makes them defensive and violent. Humans seek to conquer what they do not understand. We would be seen as a threat, something to fear, maybe even savages that want to drink human blood or control your world— just like in your movies, TV shows, and video games."

The students laughed uneasily. It was true.

The alien made a sound that could only be a laugh then continued: "We have come to interact with you because you are a superior subset of your race. Your minds are more evolved, and you enjoy special powers that can be used to improve your civilization and planet. When the time is right, we will make ourselves known here with your help."

Nate was seventh in the line heading toward the platform of aliens. As he walked on the soft, moldable platform, his shoes made imprints. The students entered a large, bright space that looked completely empty, but as they walked down the center, they noticed holes in the nothingness that led to well-lit rooms. They looked into each, and Nate noticed that every one of them had some sort of screen against one wall made of the same pliable material.

They walked through one of these larger openings at the end of a hallway and gasped as they entered a gigantic space. A circular electronic-looking structure took up the center of the room. Rising from the center were large, lifelike, 3-D scales of the Earth, Moon, and Sun—each of these orbiting around the other, slowly and deliberately. Nate noticed a glowing blue dot situated in the northeastern section of the United States and knew it was what they had used to guide them to this spot.

Another alien stood at the structure and demonstrated how they used it. He pushed his finger into the dot, and the image zoomed in until they saw the very ship they were in sitting in a field by a lake. The alien demonstrated by moving his finger while it was still pressed into the image. If he stopped giving pressure then pressed it again, the diagram would zoom out until it reached the full-sized Earth again.

"We are able to use your satellites without you knowing," explained the ambassador as he scrolled around the Earth. Nate and the others watched, awestruck, until the 3-D image was brought back to the Earth, spinning on its axis and orbiting the Sun. "Your planet orbits around only one sun. Ours orbits around and between two, and unlike your solar system, we are the only planet in ours."

Nate and the other dozen students at the front of the line were then led back out to the platform, passing their classmates going in to experience the same thing. Nate was in such awe he nearly tripped as they walked down the plank to the grass below.

"Wow."

It was all anyone could say as their group walked back around the main building and back to the Transformation dormitory. They walked back in silence until they'd almost reached the dorm when Erica said what they were all thinking.

"Kind of makes you wonder what else we don't know, doesn't it?"

"Yeah." Their murmurs came out as one voice.

Chapter 14
A Simple Plan

AFTER THE BLINDING sunlight of Saturday and the overwhelming events of the night before, the sky reflected the mood in Nate's room when he awoke, rather later than usual. The walls had also obligingly changed to concrete, and the room felt cold and damp. Nate didn't want to get up and face the day—there was too much to think about. After Baako's unsuspected cheery mood the night before, Nate wondered how his friend would hold up this morning.

Nate dressed right away and headed to breakfast by himself. He finished his plate of customary strawberry French toast in five minutes, downed his grapefruit juice, and sprinted up the hill and into the Astronomy hallway. He wanted to speak with Hurst right away. He stopped dead in the middle of the hallway, realizing he didn't even know where to find Hurst's office.

Hurst didn't teach any classes, so he wouldn't have an office in any of the hallways; still, he deserved a place of honor. Nate checked the entire building. Finally, he stopped, breathing heavily, by the gorge on the third floor. He leaned over the edge and noticed stairs that were barely visible. They led from a bridge that crossed the gorge to the solid wall of the gorge. Nate crossed, nervously looking around at the seemingly endless depth below him.

The stairs seemed to go downward forever until they ran into a solid wall. There was no door. Nate searched the walls then pushed on the smooth surface. He almost fell forward as the stone slid back slightly and then right into the wall. A brightly lit, hexagonal room of diamond lay before him. Diamond stairs led out from a thick golden pole in the very center and without hesitation, Nate began to climb—fifty feet then one hundred feet. Soon, he reached a landing made of diamond. A rectangular entrance led to a golden door at its center. The door had been left partially open, and Nate could hear two men talking inside.

"We can't keep covering these up, Carter," Hurst said. "The students are bound to realize something's up during break. I mean, some of them have parents who are naturals and who must notice the pattern."

"We need to wait. Please listen to me," begged Carter. "What they want is publicity in our community, and therefore, publicity to cause panic. Do you ever read the normal's newspaper?"

"Occasionally," Hurst said indignantly.

"So, you've heard about these terrorists who cause fear and panic by attacking rarely, making threats, and simply existing?" Without waiting for an answer, Carter continued. "John, seven of us have been assassinated since school started, and when you consider how many of us there are, it's almost impossible that it's a coincidence."

"I hear what you are saying, Charles, but if we don't inform the students before they find out through rumors, it could create a much larger problem. The Special Police is on it. They are close to finding," he lowered his voice, "The Bat."

"You know as well as I do that the Special Police isn't any

closer to finding The Bat as we are to beating England this Wednesday."

"So, very close then?" said Hurst with a hint of laughter in his voice.

"You saw the Germany game?"

"I did. They were slaughtered, but the last couple of practices have gone well. Baako and Nate are strong players, and they will bring the team back to where it is supposed to be.

"Enough about sports. There is a more urgent problem at hand. How the hell did he get out anyway?"

"I don't know. No one can make sense of it. I'll have to ask Joshua."

"Just wait. That's all I'm asking. You can tell them after Christmas. You'd better just hope that the rumors don't start before then. You know what they are after, of course?"

"Of course." Hurst sounded slightly offended. "It will be fine."

There was a pause in the conversation, and Nate considered it a good time to announce himself. He knocked lightly on the door.

"Come in," said Hurst.

"Good morning, Professor Hurst. Professor Carter." Nate nodded to the two of them. Upon entering, Nate stopped dead in his tracks. He stood in some sort of entryway. The walls were still diamond, and the stairs ahead of him were golden. Five of them led up to another area that Nate could just see into. He began climbing the stairs and a look of wonder broke out over his face as he reached the top.

He was standing in an entirely circular room with a twenty-five-foot diameter. The walls were completely glass, and Nate looked out over the entire campus. The office was situated two hundred and fifty feet in the air. To the other side, Nate followed the downward slope of the roof of Noble. He could see the lake and the waterfall pounding away at its surface.

"Good morning," Hurst and Carter answered back, looking slightly startled to see him there.

"Quite spectacular, isn't it?" Hurst smiled.

"Yes, it is. Professor Hurst, do you think that I could have a word with you?"

"Of course, Nate. Charles, can you excuse us for now? I will come by your office later this evening."

"Yes. Of course. Goodbye, Nate." Carter left the room in a hurry and Nate assumed he had many things to go over so he could convince Hurst to change his mind.

"Something on your mind, Nate?"

"Yes, sir. I'm sorry to disturb you on a Sunday, but I was wondering if you could give me some advice and answer a question?"

"Of course. And as for it being Sunday, every day is a work day for me." Hurst smiled.

"Right." Nate tried to smile back, but failed. "Well, have you ever known someone who has lost a family member?"

"Yes, I've had the displeasure."

"Well, my friend Baako. His sister, Imani, has brain cancer. He found out yesterday, and I'm not sure how he is taking it."

"Ah, cancer—the silent killer. It's hard for even the best of us to deal with cancer."

"Yes, well, the main reason I came to you this morning, sir, is because I wanted to ask you whether we, I mean naturals, can we cure cancer? I know Imani. She is very young, innocent, and happy. I don't want to see her die. It would tear her family apart."

"Nate, I understand what you're going through, and it makes sense that you would think we might help. We can, but there are just several problems that get in the way. There are only three people who've successfully cured cancer in our history. It takes extraordinary brainpower. Would you like me to tell you how?"

"Yes!" The world exploded out of his mouth. "Sorry, sir."

"You must learn everything you can about cancer in general, as well as brain cancer—Imani's cancer. Where it is in the brain and so on. Read, ask anyone you can think of, and research, research, research. There's a lot of information, but once you know it, you might be able to direct certain cells of the brain to kill the cancer. It'll take at least two years to learn this, and if you are strong enough, you may be able to do it. I suggest you go to Professor Mathews and ask him about it. He may be able to help you or at least point you in the right direction."

"Thank you very much, sir." Nate got up to leave, but Hurst called him back.

"Nate, wait a minute."

Nate turned. Hurst had gotten up from his desk and was now concentrating on the floor. It moved and slowly a circular bookshelf divided into four sections rose to the surface, surrounding them and Hurst's desk. There were gaps of five feet between the bookshelves, but otherwise, they formed an uninterrupted circular bookshelf about Nate's height. Hurst smiled at Nate's amazement. He went over to a bookshelf and pulled out a slender volume.

"Take this," he said, walking forward and holding the book out to him.

The Body's Reaction to Cancer. Nate took the book and looked back up to Hurst. "Thank you, sir."

"No problem." Hurst returned to his desk.

Nate saw himself as dismissed and began to leave, but then he heard his name once more. He turned.

"Nate, good luck."

"Thank you, sir," Nate repeated. *Why can't all teachers be like that?* Nate thought as he made his way back down the diamond stairs.

Chapter 15
England

THE BRITISH PRIDE themselves on their soccer. It is no different with Jeka. Nate and Baako spent half of the next week's practices in the screening room, watching English games. What they saw wasn't good. The British were right to pride themselves in Jeka—their players were superb and their teamwork was flawless. They had won their first game against Egypt 36-9, and Egypt was supposed to be the second best team in the league.

Noble had improved greatly since the game against Germany. Their offense was flawless, but their defense, aside from Baako, needed a good amount of work. Nate and the other offensive players spent most of their field practices helping the defense get into shape. Baako had been distracted for several days, but he improved.

The days sped by and before anyone was ready for it, Wednesday arrived. The weather took a turn from its usual freezing temperatures, blustery winds, and clouded skies, and the sky was glowing with promise of the morning's sunrise.

Nate's room faced the opposite direction of the rising Sun, but he noticed the distinctive pinkish glow on the deep-blue horizon high in the sky above him. He lay in bed, looking up at the ceiling, until he could find nothing else interesting in the mahogany. Reluctantly, he rolled out of bed. It was too early for anyone else to be awake, so Nate walked downstairs, hoping his feet would tread as softly as possible. He headed over to his desk and opened his computer; now was the time to finish the half-completed animal essay on the differences between the languages of predators and prey. It was due in an hour and a half, but Nate didn't mind. He had kept a solid B in his writing class last year and could whip up a decent essay in about thirty minutes.

Light had fully breached the landscape outside Nate's room by the time he confidently tipped back in his chair. He heard Baako and John stirring as the first real light fell upon their beds. He looked up at the clock: 8:15. He printed the essay and left it sitting by the printer while he took a shower. John stumbled down the stairs, half-asleep, picked up Nate's five-page essay, glanced at it, and cursed in a muffled tone. Baako stirred and looked groggily over at John. "You didn't do the essay, did you?" Baako tried not to smile.

"No." After another minute, John snapped back to life. "I have to get it done in forty-five minutes."

"Come on, John. There's no way you're getting that done."

John didn't answer, but swung himself onto his desk chair and, after waiting for his computer to load, began typing furiously. Baako smiled to himself and looked over at the seven-page animal essay lying in his bag. Nate walked into the room with soaking wet hair and looked at Baako lying lazily in bed and John typing with intensity.

"Did I miss something? No breakfast?" he asked.

"No." Baako rolled out of bed and sauntered over to his dresser. "John forgot about the essay and is trying to get it done before nine. So, I figured we might as well not."

"I guess. I was kind of looking forward to good food." He headed over to the fridge and poured himself a bowl of cereal. "This can't be healthy."

John snorted in the background and continued furiously typing away. "You know what else isn't healthy? Not turning in an essay when you have an A average."

"True." Nate would've said something more but kept his mouth shut, because he knew John was someone who cared and put forth more effort than he and Baako together toward his studies.

By the time Baako and Nate had finished their third bowls of cereal, John pushed his computer back and the printer beeped on. "Six pages," he announced with a huge sigh. He caught a look at the clock: It was ten to nine. Swearing loudly, he dressed, ran over to the fridge, and wolfed down a bowl of cereal. Baako and Nate smirked as they watched.

When John was ready, they all grabbed their bags and left. They hurried down the stairs and almost slipped on the smooth mahogany that felt more like a slide than stairs. At the bottom, they ran into Jasmine and Olivia, stumbling out of the first floor doorway.

"Forget the essay?" asked Nate as they all hurried outside.

"It's like Mathews is messing with us," said Jasmine, disgruntled as they ran through the melting snow.

"Maybe he is." Baako grinned. He reached the door first and held it open for all of them. They said thanks as they rushed in and up the stairs. They walked in barely a minute late and took their seats in the front left table. They looked expectantly at the scarlet macaw perched on the back of the teacher's desk. It was then that Nate noticed they were the only students in the class. The macaw nodded to the pile of papers on the desk and then toward the board: "No Class."

They all sighed and pulled out their papers. Leaving them

neatly on the desk, they exited out into the middle of the yammering Amazon. No one could be expected to hear what anyone else was saying over the chattering of early morning monkeys.

The monkeys' screeches didn't die down, so none of them spoke until they left the hallway. As they stepped out onto the field, Nate said, "I wish we'd known that before we rushed here. Why couldn't she have shot us an e-mail last night and told us just to e-mail it in and get some extra sleep?"

"Dunno." John looked careworn, which was a rarity for him.

"What do you think of a second breakfast?" asked Baako.

"You've already had a first?" Jasmine shook her head.

"I don't know how we'd survive without cereal in our room." Baako laughed.

"Where's Rebecca?" Nate hadn't listened to a word of the previous conversation and was asking about the most important thing on his mind.

"She checked herself into the infirmary last night. She wasn't feeling too great. Nate? Where are you going?" Jasmine asked as he dashed off. Soon, he was out of sight.

"Checking on Rebecca, no doubt. I'll take that second breakfast," said John.

"That was quick. Did you sprint?" asked Jasmine, when Nate returned.

"Yeah, she's fine." Nate panted as he sat down at the breakfast table. "Eggs and bacon please," he said to the small fairy. He looked across the table and caught Baako's eye for a second and knew he understood why Nate had sprinted to get there.

"You should eat more than eggs and bacon." Olivia watched him through long lashes. "You've got a big game coming up."

"You know? You're right." He proceeded to order pancakes, waffles, sausages, and toast.

"I didn't mean empty the kitchen." Olivia giggled.

The conversation turned to the England game later in the day, but every now and then, one of them looked over in amazement as Nate ate continually until every one of his six plates were scraped clean. He then downed three glasses of orange juice and sat back leisurely.

"I also didn't mean eat it like it's a race," said Olivia. "You don't want to overdo it."

"Thanks for the afterthought," said Nate, grinning. "I was hungry."

"Plus, the English players look more like football linemen than Jeka players. He will need all the energy he can get," said Baako.

"So about ten of you?" asked Jasmine, laughing.

"Just about, yeah."

For the rest of the day, the other teachers were not so forgiving. Mathews gave a lecture then quizzed them at the end of class. They had a pop quiz in Transformation, but half of the questions had less to do with the actual subject than obscure things like their hair color. It was a good way to lighten the day because by lunchtime, Baako and Nate had begun to feel the pressure of the upcoming game.

People kept thumping them on the back in hallways and saying encouraging things to them as they passed. They pushed through the last of their classes and headed down to the fields with nerves, but good spirits.

The locker room was silent, which was a first. When they were all dressed, the players looked expectantly at the captains.

"We trained all year for this! Hands in!" shouted Chris Johnson.

They all got up and regained their voices at once.

Placing their hands on top of one another's, they shouted, "We are Noble!"

They ran out onto the field with new determination to the

tremendous uproar from the unseen fans. Ninety percent of the voices were cheering, but England had brought along its own fan club and they added in their fair share of boos. Nate heard the noises as if through a tunnel; it was always like this for games. Once on the field, he focused on nothing else and would not be deterred until the game was over.

The four Noble forwards ran out and joined the four English forwards in a small circle four meters wide. Nate looked up at the unnatural light that emanated from every corner of the giant dome. He heard the roar of the invisible crowd and imagined he could see them as he positioned himself in the center of the field. They spaced themselves equally around their half of the circle, and the English players did the same. When the whistle blew, the ball dropped from the referee's box into the middle of the circle, and they could use any means to get it.

Nate looked up and saw the enormous clock on the wall count down from ten: Eight. The gold stripes on the American's blue jerseys shimmered in the unnatural light, as did the silver stripes of the English players' red jerseys. Six. Nate heard the cheers from the crowd very faintly. Four. He looked back toward the center, noticing the fixed looks on the other players' faces. Two. Nate set his jaw and waited for the worst. The sound of the whistle blew unnaturally loud from all sides, and Nate dove for the center.

"A violent brawl at the center, and this barbaric match has begun."

He knocked a tall, skinny British player to the ground and looked around to see Johnson ripping the ball from another player and tossing it over his back to Corey Parker. Corey grabbed it with astonishing ease and dropped it to his feet. He began dribbling it until a British player caught him unawares and sent him flying backward. Now the British had the ball. The red player had flipped it up to his hands and was sprinting in-between diving blues.

"The English have a clear path!"

Before anyone had time to register what had happened, the British were running into the score zone cheering. Nate heard a metallic click as the AWAY on the scoreboard shifted from zero to three. He swore. He heard his fellow team members do the same as they trooped back to their positions, dejectedly. The English offense worked flawlessly and soon increased their lead.

The first thirty minutes of the game raced by, and before they knew it, the halftime whistle sent the Americans back into their locker room, dejected. Their coach, the limo driver, spoke for the first time, once they had all seated themselves.

"Listen to me!" His voice boomed. "You're playing a great game, but there's a problem: The English are playing a better one. The English have a comfortable lead so they'll get cocky ... and careless. Look for the gaps and use them to your advantage! Got it?"

"Yes, sir!" they all shouted.

"Hands in!"

"We are Noble!"

The English did as the coach predicted, but they still played almost flawlessly. When the ball fell, it landed straight into English hands. They passed, and the next pair of hands grabbed the ball and started dodging players. An English player was almost to the scoreline when Baako nailed him.

The English player flew backward, and the ball flew into the air. Baako caught it and sprinted forward. English players dove for him, but he pushed them aside. Then he saw three players in red converging on him and searched the field to find Nate. He tossed him the ball just as the English players floored him.

"Who is this kid? He's good."

Nate had the smooth yellow ball in his hands, but he was a soccer player. He dropped the ball to his feet and was off through the bewildered red players. It was here where his speed shone, and he raced past the opposing team, dodging their tackles. He kicked the ball up to his hands and before he knew it, his feet had crossed the white line. The American side of the scoreboard clicked to life: Home: 3, Guest: 9.

Bolstered by Nate's score, the Americans became confident and fearless. Assisted by Johnson, Nate managed to get another three points on the board, but the clock was ticking away. Henry got the ball and headed for the scoreline, but a British player tackled him and the ball was free. Another British picked it up and with seamless teamwork, they had the ball through the scoreline within seconds: 12 to 6. The Americans didn't let it get to them, and when the ball was released, they began their work. The British couldn't touch the scoreline as Baako and the defense kept hammering away at them.

While the defense was playing their A game, the offense was playing better. They passed seamlessly with their hands and feet and could not be brought down. The American offense penetrated the British defense and scored two more times. With the score tied, the match got even more physical as boys from both teams used any method to get the ball. Every minute or so, the game was stopped and a stretcher rushed another prone figure off the field. Neither team was playing well—or fair—and the fight continued until there was only one minute left.

Every player on the field—no matter the color of their uniform—was painfully aware of the clock ticking away and the tied score on the board. The whistle blew, and the ball dropped one last time. A British player wrestled away the ball and dove over Johnson as he rambled down the field. He dodged or pushed aside every player who tried to take him down. Baako was the only Noble left. He stood resolutely, ten yards from the goal line, watching the English player sprint toward him. When he got close, Baako made as though to run straight for the English player, slowed and then nailed him to the ground. The ball rolled onto the grass, and Baako grabbed it.

For a second, the English thought they'd won, but then they

noticed the blue player sprinting up the field. Twenty feet from the goal line, Baako noticed two English players closing in on him. He scanned the field and saw Nate was already running around to his right. Baako dropped the ball to his feet and kicked it to Nate, who got the ball and flipped it up into his arms. He turned and saw the line and ran faster and harder than he had ever in his life. Nate crossed the goal line as two desperate English players dove at his feet. He heard a roar then saw a wave of jubilant fans pour onto the field, jumping with excitement and pumping arms into the air. The team members charged Nate and piled on top of him in a mound of celebratory joy.

Baako and Nate changed and showered in the locker room and were the last two players to leave. When they emerged, Erica and Rebecca, the only two people who had stayed behind, greeted them. Rebecca hugged Nate. Erica caught Baako in her arms and placed a kiss on his lips. When they finally broke apart, he was grinning. The four of them set off down the tunnel, toward the town.

"I like this girl," Rebecca whispered into Nate's ear. He smiled in agreement.

Chapter 16
The Black Box

NATE AND HIS friends struggled through the wind and stored their bags under the bus then thankfully climbed the stairs to the second level. Nate passed a Special Police officer as he entered the bus. The man looked more like a SWAT team member than anything else. Dressed in all black with a helmet and a heavy machine gun, he nodded to Nate and gestured for him to be on his way.

It was warm and dry inside. On each side, there were two leather chairs facing a table that was anchored to the floor. Two more leather chairs faced the same table and these groupings of chairs continued to the back of the bus. Nate, John, Jasmine, and Rebecca took the second one on the right. Baako, Curt, Olivia, and Erica took the grouping second on the left, leaving Sam and Isabella to take two seats on the third grouping on the left. Nate watched the officer leave the bus and walk around it, trying to take stock of everything around them. Nate could only imagine how difficult that must be. Eventually, he met with another officer coming from the bus ahead and went to meet with the one behind. Slowly but surely, the buses rumbled down the mountain road and through the countryside. Nate looked out the window and laughed to himself as he watched the eight identical buses moving like a seamless train. The occasional person that passed had a hard time keeping their eyes on the road in front of them. The buses wound down through the valleys and out onto the highway. Nate drifted lazily off to sleep with his head on Rebecca's shoulder. It felt like only seconds later when he was jolted awake by the bus gliding to a stop. He glanced out of the window and noticed that the ground was no longer moving. Students were stretching and standing.

John tapped him on the shoulder. "Ready to go?"

"Yeah." Nate stood quickly and swayed before regaining his land legs. They left the bus and dragged their bags to the terminal. Desmond had sent the larger family jet this time because Nate had told him that Rebecca, Olivia, and Jasmine all lived in his city as well. He had also informed him about the recent threats and wasn't surprised at all to see four familiar members of Desmond's Guard when he boarded the jet. Nate exchanged a few words with one of them, and then took a seat. The others, especially the girls, looked quite intimidated by this show of force.

Nate sat back in his seat and waited until he felt the plane move. The ground sped away underneath them, and he felt the familiar light feeling as the jet lifted off the ground and they became airborne.

For the first half hour or so, the girls wandered around the jet, examining every bit of it. All of them had flown coach to Noble. They'd never been in first class, let alone a private jet. They were enamored by the luxury with which the other side traveled, and it took Nate several attempts to get them all to join in a coherent conversation.

John brought out his poker set, and they began a game of Texas Hold 'Em. After several minutes, it was clear to the three boys that the girls had no idea what they were doing, so they switched to teams: Rebecca and Nate, Jasmine and John, and Olivia and Baako. The game went more smoothly after that and soon, they were arguing enjoyably about the bets on the table.

The game lasted almost all the way home, and by the time Nate had finally grown tired of John going all in every hand—and then winning—they were fifteen minutes from the private airport. Nate looked out the window and noticed how clear the sky was. It was bright blue and the Sun was shining. He listened to Baako and John arguing about the last hand and to the three girls talking about which actor was the hottest.

Nate noticed a shadow cross over Baako's face as he glanced down at the runway. He could only begin to try to understand what he was feeling.

The plane touched down on the tarmac and headed toward a close-knit grouping of six cars. Three of these cars were large luxury SUVs and the other three were more modest sedans. When the plane stopped and the stairs unfolded, Nate led the group out the door and down to the pavement. He then proceeded to introduce Rebecca to his father. Desmond greeted her warmly and bounced over to meet her mother, who was standing shyly by a little gray car.

They talked for several minutes before Desmond returned to his vehicle. Nate kissed Rebecca goodbye and waved to his friends. Mid-wave, he caught sight of a girl standing by the door to a black Escalade. She had on a wool cap, which was doing its best to conceal her sparse hair.

Nate caught his father's eye and ran over to the car. Imani smiled broadly at him. Nate noticed how thin she was. She had been thin before, but it was startling now. Her face still had signs of life and happiness, but these were marred by shadows of pain.

"Hi, Nate!" At least her voice hadn't changed.

"Imani," said Nate. He closed the distance between them and hugged her tightly. He noticed how frail she was in his arms. She was like a little sister to him, and Nate felt tears begin to settle in his eyelashes. He ached to tell her they might have found a cure, but he kept his mouth shut. He was smart enough to know the damage that could be caused by false hope being ripped away. It was why he had told John, but not Baako, about his conversation with Hurst. They'd agreed to tell Baako when they returned home for Christmas break. Nate felt it was too much of a danger for Baako to know and to get his entire family's hopes up on something that was so unlikely and difficult. John partially agreed. He had argued that Baako would not be happy that they'd held it back for even a minute, but he had grudgingly followed Nate's lead.

Nate released Imani and smiled at her, trying to will away the tears. "I'll see you on Christmas," he said, his voice cracking.

"Of course."

Nate turned and headed back to the car. Desmond changed the subject upon his return. "I take it you haven't driven in a while?"

"Far too long." Nate laughed away the tears.

Desmond threw him the keys to the Rover and headed around to the passenger side. Nate had forgotten how good it felt to drive. He liked the feeling of power as he controlled the vehicle. Desmond, on the other hand, hammered him with questions about school. When he heard about the England game, he swore so loudly, Nate almost crashed.

"Wish I'd been there."

Nate let those words hang in the air as he turned onto their driveway and headed through the bronze gate. A black Audi pulled in right behind them, and the Guard exited. Emma and Sofia greeted him with radiant smiles. He hugged and kissed them both and then turned to look at Sofia, who was bouncing up and down excitedly.

"What is it?"

"I am in *The White Night*!" Her enthusiasm was infectious. "I have a two-minute scene with Mom."

"That's great, Sofia!" Nate winked at his mother.

Desmond led them into the house carrying Nate's bags and the rest of the family followed.

The week leading up to Christmas was very enjoyable. Nate spent most of his time relaxing and catching up with his sister. Sofia talked extensively of her acting, and there were times when Nate thought it became a little much. Sofia had played a young girl who had to keep the police busy while Emma got away. The movie was to premiere in the middle of January, and Nate would be flown to New York for the night.

Nate reminded himself constantly that he was supposed to invite Rebecca to the premiere, but he hadn't seen her since he'd been home. Baako and John came by almost every day, and Nate almost forgot that he was home. Snow fell continually, reminding Nate even more of Noble. Sometimes he caused a small blizzard in the living room, which caused the entire family to run around for minutes trying to find the open window. He decided he would have to tell them sometime soon that he was causing the sporadic weather in the living room, but he was having far too much fun with it. Every time he did this, Desmond gave him a knowing look, but played along.

Nate spent most meals describing Noble to his family. He gave them a play-by-play account of the game against England. He told them about every class and what he'd learned to do in them—that was, except for Weather. He told them about the fields and the village. They listened, captivated, and in Sofia's case, with jealous attention.

Early on Christmas morning, Nate woke and looked out the window to see the Sun, but the sky was overcast and the snow was dull. He showered and dressed before he remembered it was Christmas. He withdrew four wrapped gifts from the back of his closet. The first was also long and thin and contained a diamond necklace for Sofia. The second was small and square and was also for his sister. The third was small and square and contained a pair of emerald earrings for Emma. The last was for Desmond, who was the most difficult person to buy gifts for. Desmond owned most of the city and was able to buy anything he wished. Nate's box for Desmond contained tickets to the Dodgers' season opener. Desmond was a die-hard Dodgers fan and talked about buying the team on more than several occasions.

Nate headed downstairs with the four gifts in his arms, expecting to make himself a quiet breakfast but finding Emma making pancakes.

"Mom, it's six-thirty," Nate said, surprised.

"I know. I just woke up early." Emma gave Nate a dazzling smile. "Merry Christmas."

"Merry Christmas, Mom." Nate gave her a hug, then headed over to the glowing Christmas tree and set down his gifts next to a small pile. Emma continued cooking, and Nate took a seat in Desmond's usual chair by the window.

Half an hour later, Desmond came down with Sofia. Desmond looked at Nate. "Can you go upstairs for about five minutes? I'll call you when I'm ready."

"Yeah, sure." He got up, wondering what on earth was going on. He headed up the stairs to his room. He wondered what Desmond could be setting up, but he decided not to dwell on it. It was more exciting when he was completely surprised. Nate paced his room until Desmond called him down.

When Nate reached the last step, he stopped. Four small boxes sat evenly spaced on the kitchen counter: A jet-black box, a shining silver box, a snow-white box, and a golden box. Each box was exactly the same size. Nate looked sidelong at Desmond. "What's this?"

"I had a little more fun with your Christmas gift this year. Come look."

Nate looked more closely at the boxes. The black box had four rings embossed on the top. The silver box had a set of embossed wings. The white box had a black trident, and the last golden box had a crest with a stallion in the very center.

"Open them." Desmond could hardly contain his excitement.

Nate opened the black box and held up a white card that read: Audi R8. Nate's eyes filled with wonder. Desmond nodded, smiling. Underneath the card were the keys to an Audi R8. The silver box contained a card that read: Aston Martin Vantage and contained another key beneath it. The white box contained a card that said: Maserati Gran Cabrio and had keys beneath it. The last box contained a golden card with red lettering embossed on its surface. It read: Porsche 911 S, with a fourth set of keys beneath it.

"Whichever you want, it's yours." Desmond's grin widened.

"Honestly?"

"Honestly."

Nate looked down at the four sets of keys on the table. He picked up each, weighing them individually in his hand. Finally, he stopped for the third time at the black box and held up the Audi keys. "This one."

"I was hoping you would choose that one." Desmond closed the other boxes and pushed them into a bag. "After breakfast and other gifts, we'll go for a ride."

Nate just smiled, dumbfounded. He smiled when Sofia opened her gift and thanked him profusely. She asked why he had given her a piece of granite, but when he told her it might be diamond the next day, she became ecstatic. He smiled again at Emma's small squeal of delight over her earrings. Desmond brought him mostly back to life by clapping him on the back for the Dodgers tickets, and took him completely out of his revelry when he announced the meaning of his meeting in September in L.A. He had gone to buy the Dodgers and would be the official owner by March.

"Dad, that's great! I guess you won't need those season openers then?"

"Well, I will definitely be sitting in these seats." He smiled. "But after that, I'll probably spend most games in the boxes."

"That must have set us back a bit," said Nate, laughing.

"Just a bit."

The Sun was barely breaching the cloud cover when Nate and Desmond left the house. Desmond drove him to the Audi dealership and Nate got out of the car. He stopped in awe at the sight. A pristine black Audi R8 with a carbon side blade sat in the almost-empty parking lot. Nate walked over to the car. He felt his feet hit the cobblestone as he walked, listening as the resounding noise of his footsteps echoed throughout the property. He reached the car and stopped. The car's sleek black finish shimmered in the beautiful late-morning light. Nate pulled the signature keys out his pocket and slid into the leather seat, which felt as though it molded to his body. He explored the controls, feeling the wheel and pedals. The leather trim throughout the car was smooth to the touch. He ran his fingers over the large numbers on the speedometer and the smooth wheel.

Finally, Nate put the key in the ignition, and the car roared to life. The sound it made was even better than Desmond's Aston Martin. It roared like a caged beast. Nate relished the noise and was startled when he heard a beep. He looked up, and Desmond pulled up close to him with the window rolled down.

"Race you to the new building and back," he said with a smile. He rolled up the window and drove slowly out onto the road, where he stopped.

Nate drove up alongside Desmond, and at the exact same moment, they both sped forward. Before Nate could think twice, he had reached sixty miles per hour, and his speed was still climbing. The red hand flew over the numbers, stopping at around a hundred miles per hour. As Nate drove, he felt calm and focused instead of excited. They did a circle around Desmond's colossal building then headed back. They raced through the nearly deserted streets, staying neck and neck until they reached the country road. At this point, it became a little more difficult. Desmond shifted up and overtook Nate up the mountain. Nate shifted up twice and watched his speed hit a hundred and twenty. He flew up the hill and passed the Aston Martin in seconds. Nate could see the Aston hot on his tail as they whipped around dangerous corners at breakneck speeds. The gate to their house came into view and when it sensed the cars, it opened automatically. Nate sped through and parked in the middle of the driveway in a screech of breaks and rubber. Desmond flew through the gate and stopped parallel to Nate.

"Wow," they both said as they exited their cars.

"Dad, I can't thank you enough." Nate still felt the pedals beneath his feet.

"You don't need to." He grinned. "Too bad it will have to collect dust for the next couple months. Mind if I take it for a spin every now and then?"

"No problem. You bought it."

"True, but it's in your name."

They walked toward the house, but as they neared the door Desmond pulled him aside. "I wanted to ask you about the murders without your mother hearing."

"What about them?"

"They make me nervous, Nate. What is Hurst doing to keep you safe?"

As Nate looked at his father he got the odd feeling he knew the answer to his own question. "There is a special police force of our kind for our security."

"I was thinking of sending Clyde and a couple others back—"

"No, Dad. We're perfectly safe."

"I'll take your word for it, but if you even get the slightest hint that is not the case, you tell me, you got it?"

"I will. I promise."

Desmond nodded and clapped him on the back. "And not a word to your mother or sister."

"I wouldn't dream of it."

Chapter 17
Whispers

WHEN SCHOOL RESUMED, Nate felt something had changed. Everyone noticed it. There was an air of uncertainty and even fear throughout the entire campus. The teachers' faces were strained and none of them smiled. The students spent the entire day trying to figure out why such a sinister mood had gripped the school. Their best guess was that the Special Police was not at all closer to catching the vampire. Even the weather seemed melancholy. The clouds were a menacing dark gray and a frigid wind sent the snow into drifts several feet high. Nate knew it wasn't a coincidence that the weather was the same as the teachers' moods.

On a happier note, Rebecca was ecstatic at the thought of going to the premiere in New York, and during break, she and Nate went to see Hurst to ask permission to go. Nate felt it might not be the best day to confront Hurst with something as mundane as the premiere when he clearly had something more irksome on his mind, but Rebecca's excitement won him over.

Nate had passed Hurst in the hall when they'd left breakfast, and the look on his face had terrified Nate. It was the look of a fearful and confused man. Rebecca hadn't seen his expression and was under a different impression that something mundane would take his mind off of whatever was so serious. That was the great thing about Rebecca—she was extremely positive. At first, it'd gotten on Nate's nerves a bit, but as he spent more time with her, he began to like it.

Rebecca turned out to be right. Hurst greeted them warmly, and although he didn't sound too enthusiastic about them leaving for a weekend, he finally approved.

He just had one question. "Nate, what about security? I can't very well let two of my students travel without protection in the present situation." Hurst looked Nate full in the face.

"My father has security guards. Three of them will be in the limo when it picks us up. Don't worry about our safety."

"Of course. I should have known."

Nate hesitated. "What is going on, sir?"

"What do you mean?"

"I mean the mood since we have been back has been so bleak. Has something gone wrong with the vampire?"

"Don't worry about it, Nate. Everything is under control." Something about his tone told Nate they were being dismissed.

I wish I could believe everything is under control, Nate thought. As they left, they could almost hear Hurst's face go back to being a firm mask of fear and uncertainty.

"What do you think it's about?" Rebecca asked as they climbed up the gorge stairs.

"It's gotta have something to do with the vampire." Nate had been about to say "The Bat," but he cut himself off just in time. Only he and John knew about his visit to Hurst and about Imani, and he wanted to keep it that way, for now. He had to remind himself to start working on what Hurst had told him.

"You think? It couldn't be something a little less serious?"

"I doubt it. I mean, have you seen their faces? They're pretty much terrified. What made that happen? I think the problem is becoming much worse. Hurst is bound to tell the school something before long. They can't go on thinking we'll believe all the teachers' partners cheated on them or something."

"What? Where did that come from?"

"No idea." Nate laughed. "Just trying to lighten up the mood."

"Careful," said Rebecca seriously. "There are enough rumors running around as it is, and it's only the first day back."

"Good point."

It wasn't long before the rumors really started to fly. According to one convinced lower senior, the vampire had broken into the school over break and almost killed Hurst. Another student was almost as convinced that the vampires were amassing an army to destroy the school. Another was surprisingly close to what Nate had heard when listening to Hurst and Carter's conversation— the vampire was actually a bat. At this point, however, the theory took a complete left turn and, according to the student, the bat had carried off Hurst's son during the night.

Nate knew Hurst wouldn't allow rumors like this to spread for too much longer before he called an all-school meeting to explain. This came true sooner than Nate expected.

When Nate and his friends reached Astronomy class, they found it empty except for a note written in large, straight letters on the board: ALL-SCHOOL MEETING IN PLACE OF FIFTH PERIOD.

"Well, I guess we will be finding out sooner than we expected," said John as they left the hallway and joined the growing stream of students heading in the opposite direction. The assembly hall was packed, but despite all the people who sat waiting expectantly, not a single noise could be heard. The atmosphere had turned even more sinister. No monkeys hung from the rafters, and the usual loud chatter was nonexistent.

When the entire school was seated, Hurst stepped up onto

the stage. There was something foreboding in his step, and he didn't even need to raise his hands for silence; the entire school stared at him with curiosity and respect.

"It would be hard not to notice that the teachers and I have been somewhat distracted today." There was a general mumble of assent. "The assassination of the renowned senator in the fall was the beginning of a long list of deaths that would be impossible to string together if not for our knowledge.

"I know I first told you back when the senator was murdered that we are dealing with a vampire. This is only partially true. This creature is one of us and his animal is a vampire bat. Our government officials and those in other walks of life are disappearing and dying. You could say we are at war. The attacks, however far away they may have moved since the first in Albany, have moved closer and closer to Noble School in these past weeks—the most recent one being in Albany again, just the other day.

"I will update you with whatever news we may receive over the next couple of weeks, but it is now more crucial than ever that you obey the new rules and curfew and be careful. I called this meeting to give you the facts because no matter how harmless a rumor may seem, it fails to be harmless when it spreads fear and confusion. It is most dangerous when it spreads false facts. I know I cannot stop you from talking about these things; it is only natural. But I hope you stick to the facts and don't make anything more difficult than it has already become.

"Life is precious and rare. When you look at the anatomy of a human body, or even the makeup of a tiny ant, you realize how amazing and precious life is. If you consider life precious, the lives of naturals—and your lives—are a million times more precious. There are billions, perhaps trillions, of ants crawling in the forest. There aren't even fifty thousand of us in the world. Treasure your gifts and your lives and do not attract trouble. Be careful but not paranoid. Now, return to your fifth-period class."

The students stood as one, but there was no sound. Hurst's exiting words to them had been strong, and each one of them was thinking. It was not until they were out in the forest that the debates began rolling and noise exploded to decibels that made Nate's ears throb. He thought that, although Hurst's warning had been a good one, it would not stop the flood of rumors that were formulating in people's heads this very instant. Rumors were inevitable. People hypothesized and wondered out loud, and their wondering would become fact to others. It was like an infectious disease.

It took no time for Professor Wilson to realize that her students weren't listening to a word she was saying, so she decided to let the class out just five minutes after they'd arrived.

Professor King also realized their minds were elsewhere, but instead of letting them out early, she decided to make them focus on something to take their minds off what they'd just heard. She decided to teach them how to make something grow. The class had been begging to learn this since the year began, and they jumped at the opportunity. Soon, there were trees and flowers in bizarre shapes and sizes. Nate was particularly proud of the wolf he'd grown out of bluebells. It was beautiful, and Nate didn't care that it wasn't black or gold like his fur. He compared his creation only to Curt's daffodil-grown golden eagle.

"Nice." Nate stared at the magnificent living sculpture.

"Thanks." Curt paused and swallowed. "Nate, I really am very sorry."

Nate clapped Curt on the back and said, "I know you are. Thank you."

After class, the rumors and speculating resumed. Nate heard one student suggest to his friend, "What if Hurst is The Bat?" but the friend stamped on that one by pointing out, "Hurst is a bear, you idiot."

Nate wondered about that. Hurst was a bear, but this raised a difficult question. "Do you think it's possible to have two animals?"

"I guess it should be, shouldn't it? I mean, I think it's impossible for you to have two animals with two different triggers, but we're able to change substances and create extraordinary things," said John. "It seems logical that someone could change his configuration into an animal that was not his by default. It would take great mental power, though."

"Did you hear what that kid said back there?" asked Nate as he stepped gingerly over a fat tortoise that was lazily making its way to a small pond several yards away. "Hey, Harold!" The tortoise nodded to Nate with exaggerated slowness and continued on its way.

"Something about Hurst being The Bat. You can't be serious, Nate?" Baako's eyes were wide.

"I don't know. It's possible."

"Anything is possible, but it's not probable," Baako countered. "Look on the bright side: Class is over, and I'm personally in a mood to knock some kids out."

"Well, I don't share your enthusiasm, but it will be good to do something active."

John left them muttering something about studying, and they headed down to the Jeka fields. Practice turned out to be one of the best they'd had so far. Exhilarated by the England win just before break, the team was in such good spirits it was hard to focus on boring and routine things like drills. They ended up scrimmaging, but a lot of people ended up just rolling on the grass, laughing.

Johnson tried to pull them together after an hour and a half, but to no avail. He ended up laughing so hard he couldn't stand, let alone keep a straight face, and they left early, without any practice-ending speech. Back in the locker room, Nate looked over and noticed Baako had been hit by one of his fits of sadness.

His face was buried in his locker. It was this more than anything that told Nate he had to tell him what he knew. He knew Baako wouldn't be too happy with him, so he braced for the worst.

"Baako, I know how we can help Imani." Nate's voice was strong.

Baako turned slowly and finished pulling his T-shirt over his head. "How?"

"I went to see Hurst. He said it's possible for our kind, but it's extremely difficult to heal diseases like Imani's."

"You went to see Hurst today?"

"Well, no." Nate took a deep breath and then blurted out the rest. "I met with him just after the E.T.s came. John and I decided to wait to tell you until after Christmas."

"You decided to wait? Since when was it your decision to make?"

"I just thought it would be best not to get your parents' hopes up."

Baako stared at him. Nothing could have prepared Nate for what came next: Baako walked forward as if he were about to embrace him then raised his fist with lightning speed. Nate fell back before he event felt the blow, slamming his back into the corner of the bench. Pain seared through his body from his face and back, meeting somewhere in the middle. He collapsed against the bench. His vision blurred then turned black, and his head slumped against his chest. Baako grabbed his sweatshirt and left the room without a backward glance.

"Nate. Nate!" The voice sounded as if it was echoing through a very narrow tunnel. It ricocheted off the walls like a pinball. Then the pain came—throbbing and stabbing in his back and through his face.

Nate felt a hand grasp his arm and gently shake him. His eyes opened slowly. The pain increased, and he grimaced as he felt every part of his body scream in protest. A figure was kneeling beside him, and Nate could just make out the blond hair.

"John." Nate's voice came out as a thread of a whisper, though it echoed through his pounding head. He started to sit up, but John pushed his shoulder, forcing him back down.

"Nate, you don't look so good. I called the infirmary. They should be here any minute."

Nate groaned, not in pain, but in annoyance. He didn't want the infirmary. He didn't want to have to explain what had happened. He heard the growing chatter of voices, and his vision filled with several nurses and a doctor.

"Nate," said a young, sweet voice. "I need you to roll onto your stomach."

Nate obliged, cringing out in pain with every inch he moved. He looked out across the floor and underneath the lockers. Searing pain shot through his back and he groaned.

"What are you doing?" he heard John ask.

"We're fixing his broken ribs," responded the female voice.

The pain was soon over, and it was replaced with a dull throbbing.

"Four broken ribs. He's lucky nothing else was broken."

Nate rolled over and looked up. An elderly man with a short white beard looked at him.

"I'm Dr. O'Neil. Nate, you'll be fine. I fixed your ribs, and your nose is not broken."

Nate sat up slowly. His back hurt, but it was nothing like it had been just a moment ago.

"Nate, how did this happen? You look as though you were hit," asked the doctor.

"I *was* hit." Nate ran his hands over his face to feel if anything was wrong.

"By who?"

Nate didn't answer. He stared resolutely at the doctor.

"Nate, who hit you?" asked the pretty nurse to his right.

Nate remained silent. He stood painfully and found his shirt, leaving the doctor and nurses looking confused.

"Nate—"

"Look, I'm not going to tell you." He turned to the doctor, "Thank you, Doctor." He then marched out of the room and out onto the fields.

John exchanged a brief word with the infirmary staff before running after him. He didn't ask questions; he was pretty sure what had happened.

Nate stumbled into a bathroom on the ground floor and washed the blood off his face. He and John then proceeded to the dining hall. They sat at their usual table, which was already occupied by Curt and Olivia.

"Can you believe what some of these idiots are coming up with?" asked Curt, fighting to keep a straight face as two smaller students walked by their table, talking about the bat as though it was a misunderstood kitten.

"No." John laughed as the two students looked up angrily at Curt and hurried off. "But it makes for such great entertainment."

"Nate, what happened to you?" Olivia interjected.

Nate didn't answer. A fairy appeared by his side, and he ordered a glass of juice and toast.

Exasperated, Olivia turned to John, and asked, "Where is Baako?"

"I don't know."

Nate glanced up from the table where he had been staring and nodded toward the cliff. "There."

Baako was coming down the cliff, and when he reached the floor he made a beeline for their table.

"I've had so much fun today." Baako slid into a seat between John and Erica. "While most kids are running around scared, I'm having the time of my life."

Nate heard this but didn't look up. There was something off about Baako's voice.

"What have you heard?" John asked in a voice that told Nate he was testing the water.

"All sorts. I just passed a kid convinced the fairies are in a conspiracy with The Bat and intend to poison us. His friend said it was ridiculous. I leaned in and said you never know. That sparked quite an argument." Baako chuckled deeply.

Throughout the entire meal, Nate looked at Baako warily, all the time wondering if he was finished.

They barely had any homework that night so they spent the majority of the evening listening to absurd comments and rumors. Nate didn't hear a single thing that sounded remotely possible, and by the end of the night, he had laughed more than he had all year. It was with resentment that he headed upstairs with John and Baako to do their only assignment for the night. They finished within an hour and Curt, Sam, Erica, Jasmine, Olivia, and Rebecca all came in and they spent the majority of the night and early morning talking and laughing.

Nate spent most of the night discreetly watching Baako and subsequently, Erica. She seemed to have calmed him significantly, and Nate considered he might even get an apology that night.

When everything had died down and the others had left for their own rooms, Nate had moved up to his loft. He was lounging on his bed when he heard footsteps on the stairs below. A large outline blocked the light from entering the loft and then sat on the end of Nate's bed.

Baako looked at Nate. "How do we save her?"

Two days passed, and the mood grew heavier as daily assassination news came pouring in. An ambassador from England, an architect from Poland, and a Fortune 500 CEO had all died in the most obscure and confusing ways.

Baako, Nate, and John didn't have much time to listen, for they had begun their study of Imani's unique cancer. Baako's attitude had changed completely now that he had something positive to sink his teeth into. He became happier and forgave Nate almost immediately for waiting to tell him about the possible cure. He wasn't stupid enough to waste time being angry when there was so much work to do to save his sister.

Chapter 18
The White Night

THE LIMOUSINE PULLED up to the red carpet, and Nate heard the familiar click of cameras and saw the flashing of many bright lights. The excited murmur of journalists fighting brutishly to be the first to interview the guests filled the air.

Nate looked at Rebecca. "Ready?"

Beaming, Rebecca got out of the car. Nate took a deep breath and followed, surfacing somewhere on her right. The cameras blinded Nate as he and Rebecca made their way slowly down the carpet. All of his senses were being accosted. Halfway there, Nate spotted the rest of his family and hurried to bring Rebecca to them. When he finally reached them, a huge smile graced Desmond's face. He hugged and kissed Rebecca on the cheek, and then embraced Nate in a tight hug.

"How was the flight?" Desmond shouted over the roaring of the reporters.

"Short and comfortable!" Nate shouted back.

Desmond nodded and winked at Rebecca then turned to

notify Emma, who was being interviewed by an eager *Vanity Fair* journalist, that Nate had arrived. Nate hugged and kissed his mother as well as his sister. Rebecca smiled at the two of them, and they continued along the carpet together at a slower pace. Nate felt a little more comfortable now that he was with his family, and he was more apt to answer some of the questions being shouted at him and smile for the cameras that were shoved at him from every direction.

Unlike Nate, who had to force himself to smile at these types of things, Rebecca greeted everything with a broad, realistic smile and talked enthusiastically to anyone who approached her. Her long, billowing blue dress rustled with the slightest movement, and Nate caught Sofia casting jealous looks in her direction, yet he had no idea why. Sofia was dressed in a red strapless dress with the diamond necklace he had given her glistening around her neck. Her hair shone in its bun, and she looked beautiful.

It took about an hour to make it all the way to the door as reporters hammered them with useless questions, often repeating what the last one had said.

Nate breathed a sigh of relief when they entered through the gilded doors. The noise level lowered considerably as they walked into the theater. The seats were red velvet, and Nate, Rebecca, and his family sat in the front. Arches painted in gold made up the ceiling and the walls. The floor sloped gradually down to an elegant stage, where a red stage curtain was hanging, waiting to unveil the movie. The theater continued to fill over the next half an hour. Emma got up frequently to hug and introduce various movie stars and directors. Soon the theater was full, the lights had dimmed, and the movie had begun. Nate immediately lost himself in the rapid plot.

Two and a half hours later, the lights came back on and thundering applause filled the theater. It continued for minutes, and Nate turned to see his mother with two tear tracks framing her nose. As he watched, Desmond rose to give her a hug. Nate turned to Sofia. She was sitting still with a smile etched onto her face.

Nate put his hand on her arm. "Great job, Sofia."

Her voice was in her throat, so she simply stood and held him tight.

Nate could never have anticipated how long it would take to actually leave the building. He and Rebecca nodded, smiled, and answered questions as the majority of people swarmed to Emma. Sofia was standing next to Emma and was almost getting as much attention as she was as directors, producers, casting directors, actors, and actresses greeted and complimented her and handed her their cards.

After an hour or so, Nate was getting a bit impatient, and the door was barely creeping closer. After another hour, Nate and Rebecca reached the door and burst through it. They began down the red carpet to the limousine. They were to meet Nate's family at a hotel for the night, and Nate was eager for peace and quiet.

An explosion shattered the air. Pain ripped through his chest, arms, and legs, and he flew backward. He hit the ground with a thud. Ringing filled his head, and his vision went white. Nate closed his eyes. The light flashed brightly and then everything went black. The last thing Nate felt was pain—gut-wrenching pain in every part of his body.

"Where? Where is Rebecca?" Nate muttered as he regained consciousness for the first time since the explosion.

Desmond moved aside, and Nate saw Rebecca sitting up in bed with tears streaming down her face. When she caught Nate's eye, she lay back and smiled. Nate breathed a sigh of relief. Pain shot through his chest, and he gritted his teeth in anguish.

A doctor gently moved Desmond aside to get up close to Nate. "Nate, your lungs are still healing. Try not to take deep breaths. Shrapnel tore through your body, but we were able to get all of it out. It missed most major organs, but sliced through your left lung slightly."

"I'll live?"

"Yes, you'll live. You're a lucky young man."

The doctor gestured for Desmond to meet him outside. Desmond grasped Nate's hand tightly then followed the doctor out of the room. Nate barely noticed as they whispered just outside the door. Emma and Sofia came closer.

"You were great, Sofia." Nate smiled at his little sister. He could only speak a few words before his lungs throbbed in protest.

"Thanks." Nate could tell she was still in shock.

Emma just smiled and squeezed his hand in a viselike grip. It was clear she didn't trust herself to speak.

"You too, Mom."

Desmond came back in and gave Nate a broad smile. "Nate, you truly are one of the luckiest people I know. When they brought you here, they weren't so confident. They will have you out of here in less than a week. You're going to be fine."

Nate smiled up at his father then closed his eyes. He was exhausted. He simply let go and slipped into a deep sleep.

Chapter 19
Recovery

REBECCA HAD REFUSED to leave Nate even though all she had suffered were a couple of scratches. She stayed in his room night and day with his family until they both went back to school. She arrived back on campus in the same limousine as Nate, and they emerged together. The campus was deserted, but Nate couldn't blame anyone, for it was extremely cold and windy. He and Rebecca hurried inside, and Nate held the door for their chauffeur who carried in both of their bags. He smiled then headed back out into the Arctic-like temperatures.

Baako and John hugged him tightly when he entered. Nate had barely laid his bags on his bed before there was a knock at the door. John opened it and Nate heard him say, "Professor Hurst."

"A minute, you two."

"Of course." John and Baako left silently.

"Nate, how are you feeling?" Hurst came over to shake his hand.

"I'm shaken and hurting, but glad to be back."

"Under normal circumstances, I would have waited until I saw you in the main building during classes tomorrow, but I thought this would be something you needed to hear. Have you suspected anything about the failed attempt?"

"I don't really understand why they targeted me. Is it something to do with our world?"

"Well, yes. Do you remember The Bat?"

"Of course. Hard to forget."

"None of our students are ever taught how to create an explosion, but that doesn't mean there are not books that teach it. We believe that The Bat must've been near you and he remote-detonated the bomb with his mind. Clearly, he didn't judge the distance well because you are still standing and talking."

"Why me?"

"Before we touch on that, do you realize how unlikely it is that you had no shrapnel punctures to major organs or your head?"

"The doctors told me I was very lucky."

"More than that, Nate. Only one of us could have been so lucky. We train and use our mind so much more than the normal population that it automatically protects itself and the body it lives in. It would have been nearly impossible to stop all the shrapnel from hitting you, but the brain is so strong, it repelled the shrapnel from areas like your heart and face."

Nate had expected as much, but kept silent.

"I just wanted you to know that. Now, on a different note, we don't know why. I have farfetched theories that are as likely as the next, but nothing more. I am sorry, Nate, but there's no way of knowing why The Bat wants you dead. I'm convinced that he cannot reach you here, but even so, you must be extremely careful. Most importantly, do not stray outside past curfew! And always remain within the confines of campus."

"I will do my best." Nate was surprised by the intensity of

Hurst's voice.

"I wouldn't expect anything less. I hope you make a full recovery soon."

Then, as Nate turned away, Hurst added, "Oh, and Nate, I am assigning three Special Police agents to this dorm. I would like you to check with one of them every time you leave or return. There will always be one by the main door." With that, Hurst left.

Several minutes later, John and Baako came in.

"So what did the boss want?" John cocked a brow.

"Basically to tell me to be careful."

"So, who was it?" asked John.

"The Bat."

"The Bat?" asked Baako.

"He doesn't know why, but yes, The Bat tried to kill me."

John and Baako looked on in horror.

"Why didn't he get away with it?" asked John solemnly.

"Stupid bastard was impatient and blew up the car with his mind before I was within range. Even so, I should have died. But Hurst said that we are different, and our minds protect our most valuable organs from attack."

"Wow," said Baako. "Makes me more grateful than I've ever been in my life."

"Yeah, you could say that," said John.

"Do you think he knows more than he's letting on?" asked Baako.

Nate looked over at him and something dawned in his eyes. "Come to think of it, he probably does. Why would he tell me the whole truth, anyway?"

"He wouldn't. Who do you think he tells the truth to? Better yet, who knows the truth?"

After an hour of restlessness, Nate heard a sound. He sat up and heard the light tread of bare feet on sandstone. The sound traveled up the stairs to his loft and then his bed. He felt a weight by his feet. The weight moved from his feet to his waist then settled near his chest. He felt a hand grasp his and the cold shock of lips on his cheek. Nate smiled and held up the covers to let Rebecca slide underneath.

"It's hard to sleep," she whispered in his ear.

They fell asleep, comforted by each other's arms.

When Nate woke the next morning, Rebecca was still there, and he breathed a sigh of relief.

Rebecca felt him wake, and opened her eyes. She glanced over at the clock and, noticing the time, gently pulled the covers back. She turned to Nate and kissed him then tiptoed down the stairs to the door. When the door closed, Nate heard a slight cough.

"I slept well."

"Yeah, me too," said Baako.

"Nate?" They both smirked.

"Not too bad." Nate grinned and rolled out of bed. He lazily stumbled across the bamboo floor to his dresser.

As Nate pulled on his jeans and struggled to get a shirt on, he looked outside. It was another dull, cold day. He turned with regret back to his dresser and pulled on a coat over his polo shirt. He nearly received several painful-looking splinters as he made the mistake of running his hand down the guardrail. Each time he felt one beneath his hand, he swore then forgot and put his hand back on the rail.

"Breakfast?" asked John, walking out of the bathroom with wet, wild hair and a boyish look on his face.

"Well, we have the dining hall or our gourmet selection," said Baako sarcastically, looking over at their fridge and boxes of cereal.

"I'll take option A," said Nate. "I've had just about enough of cereal and hospital food."

"Good point," said John. "Let me get dressed."

If there was one thing that John Reynolds had going for him, it was his speed in getting dressed. Within a minute, he was dressed in a sweatshirt and jeans and had beaten Baako and Nate to the door.

When they reached the bottom of the stairs, they joined Olivia, Jasmine, and Rebecca. Rebecca gave Nate a shy smile, and they all headed out into the frigid weather.

It was a relief to enter the humidity of the rainforest. Nate shook his head as he stepped through the doors, trying to get the snow out of his hair. He heard the familiar sounds of tropical birds and other sounds of the forest as they walked along the earthy path to the Astronomy hallway. To their right, an upper senior ran at a tree and began to climb. Mid-climb he changed into a monkey and swung off through the branches.

When they entered the astronomy hallway, they found that a supernova had just exploded once more, and one side of the wall was a blur of colors and vapors. They hurried through the stormy conditions and barely stopped in time to turn and head down the cliff. Nate could just see the Sun poking through the frigid clouds as he took a seat on the far side of the dining hall.

Everything outside looked so fragile. It made Nate wonder what protected the school. Now that he thought of it, he had seen the Special Police, but the canyon that the school was in was huge. Sheer cliffs ran parallel, three miles apart, down to the end where the waterfall pounded away into the lake. The campus was at the epicenter of a natural fortress.

Olivia brought Nate out of his revelry. "Nate, how are you?"

"What? Oh, I'm great. Thanks, Olivia."

"So, what happened? We never really got the full story from Hurst," said Jasmine in her loud, inquisitive voice.

"What story did you get?" Nate was curious.

"Well, he said that you were near a terrorist bombing in New York City, but no one believes that. Even the normals know it was a targeted attack. So what really happened?" Jasmine's eyes were wide.

"Well," said Nate, notching his voice down several levels from Jasmine's. "Hurst said it was The Bat who tried to kill me. He doesn't know why."

"But we're not sure that's true," said John, cutting in.

"Well, it's likely." Baako defended Nate.

"It's true that he has no reason to tell you the full truth, but I mean, he is a good guy. Hurst is so likeable and honest. It's hard to picture him leaving someone in the dark on purpose," said Jasmine, almost shouting.

"Good point, Jasmine," said Rebecca. "Maybe dial down your voice a bit."

Jasmine glanced around and saw several people looking at her. "Oh yeah. I guess I should," she said apologetically.

Nate smiled to himself as he cut his pancakes. Jasmine's loudness never bothered him; in fact, it always managed to make him laugh. He looked up and caught Jasmine's eye for a fraction of a second. She smiled and turned to her food.

Out of the corner of his eye, he could see Rebecca looking at him reproachfully. Now wasn't really the time, Nate reminded himself. Jasmine was with John, though when Nate looked over at the two of them sitting side-by-side, he thought that they seemed rather awkward. He leaned to his right and whispered to Baako, "What's up with Jasmine and John?"

"Oh, yeah. Sorry. I forgot to tell you they split up over the weekend. No idea how they ended up sitting together. I don't even know what caused it. It just sort of happened."

"Bad weekend for romance." Nate smiled and Baako laughed. The others looked around curiously, but Baako's laugh became a cough, and their eyes turned back to their plates.

When Nate looked up again, he saw Isabella edging through the tables toward them. Nate had never really noticed how young and beautiful she was. She almost glided when she walked and seemed to be able to cheer up everyone around her. When she reached them, she took a deep breath. "Have you heard?"

"No." All eyes swung to her.

"By the way, glad you're back, Nate." She looked down at him shyly. "Anyway, a family was found dead in their house in L.A. Everything points to The Bat."

John and Baako glanced at Nate. He just shrugged. "When?"

"They think it happened about a week ago, but they just found them." A friend waved to get her attention, and she moved off with a shy smile.

Just then, Erica dropped in to take her place. She greeted Nate then took the empty seat beside Baako.

"Nate, that doesn't make any sense," said John, trying to wrap his head around the information.

"I know, it doesn't. A week ago it tried to kill me. I don't understand how it could get all the way to L.A. that day."

"There could be more than one," said Rebecca. "Think about it. All these murders have been so widespread, it seems unlikely it's just one person."

"You know, you're right. One person couldn't elude the Special Police for so long. Sounds like this is bigger than Hurst is making it out to be, which means he definitely didn't tell you the whole truth, Nate." Baako shook his head.

"That's not all." Olivia jumped into the conversation. "Hurst called a meeting the Monday after the premiere to tell us about a murder in Texas, so there's no way just one person did all of that."

Before anyone else could contribute, the hall fell silent, and Nate noticed Hurst standing at the far end. He looked almost triumphant. "I have good news," he shouted in a steady, clear voice. "The Bat was caught by the C.I.A. early this morning on the outskirts of Las Vegas. The Special Police have taken over the case and The Bat is in custody. Therefore, all imposed safety rules have been lifted and most importantly, curfew is pushed back to midnight."

A cheer went up in response, except from Nate's table. They all stared in shock.

"Didn't we just decide there was more than one bat?" asked Curt, who'd been absent from most of the conversation.

"We did," said Nate darkly. "Either they caught the others and don't want us to think there was a huge threat, or they haven't pieced it together. Either way, it's not comforting."

"I can't believe he'd be so quick to get rid of the rules." Jasmine was also concerned, but her loud voice was back.

"Yeah, it's odd." Baako looked over at one of the teacher's tables where Hurst now sat, chatting to Professor Wilson. "Nate, I'm not sure I trust him now. Something just doesn't feel right," Baako whispered in Nate's ear.

Nate didn't respond. Everyone was looking at their table, their eyes showing that they ached for fresh rumors.

Chapter 20
The Phantom of the Night

A HIDEOUS FORM stared at Nate. He couldn't make heads or tails of it. It was misshapen and ugly and leered over him, extending one scaled arm out toward him. Its arm was the size of Nate's torso. Nate backed away from the creature as far as he could go, but the arm kept on coming, elongating. Then Nate felt something give behind him, and he tumbled backward into a hole. The entrance resealed, but Nate was still falling. He fell down, down, and down, then crunch! He hit something that cushioned him slightly. Light permeated the tunnel, and Nate turned and looked down upon something the likes of which he could never have imagined.

He was lying on a layer of bones, but the layer was thin; he could see through them down into what seemed to be a pond. A face floated to the surface—it was unrecognizable. A second face floated up—a woman's face this time. Then Desmond's face broke the surface. Nate screamed.

He sat up, sweating violently. He turned and put his clammy

palm on the wall behind him. He lay down on his pillow and took several deep breaths. Fresh air. He needed fresh air. Nate jumped out of bed and was about to pull on his clothes when he realized what he really needed. The pain came and the transformation ensued.

The wolf bounded from his landing and out the door. He reached the deserted common room. He left the building and immediately breathed in the fresh winter air. He stood there, outside the building for several seconds, just breathing. The moonlight lit the land in the eeriest of ways.

Nate began to breathe more steadily. It had been just a dream—a very weird dream. He glanced around. Now that he was awake and out, he might as well look around. Nate turned quickly to check behind him, and when he was positive nothing was there, he turned his attention ahead. There was a huge form directly in front of him. A gigantic grizzly bear stood in front of him. Its eyes were almost level with Nate's, but its back rose up much higher than his. It stared at him quite pointedly then gestured with its head back the way he had come. Without question, Nate turned and headed back to the dorm.

Nate noticed figures following him and several guarding the doors. Impressive and imposing, everything from lions to cougars to bears and dogs scowled at him menacingly. The security had not lifted—it had simply become invisible. Nate hurried inside and up the stairs to his room.

Chapter 21
Time for a Change

PEOPLE WILL TIRE of each other given enough time, unless there is something that bonds them together far stronger than love. Spring approached, and Nate began feeling this way about Rebecca. She was great—beautiful, sweet, friendly. Nothing about her bothered him, he just found he didn't enjoy her company as much anymore. There was nothing wrong with her. In fact, Nate had spent the four months they had been dating searching for some sort of imperfection. He now concluded that her flaw was that she was flawless. He loved all the good things about her, but decided that loving the flaws makes two people especially close. Rebecca made comments on how she didn't like his impulsive attitude, slight anger issues, and arrogance. Clearly, she knew his flaws, but didn't love them. Unfortunately, this was not the only thing Nate was feeling; over the next two weeks, he began to feel closer to Jasmine. He found himself spending much more time with her, and he could tell Rebecca had noticed. She might have begun to feel the same thing about Nate, but it was always hard to tell with her; she kept her true feelings well hidden.

Nate was also very busy. He had Jeka, homework, and now research for Imani. Only he and John knew anything about Imani, and they worked tirelessly to help Baako with the research. Nate knew the others were bound to ask questions eventually, but for now, they just assumed they were working particularly hard on their studies, and that was good enough for them.

Although they were creeping slowly through February and nearing March, Nate couldn't help noticing that the weather had not changed in the slightest. If anything, the beginning of the new month brought more cold, wind, and snow. Although worries of The Bat and possible allies had been quelled by Hurst's announcement, the students of Noble couldn't help feeling on edge. Most people still obeyed the safety rules out of habit and uncertainty.

The Special Police had melted away into the shadows and now were only recognizable by Nate as he noticed several animals that paced certain areas. Everyone else just assumed that these animals were students in the vastness of the school. The thing that nagged constantly on Nate's mind for the majority of classes and practices was his relationship with Rebecca. Only after he had received his first D in his life and had been reprimanded for not trying at practice, did he decide that he had to talk to her. They'd been growing apart, and Nate knew that the feeling was mutual. He wanted to do it right so he didn't just go up to her during dinner and ask for a talk. He asked her whether she wanted to go into town and get a coffee with him Sunday morning. She agreed with a knowing look that made Nate feel even more uncomfortable.

When Sunday morning finally arrived, Nate dressed nicer than usual. He put on dark jeans and a button-down shirt. He tucked the shirt in and threw on a jacket. After spending several minutes fiddling with his hair in the mirror, he headed downstairs to meet Rebecca. She looked stunning in tight jeans and a plain blue shirt. She was staring out at the swirling snow and looked around when she heard Nate's footsteps on the stairs. She smiled up at him.

"Good morning. Sorry I'm a couple minutes late."

"Nate, how much time did you spend on your hair?" she asked, laughing.

"Some. How does it look?"

"Spectacular." Her eyes sparkled with mirth.

They met at the door and after they exchanged an anxious look, burst out the doors and almost sprinted through the rapidly accumulating snow to the main building. When they reached the rainforest, it was such a sudden weather change that they blinked, for no other reason than shock. Once they gathered themselves, they took one of the winding paths that led down to the fields.

The walk to the fields was quick without the usual crowds of students to slow them down. A comfortable silence surrounded them.

Because their livelihood depended solely on the Noble students, the villagers normally slept late on Sundays. The streets were deserted, and all the shops were black. In fact, the only exception was the coffee shop whose windows were cheerfully lit. A smiling elderly woman sat behind the counter, reading a magazine. The shop was warm and cozy. Nate and Rebecca took two leather seats by the window and before they knew it, the woman was standing next to them.

"Tea, coffee, pastries, juice?" she asked expectantly.

Nate gestured that Rebecca should go first, and she smiled at his manners. "Green tea and a blueberry muffin, please."

"And you, dear?"

He hesitated, scanning the menu scribbled on a blackboard above the counter. "A medium mocha, and a ... apple turnover."

The woman bustled off to prepare their orders, and Rebecca turned her attention to Nate. She looked expectantly at him.

"I guess I might as well just jump into it. I've noticed that we are growing apart." He stopped and looked at her, trying to guess what she was thinking. As usual, her face was expressionless. "Something happened after the premiere. You must have noticed it too?"

"Yes, I've noticed it. It's mutual, Nate. After the premiere and when we came back, you were just ... different. You're still a great guy, but the difference just doesn't make us work together anymore. We were never really meant to be."

Nate breathed a sigh of relief when he heard it was mutual, but he also felt a sense of abandonment. Her last statement had stung a bit. "So it's over?" he asked tentatively.

"Yes." There was no need for her to say anything else, but she continued, "If you don't mind, I noticed you at breakfast yesterday looking at—"

Nate cut her off before she could say Jasmine's name. "Yeah, I thought you had," said Nate, feeling guilty. When he looked up, Rebecca was smiling. He furrowed his brow.

"You'll be great together." Noticing how surprised he must've still looked, she smiled again. "She's had something for you from the beginning. She took John as the next best thing and let me have you. Then again, we didn't give her much of a choice, did we?"

"Yeah, I guess we didn't." Nate laughed. "I hope it won't be too awkward."

"You know we are both too mature for it to make much difference." Then, after catching the doubtful look on Nate's face, she added, "I promise."

Over the next week, Rebecca maintained her promise. Nate and Rebecca remained good friends while Nate showed his interest in Jasmine. Jasmine, delighted at Nate's attention, had almost immediately fallen head over heels. Within five days, they were inseparable, and Nate was as happy as ever.

Jasmine was a great comfort to Nate over the next weeks. Bogged down as he was with Imani, Jeka, and homework, she kept him sane and smiling. She had blond, wavy hair and bright-blue eyes full of cheer and adventure. She was almost a head shorter than Nate, but when the two of them were together, they just looked right.

The others hadn't failed to notice that Nate, Baako, and John's obsessive studying cut into the limited time they had to hang out.

"What have you guys been up to?" asked Curt. They'd just ordered dinner, and he had been the first one to start up a conversation.

"Working," said Nate.

"Nate, we don't have that much work. You guys are studying most of the day. What are you doing?"

"It's personal," Baako answered, giving Curt a look.

"Very personal," said a sneering voice. Ryan was sitting at the table next to them and had overheard their conversation.

"Don't start," Nate warned.

"I don't mean to pry, but we're your friends," Curt said, looking around at the rest of them grouped around the table. Sam, Rebecca, Jasmine, and Olivia nodded. John glanced at Baako. He shot him an approving look and John proceeded, "Baako's little sister has brain cancer. We're working on a cure."

"A cure for brain cancer. Yeah, right," said the irritating voice.

Baako turned and looked at Ryan. "Do you want to make a thing out of this?"

"No. Sorry." Ryan squeaked and quickly returned to his plate.

"Hurst told Nate that it's possible for our kind to cure it, but it takes years of research, so that's what we are doing," continued John, as if there had been no interruptions.

"I'm so sorry," said Curt.

"We can help!" Jasmine piped up, loud as usual.

"Thank you, Jasmine," said Baako. "We've got a handle on it and the more people we have, the more spread out and confusing the research. But I appreciate the offer."

It came as something of a shock later that night when Nate and Jasmine walked in on John and Rebecca hooking up. After a split second looking at each other, they all burst out laughing. Nate gestured to Jasmine that they should find another room, and the two of them left, still laughing at the irony.

Life at Noble returned to normal as the spring semester wore on. The threat of The Bat subsided as reports of murders had slowed with The Bat's arrest. Nate, however, knew better. He paid very close attention to news about unusual deaths of notable people. The murders occurred in the south or west, far from Noble.

Spring break had arrived, and the students were anxious to escape the cold and dampness of Noble. On the morning they were to leave, Nate and his friends piled gratefully into the waiting coach buses.

Nate, Baako, and John shared a jet with Rebecca, Olivia, and Jasmine back to the city, as before. This flight was almost as good as the last one, and Nate almost felt sad as he departed the plane to a waiting, beautiful black Audi R8. The sadness vanished when he slipped into the leather sport seat and felt the leather of the wheel beneath his fingers. After relishing the feeling for several seconds, Nate started the car. It roared to life, and Nate drove out of the airport. He sped up the mountain and turned in through the gate, up to his house and waiting family.

Chapter 22
Family of Four

WHEN THE STUDENTS returned on the first of April, they found welcoming warm weather. They were able to enjoy it for several hours, and then it began to rain. That was the last time without rain for the next week. The academic year at Noble ended at the beginning of May so there would only be one month left at school. With the warmer but duller weather came spring exams at Noble. Tests, essays, and papers consumed afternoons and nights.

Weekends offered little break—usually they just meant more studying. Almost no one was making it to the town and between Jeka practice and all their work, Nate and Baako found that they had barely an hour free a day.

Their game against Norway resulted in a staggering win for Noble. Their record was now 3-1 and their confidence had been bolstered. Many people were hoping for the World Cup slot this year. They had one last game against Brazil. The Brazilians were perhaps one of the best teams in the world and practices were becoming longer and harder as the captains pushed their players to excellence. Nate didn't resent the long practices, no matter how much work he had to do. It was good to have something to focus on other than how birds communicated or how to make the air humid.

Test weekend was approaching, and it was not just an exam on paper. Each student would be released into the wilderness. They would have to use the skills they'd learned throughout the year to survive a weekend on their own, and the teachers would monitor their progress. Nate was surprised these tests were still going to take place, considering the very real danger they stilled faced.

One sunny afternoon, Nate walked with John back to the dorm after dinner. Baako had said he needed to "study" in the library with Erica. They both knew what that meant but had humored him. It was nearing sunset, and the land was glowing with reds and golds. The paths were almost deserted except for the odd animal.

"How're your prospects looking against Brazil?"

Nate kept his eyes on the horizon. "All right. The annoying thing is that we are almost positive they will change their strategy completely for the game against us. So all our studying of their game tapes is probably going to end up being pointless. We could have used that time for some solid practice."

"If you are so sure about that, then why study the tapes?"

"Because we are not positive. This will be an easy game if they play the same way they've been playing all year."

"That's a pain."

Nate worried, constantly, about the hidden threat that was seemingly being covered up or—at the very least—ignored at

Noble. It had become a constant distraction during a time when Nate needed all of his focus.

Nate walked along the gorge, looking nowhere in particular. His eyes alighted upon movement to his left, and he saw Professor Hurst heading up the hidden stairs from his private office. "Professor!" he shouted as he closed the distance between the two.

Hurst stopped and waited for Nate to reach him. "What is it, Mr. Williams?"

"I just need to speak to you."

Hurst nodded. "Can you wait a minute?"

Like Nate had a choice. "Of course." A flood of concerns ran through his head.

"Great. Sorry, I have to go check with Professor Mathews on something. Could you just head up to my office now? I'll be there as soon as I can."

"Sure. Professor, I have a meeting with Professor Wilson."

"I'll tell her to expect you when I'm done with you."

With this last, rather ominous statement, Hurst nodded and hurried off toward the stairs. Nate followed the hidden staircase down into the wall then climbed the long, winding, diamond stairs. He reached Hurst's office and looked around. The office was spotless. The view out over the entire campus was stunning, especially since the rain had just stopped and everything was glistening with droplets of water.

Nate made his way to Hurst's desk and was about to sit in one of the guest chairs when he noticed an open drawer. He dropped his bag and edged around the desk to get a closer look. The drawer was filled with papers, but there was one at the very top. It was an old newspaper headline, yellowed slightly with age.

"FAMILY OF FOUR MURDERED IN HOME."

Nate pulled out the article and focused on the picture. There was a beautiful woman, smiling, with her arm around a tall, handsome man. Two small boys stood below their assumed parents. One looked about five, the other around three. The three-year-old was holding the five-year-old's hand. The five-year-old looked oddly familiar. He reminded Nate of pictures of himself and Sofia just after Nate had been found. The little boy was smiling broadly. Nate ran his hand over the delicate picture and then, slightly shaking, proceeded to read the article.

> *The Banks family has been missing for four days. Police arrived at the Banks' estate mid-afternoon yesterday to find four bodies. William Banks, his wife Nadea, and his two small boys, Nate and Andrew, were murdered brutally. Investigators are at a loss as to who the murderer was and what the motive might be. The bloodless bodies could have been submitted to some sort of torture. The look on the youngest son, Andrew's, face was one of absolute fear and confusion.*

"Nate," said a voice behind him.

Nate looked up from the article, his hands shaking. "Family of four," he said, barely getting the words out.

"Nate, I ..." He spotted the article in Nate's hand and his face fell. "I was going to tell you."

"Family of four! Four!" Nate shouted. "You. Desmond. No one ever told me!"

"We would have, Nate. Please, sit." He hurried to his desk and helped Nate into a chair on the opposite side.

"I had a little brother." Nate's voice trembled.

"Yes. Andrew."

"How is this possible? I don't remember anything!" He stared down at the picture of his family.

"The mind blocks out more than it can handle, Nate."

"You had no right to hide it from me. My father." Nate paused. "My foster father had no right to withhold the truth from me."

"We didn't, Nate. It was a mistake."

"Wait a minute. Four. Four bodies." Nate's mind was on fast-forward.

"Yes, four. Someone from the Hidden World created a mirror image of you ... dead."

"Someone?"

"Me."

"Did you murder my family?"

"Of course not! Nate, please. It was for your protection."

Nate was breathing heavily. He felt a familiar pain going through his body. He looked down at his hands and saw they were covered in fur. The transformation took less than a minute, and the huge wolf landed on the floor. Anger and confusion coursed through his powerful body. Nate felt a new and unfamiliar sensation—a tingling. He growled in protest and fought against the coming blackness. Hurst moved toward him, and his vision tunneled. He looked up at Hurst one last time before the gold wolf crumpled to the ground.

Without opening his eyes, Nate could tell he was in a hospital bed. He groaned. He was still the wolf. Focusing as hard as he could, and trying his best to ignore the pain, he slowly changed back into his human form. He covered his naked body with the sheet at the foot of the bed and looked around.

Just a moment later, there was a knock on the door. It opened. Jasmine stood frozen for a moment before she rushed over to Nate and kissed him. "Nate! How are you feeling?"

"Fine. Where's Hurst?"

"He's not here. He said you passed out in his office."

"Because of him." Nate was still furious. He was no idiot; he knew when something was being induced. Hurst had used his mind to make Nate fall asleep. "I'm tired of his lies. I'm tired of him covering things up time after time and only telling me some of the truth. Why can't he just tell me the whole truth for once?"

"I don't know." Jasmine looked shaken. She put a comforting arm around him. "Breathe, Nate. Now is not the time to dwell on it."

Nate grasped her hand gently and gave her an apologetic look. The door opened once more, and Baako and John pushed in. "Nate, you have got to stop ending up in hospital beds. As your friends, it isn't the easiest thing."

Nate smiled. "Sorry, I'll try and put a stop to this bad habit of mine."

"So, what the hell happened?" asked John, sitting on the bed next to Nate. "We heard some bull story about how you fainted due to stress in Hurst's office."

"I'm not sure I trust Hurst anymore."

"Why not?" asked Baako.

"I had a brother. Hurst and my father never told me. I found a newspaper article in his office with a headline that read, 'Family of Four Murdered in Home.' He fabricated my broken body for the police. Why was he even there that night? According to records, I don't exist. I am an unknown orphan adopted by Desmond Williams."

The other three just stared at him, at a loss for what to say.

"I'm sure he had his reasons, and he'll tell you eventually," said Baako reasonably.

"I guess so." His head was exploding, and he couldn't think or speak. Baako, John, and Jasmine noticed his discomfort. Baako and John got up.

"You need your rest, Nate. We'll check in on you later." John grasped his hand and then Baako followed him out, leaving Jasmine to help him relax.

She got on the bed beside him, lying on top of the sheets, and put her arm around him. Slowly, Nate calmed down and emptied his mind. Then he fell asleep.

Chapter 23
The Roar of the Crowd

EVEN THOUGH NATE could not see the crowd of Noble and Brazilian students, he heard their roar. It echoed all around them and the players now practicing on the field. On one side of the field swarmed players with green and yellow. Even from a distance, Nate noticed their passing and running skills were superb. On the other side were the Noble players in their customary blue. They looked almost as good, and as Nate joined his teammates, he knew they had a long afternoon ahead of them.

Johnson looked over from where he was discussing tactics with the coach and beckoned Nate off to one side. "Nate, I just wanted to tell you that you always do a good job of pulling yourself together. You're probably the best player on this team and they need you today more than any other. I know I'm the captain, but there is nothing like a young, new player to give the others motivation. Noble hasn't reached the World Cup in over ten years, and it's about time for another one. Just play your best and help the others to do the same."

"I'll do my best." Nate almost expected Johnson to add "no pressure."

"I wouldn't expect anything less. Come on. We don't want to miss the most important part."

The Brazilian players were still in their huddle when Nate walked out to his forward position on the field. When the Brazilians took their positions they appeared even older and larger than Nate had envisioned. These were men, not boys. Every one of them was at least six and a half feet tall. They also weighed about two hundred pounds each. They would be stronger and hit harder, but they might not be as nimble or quick. Being light and fast had served the Nobles well in other matches. The whistle blew, and the bright yellow ball dropped from the ceiling. The players at the center dove for it and scrambled on the ground, pulling and tugging and shoving. Suddenly, a Brazilian player broke through the pile of bodies and sprinted to the opposite side with his arms clasped around the yellow ball. It looked so tiny in his huge arms. Corey and the other mids converged on him.

"They're off!" The announcer's voice boomed out over the field.

The game progressed evenly, both teams charging up and down the field jockeying to score. Nate wondered whether the Brazilians were saving their energy for the second half. They were either not as good as they were supposed to be, or they were sandbagging.

Nate stood at the center of the field and watched Baako knock the ball from a Brazilian's hands. The ball soon reached Johnson, and he sent it flying to Nate. Nate lost no time in catching the ball with his feet and dribbling off to the opposite team's goal line. A massive green-and-yellow player floored him and took the ball.

"That had to hurt!" the announcer sneered.

It did.

The game was scoreless as Nate joined the others heading to

the benches after the whistle had been blown for halftime. They had played to a draw in the first thirty minutes. The Nobles had taken some hard hits.

When the ball dropped at the start of the second half, a Brazilian player jumped and caught it. He leapt over the two blue players who were trying to bring him down and sprinted up the field. The opposing team blocked all of their defensive moves.

Finally there was just Baako. He didn't dive in like the others; he just waited. He was still sprinting when Baako dove left and in a second, turned and brought the Brazilian player down. The crowd cheered as Baako looked around and picked up the ball. He ran without ever looking back. He did exactly what the Brazilian player had done, but then he saw two players approaching from either side. He looked forward and saw that Johnson was wide open.

Baako passed to Johnson, and Johnson dribbled the ball up the field. He kicked the ball into his hands and began to sprint. A massive green player hit him with the force of a charging rhinoceros. Everyone held their breath as the Brazilian player regained his footing and took the ball from Johnson's outstretched arms. For a while, it looked as if Johnson would not get up, but then he rose, stumbled, and fell. Two people carrying a stretcher ran out onto the field. After two minutes, they placed Johnson on the stretcher and ran him off the field.

"Quite an unfair move, even by Jeka standards."

The Brazilians played brutally. Bruised and tired, the Americans refused to fold, digging deep inside themselves. Corey was running up the field with the ball in his hands. Nate sprinted ahead of him and to his left then he heard the whistle blow. Furiously he stopped in his tracks then heard:

"Off sides. Number fourteen. Brazilian free run at Noble defense."

The Noble players cleared the field except for their defense. Nate watched as Baako set his jaw against the oncoming mass of Brazilian players. The rules dictated that the Noble players could return only once the opposing team had scored, dropped the ball, or lost it to a defensive player.

The one with the ball was running toward Baako, dribbling quickly. Baako stood there like a brick wall and waited for the player. The Brazilian tried to doge him but Baako hit him with full force and knocked the ball away from his feet. He dove for it and then the Brazilian player grabbed it again, but it was too late—the Noble players ran back onto the field.

Someone was sure to score soon. Just then, a Brazilian player broke free with the ball and flew head first over the line. The cheers from the handful of Brazilian supporters drowned out the groans of the Noble players. The scoreboard clicked to life in favor of Brazil.

As the Noble players returned to the field, Nate heard a cheer. He looked up to see Johnson making his way to his forward position. With Johnson back on the field, their confidence swelled. With only five minutes left, the Noble players renewed their fervor. The ball was almost entirely on their side for the next five minutes as the Brazilian defense barely managed to keep the Noble players from scoring. Finally, Nate saw a gap in their strategy. Over and over, two defensive players would go for the guy with the ball. He realized if he passed sideways, they would have a clear shot. It seemed so simple that Nate wondered if he was missing something. Johnson got the ball back from a center and was about to try the same thing when Nate waved his arms in protest.

"Pass!" he shouted more loudly than he'd ever done in his life.

Johnson turned and saw the gap immediately. He kicked the ball almost within reach of the two rushing green-and-yellow players, and then whipped it to his left. Nate caught the ball with his feet and flipped it up into his arms and ran toward the goal line. A Brazilian ran at him, but Nate darted to his right. The player dove into the ground where he had just been. Then Nate set his eyes on the goal line and sprinted toward it. Two players were closing in from his left. He ignored them and dashed the last few yards over the goal line.

Nate had never heard such loud cheers as the ones now emanating all around him. He saw a mass of blue then got the wind knocked out of him as every member of his team piled on top of him, hugging him and patting him on the back. The whistle blew and the game resumed for the last thirty seconds. Both teams fought hard and when the whistle blew again, it was tied 3-3.

Nate ran over with his team to get a drink while the referees decided how to handle the overtime.

Nate felt someone clap him on the back, and he turned to see Johnson standing before him, beaming.

"That's what I'm talking about."

A voice boomed from overhead. "After further discussion, the game will proceed as follows: We will work four on three with five-minute halves."

Four on three was the closest thing to soccer. It was almost like penalty shootout. For half of a determined time, the away team would have four players on their side against three players from the home team. Then, when the whistle blew, the sides would flip. The score would go back to 0-0. Whoever scored the most would win the game.

Johnson quickly called everyone over. "All right, boys. You two play defense," he said, pointing to Baako and one other player. "I will be the forward. When the whistle blows, Nate will join me."

"All right." Johnson had lost the happy smile on his face. It had been replaced with a grimace of determination. "Let's do it."

The three he'd mentioned headed out onto the field. This was the first time Nate had ever watched from the sidelines. Baako looked determined, but calm—something he'd always admired about him. The whistle blew and play began. Almost right off the bat, the same huge Brazilian player scored. No one had even gotten their bearings.

After that, Brazil scored two more times. When play began again, a Noble player got it and passed back to Baako. Baako flipped it into his arms and ran. This was football, and it was what he was made for. He dodged every player and barreled through the last one. The goal line approached, a defensive player advanced toward him hesitantly. Baako put on a burst of speed and scored. When the whistle blew, it was 9-3.

Nate jogged onto the field, feeling really nervous for the first time in his life. He took his position on the center circle and examined the players he was up against—they were just as big. The ball dropped and Johnson grabbed it. He was off before any of the green really knew what was going on and before anyone knew it, he had scored. It was now 9-6 Brazil.

Sweat glistened on each player. The field now seemed incredibly hot. Nate tried to focus on the game.

When the ball dropped once more, Nate saw an opportunity and took it. He grabbed the ball and dodged an opponent to his right. Sprinting up the field, he quickly realized that he would not be able to get around the player ahead of him. Johnson was to his right; Nate picked up the ball to confuse his opponent and then dropped it to his feet and kicked to Johnson. Then he darted around the left side of the Brazilian, and Johnson passed to him once more. The goal line was ahead of him, and no one was blocking his way. The game was tied.

There was just a minute left, and Nate was running hard, dribbling the ball quickly down the field, but as he neared the goal line, he found himself in the same stupid position he had watched all day. He looked around and saw that Johnson was open once more. He passed to Johnson and then a Brazilian floored him. Landing on his back, Nate heard the crowd groan and then their collective intake of breath. Despite the throbbing pain in his chest and his inability to inhale, he raised his head and watched as Johnson dodged another player, flipped the ball into his hands, and ran across the goal line. The game was over. Johnson offered Nate a hand, pulled him up, and then embraced him gingerly. They met the rest of their team halfway from the benches.

Chapter 24
More than Whispers

NATE WRAPPED HIS arm around Jasmine. She turned and smiled at him then gently pressed her lips to his. Nate kissed her back. They lay in each other's arms for a few minutes. Nate checked the clock. It flashed 11:00. He rolled out of bed to get dressed. As he pulled on his jeans, he noticed the air was very cold. He went downstairs to brush his teeth and dunk his face in cold water. He grabbed a T-shirt hanging on the door and pulled it over his head.

When he returned to his bed, Jasmine hadn't gotten up. She was sitting with the covers pulled up to her shoulders. She smiled at Nate then relented and got out of bed. With her back to him, she pulled on her clothes and turned to face him. She wore her usual shirt and jeans, and they headed down the stairs together.

The dining hall was almost empty. Nate guessed that since people were so used to the hellish school schedule, they didn't wake up much later than they usually did. He knew the feeling, but it was rare that he was affected.

He and Jasmine took a small table by the left window and, as usual, a fairy hurried up to them almost immediately. They ordered drinks then looked down at the stitched-in menus. When the little person returned, Jasmine ordered a bacon, egg, and cheese sandwich, and Nate asked for his customary strawberry French toast with whipped cream.

When their food arrived, they ate in silence—both were almost completely talked out after the night before. They didn't rush because there was absolutely no need. When Nate had finished, he looked around the dining hall and noticed something for the first time. Among the crisscrossing panels of glass near the floor was a glass door that opened out onto a path, presumably to the woods or lake. Nate gestured to it, and they both rose and headed to the door.

He tried the door, and it slid open easily. The lake was on their right, but that was not where the path was heading. They stopped and looked at the lake before continuing down the path into the woods. Having rarely been in the woods lately, Nate realized he would be spending the entire weekend there along with the rest of his class, so it was time to get acclimated. The plans had changed slightly for exam weekend, and they were now allowed to be together. In fact, it was mandatory. The teachers felt it would be easier to monitor them.

The path snaked through the woods and came out on the other side of the main building. As they walked, Nate and Jasmine just talked. They didn't talk about anything important or relevant, they just chatted casually. Nate relaxed as they made their way through the waking forest together. It was quieter than Nate would have expected, but he took no notice.

The trees stood tall and ominous, sentinels to a time long forgotten. The light permeated through the canopy, making the new green buds glow beautifully. Where there were gaps in the leaves, the sunlight shone through to the forest floor and lit up the leaves and trunks of the trees. The animals of the forest seemed to be quiet, but a few rustled through the leaves in the shadows. Several birds called to each other in the distance.

When they emerged from the forest, it was obvious that something was wrong. Teachers were darting from dorm to dorm, and an orderly line of students was entering the main building.

Professor Wilson saw them and ran over. "All-school meeting. Immediately."

They took the path to the assembly hall, which was supposed to be quiet, but whispers swept the hall as students debated. Nate noticed all of his friends sitting in the first row of the last section with two empty seats next to them. Jasmine and Nate made their way toward the seats. Jasmine sat on Sam's right, and Nate took a seat on Baako's left.

"Baako, what is this?" Nate whispered.

The mood was somber. Everyone looked scared or worried as they whispered among themselves.

"People are saying The Bat broke out. There was a mass killing in New York last night. A quarter of us from New York are dead."

"Jesus!"

Baako was about to reply when Hurst stepped to the front of the stage and held his hands up for silence. A hush fell like a blanket over the students, and they looked attentively at Hurst. "The situation has become more serious. As many of you now know, there has been a massacre in New York. Eight of us were killed last night, and it seems the assassins are looking for something. Some of the bodies showed signs of torture."

The students hissed a collective breath.

"Two of them were parents of a student here," Hurst continued. "I will not give that student's name for obvious reasons, but she has been taken into protection. The Special Police and law enforcement think she has become a target. There are no indications, however, that they are making their way here." When he said "they," a flood of whispers erupted again, but Hurst held up his hands. "Yes, these killings could not have been executed by just one person. The Bat has others working with him. The rules are hereby reinstated. I urge each and every one of you to strictly abide by them. There is no need to leave your dormitory except for meals, and I don't want you going anywhere other than the dining hall. The practical exams will be canceled, and the written ones will count for the entire exam grade. Please head back to your dorms immediately. Dismissed!"

Everyone stood simultaneously.

"Jesus. I guess we were right," Baako said to Nate as they headed into the crowd that was surging up the stairs.

"I'm pretty sure they know what The Bat is after, though." Nate pushed out of the door and headed along the path. "It seems that—"

"Nate Williams." Nate turned as his name was called to see Professor Carter hurrying toward him. "Nate, you need to come with me."

"But, sir," Baako protested.

"Mr. Clark, please return to your dormitory. Nate will be along soon."

Carter marched him out of the flowing stream of students and off into the woods. They seemed to be heading for the stairs, and Nate had a very good idea about where they were going. He wasn't mistaken. They headed up the stairs to the third level and then over to the ravine. They walked down unseen stairs to the diamond staircase and stopped at the door at the top. Carter knocked. Surely, Hurst couldn't be back in his office already, but his voice said, "Come in." It was clear he had a faster route from the assembly hall to his office.

Nate and Carter entered, and Hurst looked up from a huge pile of paperwork. "Nate, I need to talk to you. Please, sit down. Thank you, Carter. If you could leave Mr. Williams and I alone for a bit, I will call you back when I am done with him."

"Of course, Professor." Carter backed out of the room, throwing an odd look Nate's way.

"Nate, I am sorry to inconvenience you, but I feel I have to just put it right out on the table."

Nate looked at Hurst, feeling as though he was missing something, but saying nothing. He still wasn't quite sure if he trusted Hurst. This would be the third time Hurst was telling him something and pretending it was the end of it.

"You know that The Bat, or someone who works for him, has tried to kill you. I am sorry for not telling you before, but I only had a suspicion and it has now been confirmed." He paused to take a sip of something then continued. "The situation has become much worse. Now The Bat seems to be after you exclusively. It's time someone filled you in on who you are."

"Who I *am*?" Nate asked, puzzled.

"Yes, Nate. We have kept it from you for far too long already, and it's the reason The Bat is after you. These types of killings were happening all over the world seventeen years ago. Your parents were very accomplished in our realm and were able to do things most of us could only dream of. Your father was the head of the Special Police and your mother worked from home to help him and to look after you. Our leaders met and decided that this had gone on long enough. Your father and mother were dispatched with a special team in Southern India just an hour after the latest reported killing. They found The Bat and took him in. He was captured and put into jail. This became a habit. He broke out and your parents were dispatched to catch him as usual.

"Six years later he broke out of the highest security facility we have and found your parents almost instantly. You were only six. He wanted to murder you for good measure, but you got away. No one but you knows how you escaped, but somehow you did. I will not ask because I'm sure you can't remember right now, but I believe someday you will. You made it to the city where Desmond found and adopted you. Soon after, the murders stopped. The Bat disappeared for the next ten and a half years until last fall when he resurfaced, looking for you. It is rumored that we captured him again, but that never happened. We assume that he traveled the world recruiting people to his cause and is now coming for you to finish what he started. It wasn't that urgent back then, but it seems he is determined to find you now."

Nate stared at Hurst blankly, but his mind had spun into action.

"We assume this time, he has gathered followers. Now, he is trying to finish what he started so he doesn't have to worry about your family ever again. He thought the premiere was the perfect opportunity, but apparently failed to research the effects of a bomb on a normal human versus a natural."

"But what is he after?" Nate's mind swam.

"There is no method to his madness. He's one of us. He actually went to Noble when he was your age. We have been trying to figure out his reasons for some time, but after he attempted to kill you at the premiere and after these killings just last night, we've come to the conclusion he's been murdering all these people to get to you." He stopped to let that sink in, then continued, "Nate, I know how painfully annoying it is to have all these restrictions, but for you, more importantly than anyone else, they are crucial. You must follow these rules to the last letter. I will not have you followed, but I will impose one more rule on you. You must not, under any circumstance, go anywhere alone, not even to your common room. I know you have a good group of friends. You must always be with at least one of them when you leave your room. Is that understood?"

"Of course." Nate felt dizzy. It was so much to take in. "What about my brother and you faking my dead body?"

"Nate, I am sorry, but someone had to. You have lived this long because The Bat believed you were dead. I had to do it, and it paid off."

"Okay, I get it. I just wish you'd told me about my brother. Can you imagine being in my position?"

"No, I definitely cannot. I'm truly sorry, Nate." Nate saw sincerity in the old man's eyes, and it was then he realized that Hurst was much older than he looked. "If I could just have a word with Professor Carter for a minute, he'll escort you back to your room. I'm sorry, but it is the only time you will need to be escorted by a teacher. Nate, I wish you the best of luck. I hope you know we all care very much about you."

"Yes. Of course, sir. Thank you, sir." He got up and left the room. When he opened the door, Carter headed inside.

Nate heard him say, "You wanted to see me, sir?" before he closed the door. Nate sank to the floor. Everything he'd been told was just too much. On top of it all he'd been rushed from the room without the chance to unload some of the many questions circling his head. His head was still swimming when Carter came out and offered him a hand.

"Quite overwhelming, isn't it?" He maneuvered Nate down the hall.

"You could say that."

"Sorry we had to tell you all at once. I know it will take a while to sink in, but soon, it will all make sense."

From the sincerity of his words, Nate trusted him.

"So, what was that about?" Nate heard five people ask as he entered the room.

They all looked at him expectantly: Jasmine, Olivia, Rebecca, Curt, Erica, Sam, Baako, and John. He walked over to the couch where there was a space between Jasmine and John and gratefully took it.

"I'm fine. Hurst just told me my life's story. I'm just a bit overwhelmed."

"What did he say?" asked Sam eagerly before the glares changed his look to contrite. "Oh, sorry. Will you tell us when you feel up to it?"

Nate laughed. "Course." He took a deep breath, then launched into the short version of the story. "The Bat killed my parents because they put him in jail. He wants to finish what he started. I don't know why he killed all those people, but he did it to get to me. Hurst says I can't go anywhere without one of you."

"I'm not letting you leave this room without at least two of us by your side." Jasmine wrapped her arm around him protectively.

Nate smiled. He listened to his friends debate every part of what Hurst had and hadn't told him. Instead of joining in, he let his mind wander and soon began drifting off to sleep. After an hour of pretending to join in their conversations, Baako bailed him out.

"All right, guys. Time to wrap it up. Nate is exhausted."

They all rose to say their goodbyes. Jasmine was the last to leave. She leaned down and kissed him. "If you need me, text me," she whispered so only he could hear. Then she turned and left, slowly closing the door behind her.

"Jesus, Nate. Are you all right after all that?" John was clearly concerned.

"I'm just tired." His voice came out as barely more than a whisper.

"You should rest. It will clear your head. We'll wake you for dinner," said Baako.

"Sounds great. Thanks." He got up and took several steps before John and Baako realized there was no way he would make it to his bed by himself.

"Nate, take my bed." Baako gestured to the first-level bed then supported him as he lowered himself down.

Nate collapsed onto it and was almost instantly asleep.

"Shit," said John.

"Yeah." Baako looked down at Nate. "He'll be fine. Nate always pulls through. I've just never seen him so vulnerable."

"I didn't think he could get that vulnerable."

"Wouldn't you be?" Baako glanced at John.

"Damn right I would."

Chapter 25
Lockdown

THERE WAS SOMETHING in the room. Nate could not see what it was. It kept fluttering around in the corner, but it stayed in the shadows. He rolled out of bed and flipped the light switch by the side of the bed. The lights went on for a split second before flickering off again. The room was plunged into darkness, even deeper than before. Nate had been used to the darkness of the room and the starlight coming from the window, but after seeing the light, his eyes became unfocused. He stumbled and fell down several stairs.

His head struck a hard corner and his ears rang, though he could just make out muffled voices coming from somewhere close by. The creature was still fluttering in the corner. Nate swore loudly and ignored the voices. He pulled out his phone and used it as a flashlight to get down the stairs. When he reached the floor, he walked across the room and pointed the light up into the corner. There was a hole there.

He could see a bit of the Moon, but he didn't feel the pain he was used to. Nothing happened. Since when was there a hole in the ceiling? Nate could only feel the throbbing in his head and not the odd tingling that accompanied his change. Frustrated, he threw his phone on the ground and heard it crack, then he swore. He realized he had thrown away his light. He tried to move back across the room, but he tripped and fell over the table.

His head swam. He rolled over, but didn't try to get up. He heard the voices again, and they were getting closer and louder. They seemed to be right over him. A light split the darkness, and he shielded his eyes against it. Nate could still hear voices, but the creatures above him were not human. Nate tried to see them. They were large and misshapen. A large, furry hand extended down toward him.

Nate opened his eyes. He was sweating violently. It had just been a dream, he told himself over and over. Everything was all right. Then a hand grabbed his arm. Another covered his mouth, and he was dragged from the bed. Jasmine lay sleeping peacefully as Nate was pulled from the room. Nate tried kicking and punching, but he could not loosen himself from the iron grip of his captor. He tried yelling, but the words broke against the hand clamped tightly over his mouth. Frustrated, he stopped struggling and let himself be dragged out of the dorm. Something came in contact with his head a split second after the fresh air engulfed him. His vision swam, his ears rang, and his mind went blank.

Baako woke up with an ache in his back. He couldn't believe he'd been stupid enough to fall asleep on the couch. He looked over at his bed and decided it was all for the best; Curt and Olivia were fast asleep on his bed on top of the covers.

When he stood, his head throbbed dully. He shook himself and stumbled into the bathroom. He pulled off his clothes with his eyes half-closed and got into the shower. The warm water was relaxing, and he could almost feel himself return to his norm. He wrapped a towel around himself and proceeded to dry off.

He had just finished pulling on jeans when a noise split the morning silence. It sounded like an air-raid siren, and it emanated from every corner of their room. Baako heard the door at the end of the hallway crash open and Professor Mathews's voice shouting, "Lockdown! Get dressed—all of you—and proceed to the common room in two minutes!"

Baako heard Curt swear as he fell out of bed. The first thing Baako thought of was Nate. He sprinted out of the bathroom without a shirt.

A second later, Mathews threw open the door with a bang. He looked around the room and spotted Baako. "Mr. Clark, where's Williams?"

"He should be in his bed." Seeing the urgent look in Mathews's face, he added, "I'll check."

Baako sprinted up the stairs and found Nate's empty bed. *Where the hell is he?*

"He is not here, sir." Baako's voice cracked. He heard Mathews swear.

"If you find him, don't let him out of your sight. I have to get everyone else to the assembly hall. Down in two minutes, Mr. Clark, and that goes for your friends too."

Mathews left Baako and John staring at each other with worried looks. Olivia broke the silence. She had gotten up, dressed, and was already at the stairs. "He spent the night in our room with Jasmine."

"Dammit, Nate!" John threw on jeans and a shirt then joined Baako. They raced down the hallway and stairs to the girls' hallway. They didn't even bother knocking on Jasmine's door. They crashed through it, frantically searching for Nate.

"Nate, don't ever do that to us ... again." John's voice trailed off. Jasmine was sitting on her bed alone, fully dressed and looking terrified.

"He's gone." She burst into tears. "I don't know what happened. I woke up and he was gone. He wouldn't have gone anywhere without one of us, would he?"

"Nate wouldn't do that to us. John, we're going to look for him." Baako's stomach clenched.

"Yeah, we are," said John.

"I'm coming too." Jasmine wiped her eyes and stood up.

"No," said Baako and John in unison.

Then, realizing how cruel they sounded, Baako walked over and put his arm around Jasmine's shoulder. "It's all right. We'll find him and bring him back. We can't risk you going missing too. If The Bat doesn't catch Nate, they'll use you as a tool to get to him. We can't risk it."

"But—"

"Baako's right, Jasmine. We have to go. Come with us to the common room, and we'll leave you with Olivia and the others."

The common room was already crowded and buzzing with activity. They'd never had a lockdown before, and the gossip mill was in full swing. The fact that Nate Williams was missing was already the new topic for discussion.

Olivia saw them as they rushed in and beckoned.

"Jasmine, are you all right? Where's Nate?" She asked, suddenly realizing he wasn't with them.

"Gone," was the only thing Jasmine could manage. She broke into fresh tears and almost collapsed. Olivia grabbed her just before she fell and held her close.

"What are we going to do?" she asked Nate's two best friends.

"We'll find him," John assured. "Don't worry about us. When we leave with Mathews, we'll break off from the group and find him. I don't care what Mathews says. He's our best friend. I am not hiding in the assembly hall while God knows what happens to Nate."

Olivia knew it wasn't a good idea for her to ask to come with them, so she merely said, "Good luck."

Before they could discuss it further, Mathews came out of the fourth floor hallway. "You're all accounted for," he said, running down the stairs. Whispers rippled through the crowd, but no one raised their voice. When he reached the bottom, he carved a path to the doorway. "Follow me! Do not leave the path. When we enter the main building, go straight to the assembly hall. Don't stop and don't talk!"

He opened the doors and the students flooded silently onto the pathway. When Baako and John were clear of the door, they looked ahead. Mathews was too busy looking around in front of him to notice the two of them edging away from the group. They sprinted around to the back of the dormitory and crouched in the grass. All the other dorms were emptying in a similar fashion. The teachers were too observant, and Baako and John resigned that they would not be able to look for Nate until all of the students and teachers were in the main building.

It took a surprisingly short time for all the dorms to empty and for the students to get into the main building. In ten minutes, the coast looked clear. The Noble campus looked and sounded deserted.

Baako turned to John. "Where the hell are we going to look?"

"There's nowhere else. The mountain."

John nodded to Baako and then pain shot through both of their bodies. For a half a minute, they doubled over as they changed shape and size. Their hair changed to fur and their clothes ripped. Within a minute, a jaguar and lynx stood above a small pile of clothes. The lynx nodded at the jaguar, and they bounded off through the grass to the path that Nate had traveled the other day.

The woods were eerie and quiet. No birds called. All the animals seemed to have left. Several rays of light breached the canopy and ran over the forest floor. Far from comforting, the rays created heavy shadows where it would be easy for someone or something to hide, unseen. Baako couldn't tell whether Nate was in the woods or where he might be if he wasn't. They ran through the trees toward the inner forest, searching wildly as they went.

A bird called through the silence. Baako and John jumped; after the silence, it was unexpected to hear another sound. The bird sounded like a robin shouting, "Watch out!"

"For what?" asked Baako. He excelled in Animal Language, and they'd recently learned the language of small birds.

"Be careful. I saw a group of men earlier."

Baako was able to get most of what the bird said. "Did they have a boy with them?" he asked to the forest-at-large.

"Yes, they were dragging him."

"How many?"

"Six or seven."

Baako turned to John. John caught the worried look in his eye and turned back to the forest. "Where are they?"

"They must be heading for the other side of the lake."

"How long ago?"

"Before the Sun rose."

Baako took off into the woods, heading for the lake. It took a lot longer than they'd anticipated. By the time they rounded the corner to the shore, the Sun was low in the sky, and the temperature had dropped considerably. Baako couldn't see any sign of movement by the waterfall on the other side of the lake. This didn't mean anything at all, but he thought he would check it out, just to be sure.

"It shouldn't have taken this long." Baako looked at the lynx.

"Something is affecting us." John jerked his head left and right. "Which way?"

"Left will be quicker. We're to the left of the main building."

They ran off around the left side of the lake. The lake was in no way small, and by the time the Sun had disappeared behind the mountain they were only a quarter of the way around it. They stopped by a fallen tree to regain their breath, and John voiced something that had been bothering him for a while.

"How did they get into the dorm to get Nate? Isn't there security?"

"I'm sure the entrance is crawling with Special Police. If we've learned one thing from all these murders, The Bat is smart. They must also be masters of deceit and stealth, considering everything they've gotten away with so far."

"He could have been let in by—"

Baako cut him off. "Don't think about that now. We need to find Nate. Nothing else matters."

"Good point." Then he was jarred back to reality. "We'd better start again."

Baako didn't answer, but they both set off around the lake. When they were finally close enough to see the waterfall clearly, the moon was on the horizon and the stars were out. Clouds and trees blocked some of them, but most of them were visible. From the distance, Baako couldn't see anything, but he couldn't trust his sight. They were still about a mile from the waterfall.

"It should've taken us two hours at most to get here. I don't understand it." Baako looked worriedly at John.

"Something or someone is playing with us. I'm exhausted. They must've done something to considerably slow our progress."

Baako nodded. "It doesn't matter now."

"But it does matter."

"I'm positive they are behind the waterfall. There's got to be some sort of cave there. It's an ideal spot." They'd stopped running and were walking slowly and carefully toward the pounding water.

John just nodded in agreement. He didn't think talking was the best idea.

Baako stopped suddenly.

"What is it?" John whispered.

"Quiet." His eyes were trained on the waterfall. He could see someone moving there. "They're there. I see someone keeping watch."

"I see him too. We'd better go carefully from now on."

They inched forward, step by step. The Moon cast a great deal of light upon the lake and the forest. Baako and John had to jump from one patch of darkness to another. At points, they had to cross an open area where the ground was brightly lit by the Moon. In these situations, they sprinted across the areas together. Every now and then Baako, had the creeping feeling the guard had noticed. He shook it off assuming he would have let someone know of the disturbance. Even if he had, it didn't matter. Nothing would stop them from getting to Nate.

Soon enough, they could hear voices coming very faintly from the cave. They also were able to see the person on watch duty more clearly. He was a large man sitting on a rock to the right of the waterfall. His eyes swept one hundred and eighty degrees in a matter of seconds and began sweeping again almost immediately. They could also see the cave; it was clear from this angle. A dark space stretched deep into the rock behind the waterfall. A dim light glowed on the wall and judging by its faintness, Baako could tell that the light was coming from deep inside the cave.

"What do you think?" asked John in the faintest of whispers.

"He's big and who knows? There might be others around. I don't think even the two of us could subdue him, let alone do it quietly."

They sat there for a long time, trying to think of what to do. John couldn't help glancing across the lake to the main building, where he could see the shimmering lights of the assembly hall. He could imagine the scene there as rumors spread from one person to another that three people were now missing.

Nate was the one The Bat was looking for, and he was the one who The Bat had already tried to kill. They must know that Nate was in danger.

Every now and then, they noticed two or three teachers with

flashlights walking around the main building. They flashed the strong beams all over the place, but they had no chance of finding anything. They were obviously looking for Nate, but also didn't want to take any chances with The Bat, so they moved carefully.

They sat and waited. After a while, John, who had been staring pensively at the Moon, said, "Hey, Baako. I still don't get how the hell it's night already."

Baako glanced up. "I think it was like two when we woke up."

"Oh, yeah."

Silence stretched on. The wait was agonizing. The Moon was near the middle of the sky before Baako saw his chance. The guard turned and spoke with someone who must've been sitting below him. He nodded to John and the two of them broke cover and crept across the ground. They made it to the waterfall and hid behind two large rocks. The guards were showing no signs of stopping their conversation so Baako nodded again. Before they could creep out from where they were hiding, another person walked out of the cave and engaged the others in conversation. There were now too many people. They'd never be able to approach undetected.

The conversation between the three wore on, but their voices were muffled. *If only we could hear what they are saying,* Baako thought. It was frustrating beyond belief to sit so close, yet be so deaf. Then an idea came to him, it was so simple that he couldn't believe he hadn't thought of it before. Baako directed his thoughts to his ears. The inner mechanisms seemed to tingle, and then he could hear. He could hear so clearly and so profoundly that he could count the line of ants moving over his paw without looking down. He could also hear what was being said.

A gruff voice was speaking. "Why doesn't he just kill the boy? I don't understand why he feels the need to talk to him."

"It's like a victory speech. He wouldn't feel nearly as good about it if he didn't make the boy realize it all first."

"I'd give a hell of a lot to have his abilities. Do you think he will try and mimic them before he kills him?"

"I highly doubt it," the gruff voice said again. "It is impossible to mimic."

"Well, I am getting tired of this. He needs to get it over with. The police are probably approaching as we speak, and we just sit here waiting for Gray to finish his chat. It's aggravating."

"Speaking of him, we better get back in there."

Baako watched as the other two headed back into the cave, and the big one was left there alone again. Baako and John crept forward once they knew the coast was clear. They moved from bushes to rocks to trees until they reached the man. Just as they reached the rock behind the man, he spun around and they dropped down. They breathed heavily. Baako knew that the man was looking directly where they had been just a moment before. They lay there hoping and praying that the man would not look down. Baako's sharp ears picked up the man's breathing and the change when he turned around. Baako jumped up and lunged at the guard, hitting him in the back. He fell forward with Baako on top of him. The man's head made a nasty cracking sound as it hit the stone. The man was out cold.

Chapter 26
Between Hammer and Nails

NATE WOKE SURROUNDED by darkness. A dark-blue circle glowed subtly in the distance. It must be late. Ever fiber of his being hurt, but he couldn't figure out why. He couldn't remember being knocked out nor could he remember how he got here. The cave wall was pressed painfully against his back. He couldn't feel any bindings, so he tried to move. It was futile— he was paralyzed.

Nothing made sense. Nate tried to figure out even the smallest details, but it was pointless. He had no idea where he was or how he'd gotten there. Instead, he tried to focus on his surroundings. He was in a cavern of some sort. It either became smaller as it progressed or the opening was the same size, but very far away. It was hard to make sense of anything else.

For the first time since waking, he heard something. Voices echoed down the length of the cave. He heard the waterfall, and he slowly realized where he must be. The voices were coming closer and now the light was almost completely blocked as several figures made their way toward him. He could only see their outlines. From what he could tell, they were powerfully built with the exception of the one who seemed to be in the lead. He was slight and a good deal shorter than the rest. They walked four abreast in the tunnel and were coming close.

Suddenly, light came on and blinded Nate. The light lit up everything around him and stabbed into his eyes. Wishing he could blink, he stared blindly into the light until he got used to it. The cavern was huge, and he could see no recognizable light source.

Nate turned his attention to the people approaching. All were men. The slight one had a handsome face and seemed to command a great deal of respect. He walked several paces in front of the others. There were six of them, including the slight figure.

"Nate Williams," the slight one said. His voice was cold but surprisingly quiet and low. "Do you know how long I have waited for this?"

The group was now only ten feet from Nate, and the smaller one kept moving forward as the others stopped and watched. Nate could now see his face in more detail. He hadn't shaved in several days and had a severe five o'clock shadow. His hair was jet black and his face was tanned. He was now nowhere near as good-looking as he had seemed from afar.

"Of course, you can't answer me." He moved closer. "I suppose you are wondering why. You cannot answer me because I have been using the power you just learned for almost thirty years now. I have paralyzed every muscle that doesn't have to do with your brain and crucial bodily functions. You are probably also wondering how you stayed asleep." He was so close Nate could feel his breath on his face. "The answer is the same. Horace knocked you out, then I triggered a deep sleep in your mind to make sure you stayed asleep until I wanted you to wake."

He seemed to notice the surprised look in Nate's eyes. "Yes, we took you. You are probably wondering why I am interested in you, but before I tell you, and yes, I will tell you, I want to introduce myself. You may know me as 'The Bat,' I rather like the nickname, for I am a bat when I change, just as you are a wolf when you transform. I was born Michael Gray. When I realized you were alive, I went on the offensive. I have spent the last year figuring out who you are and tracking you down. It was easy to locate you at Noble. I could have guessed it. In hindsight, I should have guessed it."

He took a seat across from Nate, while his companions remained standing. "I learned who you were when I murdered my first senator. Yes, there have been a lot of them." He grinned showing sharp, pointed canines. "He filled me in on the speculation and details. Your parents told Hurst when they first realized you were different. I killed your parents out of revenge, and I tried to kill you, but you were a very talented little six-year-old. You changed and bit me, and then ran off into the woods. No one had ever changed that early, and no one else will. You are different. You are special."

What about my brother! Nate wanted to scream, but the more he tired to move, the more frustrated he became. This man, Gray, was playing with him. He was enjoying this.

Everything came back. Nate remembered the night as clearly as if it were yesterday. His parents and Andrew were not getting up. Their blood had stained his clothes, and he looked up at the man who had killed them. Now that Nate thought about it, it was clearly this man who was now standing before him. With fury raging through his veins, he changed and bit the man who had ruined his life. Not waiting to see whether he would get up, Nate had sprinted off into the forest, knowing he would never be able to go back. He had picked up his ripped clothes in his mouth and run as a wolf the entire night and into the next day, when he turned back into a human and continued throughout the next day and night.

"Yes, you bit me. And let me tell you, it hurt. It hurt a lot. My leg was utterly useless, and I had no hope of giving chase. From that point on until your unlocking, you repressed it. You know by now the power of the mind and that it had the power to repress your ability for eleven long years."

Confusion joined Nate's other emotions as he listened intently to the man he hated more than any other.

"You are special, Nate, but back to why I kill these people. I don't kill just to find out more about you. I kill because it maintains the order. Our society is based on secrecy and lies. We all have to make a decision. We have to join one side or the other. There is no in-between. What do you think would happen if the order was disrupted? The answer, as you very well know, is chaos. If the normal population knew of these things, it would be all over. You must understand that what I do is necessary to our very existence. There will be no age of tolerance for us. The only way that we can thrive is to remain hidden."

Nate highly doubted this, but he couldn't help but wonder if this perverted view was in fact true.

"Now, back to you. You are the last piece of the puzzle. Do you honestly think they tell you the truth? Nate, I may have murdered your parents, but that does not mean I was responsible for their deaths. You are not a natural. You are *The* Natural. You can do anything you set your mind to. You can do more than anyone else in this world. They don't teach you those things. What if they taught you how to use your full potential and you turned on them? I cannot afford to have such a powerful adversary. I can't even afford to have such a powerful ally. If you were allowed to reach your full potential, I would never be able to kill you. No one could. This is why it cannot be allowed."

Nate felt fear creep into him. Until now he hadn't thought of what Gray would do to him when he was finished talking.

"When you had your heart attack, you didn't unlock the other ninety percent of your brain. You'd already unlocked some. Why do you think I could not beat a six-year-old? Nate, you changed before anyone had ever changed. You unlocked your brain then, under severe emotional stress and a need to survive. Then, in the coma you unlocked your full potential."

Nate wanted to close his eyes and ears and think for a moment, but the new information kept pouring in.

"Isn't it such a wonderful idea to tell the students they all have unlocked their entire brain? That they can do anything? It makes them think that whatever they learn is what they can do, and they don't question the limits of their power. Nate, when most people slip into their coma, they unlock another twenty or maybe thirty percent of their mental capacity. It varies, but it's never more than thirty-five percent ... before you. You were the first and last who has unlocked everything. I saw it with my very own eyes. You changed into a wolf. Not a small wolf. You changed into the same wolf you change into today. I couldn't catch you. I couldn't even fight you. I let you go, knowing I would have another chance and knowing at that point, I had no chance.

"For a while I was confused by the reports that you were dead. It has taken me a very long time, but I finally found you. I did the math. I knew when you reached seventeen you would undergo transformation and then be recruited by Noble. What I didn't know was your identity. That's why I killed others, to get information. It has taken a very long time. Your friend, Hurst, covered things up very well, I must say. I finally found out who and what you are through the people I have murdered. In their last moments, they told me everything they knew. The adults— they know of you. The Special Police know you very well. The adults who do know are the ones who decide our lifestyle: the big-time senators, presidents, kings, architects, and ambassadors. They decide what you are to be taught and what you are to be told. When students graduate Noble, they are told the truth. You are just getting it early because you will never graduate Noble."

How can he be so sure of himself? Nate wondered.

"I set out to find and kill your parents because they ruined me and my opportunities. My father started me on the trail, and killing your parents led me farther down it to a place I never could have imagined. These people I killed … if I had not killed them, the world would know of us. I try and keep the balance."

The Bat continued, "Tell me something, Nate. Do you trust your teachers still? Do you trust your adoptive parents?"

When Gray stopped talking, Nate noticed he could move again. He felt the tips of his fingers as he brushed them against the cold stone. He couldn't help blinking once. He knew it would be foolish to fight Gray; the odds were hardly in his favor. Deciding the best thing to do was to talk and keep Gray and his men distracted, he resolved himself to wait for help that would hopefully come. He tried to focus, but all he had just heard swam around his head. "They do it for our own good and safety," Nate said, finally able to break his silence. "You may not think it's right, but it keeps our world's order and security. Things are best left alone."

"He's a smart one," said Gray, directing his comment to the men behind him. They all laughed unpleasantly. "Yes, Nate, that is true. But shouldn't you be told how special and different you are? You are The Natural, and you are not upset that they haven't told you? And probably never planned on telling you?"

Nate couldn't help but agree in his head, but saying it aloud would allow Gray some satisfaction. "I can't know whether or not they planned to tell me, and until I know, I won't assume otherwise." Nate lifted his chin. He looked beyond the people in front of him and noticed that the hole at the end of the tunnel had grown steadily darker. A sound seemed to emanate from somewhere very far away, almost like a crack. At first he thought it was nothing, but then he saw two animals outlined slightly against the mouth of the cave. Nate saw all of this in several seconds and knew he had to keep Gray talking. "I don't understand. Why am I The Natural?"

"Nate, it just so happens that you are the lucky one. You were born one of a kind. You had a much stronger genetic predisposition toward engaging your full mind, and your change was triggered early, allowing your potential to grow. In other words, Nate, you crossed the next evolutionary rung on the genetic ladder for naturals. You are, in a sense, a new breed, a more powerful and advanced breed. When you reach your full development, your skills will surpass all others. You'll be unstoppable—which is precisely the problem. Unfortunately, it has cost several people their lives, and it will cost you yours."

"And all the people who work for you?" Nate gestured to the bulky figures standing resolutely behind Gray. "They all believe as you do?"

"Of course. I have found them throughout my travels, and they are the most determined human beings I have ever met. We are all unwavering in our commitment to fight for what we believe is right. The killings are necessary. Believe me, I wish it wasn't the case."

Nate snorted. "Of course, you're not looking for absolute power or anything like that? You don't want to do the typical thing and put lesser people into submission under your iron hand?"

"If my father had his way, that would be my ambition, but no, Nate." Gray sounded offended and made an odd twitch when speaking of his father. "I don't want anything *that* materialistic. I want our world to remain the well-kept secret it has been for hundreds of years. My work allows you and your friends to enjoy the world you have recently come to know. You could call it peacekeeping. I enjoy what I do, and it is necessary for the general balance of things. The Special Police—they do a decent job. What they don't want to admit is that they need me to help them do their job. Do you know how many Special Police there actually are?"

"No." Nate's eyes flashed to the mouth of the cave. The two figures were edging closer, and he knew he only had to stall for just a few more minutes. All he had to do was be careful not to draw attention to the fact that he was waiting for something.

"No? There are about fifteen hundred of them. Fifteen hundred, Nate, to keep our entire world in harmony."

"I would assume that, seeing as they know you are after me, they are probably all here, waiting for the right moment to strike."

Gray looked around uncomfortably. "I highly doubt that." Then he looked around again. "Horace, go check on Charles again, just to make sure ..."

The biggest man, presumably Horace, nodded and headed toward the cave entrance.

Nate realized this had been a terrible idea. All he had wanted was to make Gray feel uneasy. Now, he could only sit there, hoping that whoever was trying to reach them in the cave saw Horace coming and found a good hiding spot.

"Little skittish, aren't you, Gray?" Nate ventured to ask.

"Maybe a little. I didn't get this far being careless. We are wasting our time. I wanted to tell you why you are so important before I killed you. Now you know. So ..." As he spoke, he picked up a large, shiny silver knife from the ground. Nate hadn't noticed it before. "There is only one way to do this. I have to be sure this time. Clearly, last time didn't work so well. Pretty soon, your head will part company with your body."

It had been a minute or two since Horace had left, and clearly the people in the cave hadn't been discovered. Nate highly doubted the guard or guards outside would've just let intruders in, and knew it wouldn't be long before Horace found the guard and raised the alarm. Just then, he heard a low growl from just behind Gray's henchmen. They all jumped and turned, backing closer to Gray.

"Jesus, you're scared of pretty much everything!" Gray said, exasperated. He turned to see what they were afraid of, and Nate seized his opportunity. A thick fog rolled into the cave and surrounded Gray in a matter of seconds. Nate dove for Gray, knocking him on his back. He had been relying on his obviously superior strength and Combat lessons to keep Gray subdued but immediately realized that wouldn't be enough. Gray was surprisingly strong for his size. He rolled over and hit Nate across the face, once, twice, three times. Nate cowered and struggled to get out from underneath Gray. Finally, he pushed upward and threw Gray off. While Gray was still in midair, Nate turned the floor of the cave to ice. Gray slid almost ten feet and hit the wall.

Knowing this would be his chance to gain the upper hand, Nate lost no time in beginning the transformation. He felt a stabbing pain in all of his limbs, and he felt the fur begin to grow; but Gray was not about to sit idly by while Nate transformed. A rock from the ceiling dislodged itself and smashed where Nate had been just a moment before. The floor where Nate stood fell away, and he was left holding onto the edge with his hands, which were slowly turning to paws. As he hung there, Gray approached with his knife. A rock dropped from the ceiling and shattered the blade. With Gray distracted, Nate reached full transformation. He was the wolf. He leapt out of the hole and pushed Gray to the ground. He knew that Gray turning into a bat would not help him in this situation, and Gray had clearly realized it as well. In a last desperate act, he took a shard of the knife from the ground and stabbed it into Nate's back. Nate growled with pain and jumped off of Gray.

The pain was intense, but Nate could overcome it. He blocked out the discomfort and quickly took stock of the situation. The jaguar and lynx were fighting with a group of dogs. The lynx was cornered, but just as Nate watched, the jaguar leapt in to defend John, slashing one of the dogs across the face with its powerful paw.

Gray's foot appeared out of nowhere and kicked Nate in the side. Nate whimpered and backed away. Gray was advancing now with the repaired knife in his hand. In his other hand he held a flaming torch. He swung the torch violently, and as Nate tried to block it, the knife came from his right and grazed his right front leg. Nate was being backed into a corner. The rock behind him dropped into a pool of water, splashing it up with tremendous force and distinguishing Gray's torch. All was black now as Nate backed deeper into the cave. With his keen wolf eyes, he could clearly see Gray advancing with the knife. Gray must have realized this because at that moment, he backed away toward his thugs.

Gray's eyes had gone mad. His face was a sheet of rage. The man was crazy, swinging the knife wildly.

"All your tricks will not help you." He hissed the words. "This is a battle of wits. No matter how much of your mental capability you have available, I am smarter than you and I will kill you." With that he tossed the knife toward Nate.

Nate saw a flash of silver and ducked. The blade sliced through his fur, but left the skin untouched. It hit the wall with a resounding clang and broke in half. It was Gray who was backing up now. Nate advanced upon him, his teeth bared.

"If you kill me, it is all over. You have no idea what is in store if things continue unchecked the way they are going. I am the one who keeps it all going. Do you really want to take my place? Why not just let me go, and I can do it myself. Just let me go."

His words dug into Nate and seemed to make some sort of sickening sense. Nate shook his large head and advanced. He grinned wolfishly at Gray, and for the first time fear showed in Gray's eyes. Nate stared into the face he had come to loathe. He stared at the face that had changed his life forever. He looked into the eyes of the man who had mercilessly killed his three-year-old brother and his parents. No remorse—just pure hatred, determination, and a hint of fear. Nate felt disgust flow through him as he eyed the cowering man. Then he saw the subtle movement.

The ground split apart directly between Nate's four legs. The floor disappeared beneath him, and Nate fell. Before he had gone more than ten feet, a soft bed of grass grew below him and he landed sprawled upon it. He looked up at Gray, who was looking down at him, grinning evilly. Nate caused the grass ramp to extend up to the edge and sprinted upward as he did it. He leaped out of the ground and landed, pinning Gray against the cave floor. Gray wiggled out from underneath him before he could get a good grip and put the knife up to his neck. Nate recoiled. Gray advanced. In a second Nate was pinned against the wall, with Gray standing there holding his knife against Nate's neck. Nate closed his eyes and concentrated with all his might. He refused to think that he would be dead in a minute; instead he focused on the cave floor beneath Gray. A section of the floor shot up a foot into the air, and Gray was launched up and backward. He sprawled onto the floor. Nate jumped and pinned him to the ground.

Baako and John had managed to dispatch two of the dogs. The other two were a little more experienced, and their breed was much bigger and vicious. Baako leapt for one and John for the other, and they began grappling with each other.

Meanwhile, Gray was still pinned against the ground, and Nate was trying to make a quick decision. Gray couldn't move under the weight of an extremely strong, two-hundred-and-fifty-pound wolf. Nate had never even killed a mouse. Gray surely deserved to die. If he was caught, he would go to prison, await trial, and would escape and kill more. Death was the only choice.

Just as he was about to commit the final act, Nate recoiled, yowling in pain. Gray had sliced his shoulder with a shard of metal. Instantly, Nate transformed back into human form and fashioned a blade from thin air. He tossed it, caught it, and sliced Gray's arm. Gray lunged forward, and Nate stabbed him again. Gray yelled in pain and fell backward.

Nate advanced on the now helpless Gray and pushed outward with his hands. A huge gust of wind took Gray up in the air and threw him violently against the cave wall. Gray slid to the floor semi-conscious with his arms stretched awkwardly beneath him.

"That was for my father," snarled Nate. He walked over to Gray, who was stirring slightly and looking wall-eyed up at him. He picked Gray up by his hair and dropped him against the stone floor.

"That was for my mother," he snarled again. He then looked up at a football-sized rock sticking precariously out of the high wall. He concentrated, and it fell ten feet onto Gray's head with a sickening crunch, knocking him out cold.

"And that," said Nate, seething with hatred, "was for my brother."

Nate turned from Gray's prone form and noticed that Baako and John's previously taken-out opponents were up again. They were fighting two against four. Nate transformed back into a wolf, leapt into the fray, and slammed into the biggest dog. The dog growled and turned, baring its teeth at him. Nate jumped forward and at the same time caused fire to jut out of the rock below the dog and engulf it. The dog whimpered and yelped as it was burned alive. Nate watched, slightly sickened, until he felt a weight on his back and then pain in his neck. There was a smaller dog on him. He flung around trying to swing it off, but the dog would not let go. Then the jaguar jumped out of nowhere and pushed the dog off Nate and pinned it against the wall.

Light engulfed the room once more. In the heat of the fight, Nate hadn't realized that when he had knocked Gray unconscious, the light had faded from the room. He'd seen the others because of his night vision. Now, beams of light flooded the space, accompanied by silhouettes in black. They ran into the cave with sleek, black weaponry and forced the remaining three to the ground. There must have been at least twenty of them. Two of them stayed with each man, and the others approached Baako, John, and Nate, who were still in their animal forms.

Nate now realized they were wearing skintight suits made of some sort of hardened plates. They wore fitted black helmets.

The lead one, who was heading for Nate, pulled off his helmet as he approached. "Nate Williams," said the man. He looked to be almost fifty, but still in excellent shape. "Nate, I am Joshua Black, head of Special Police. I replaced your father more than ten years ago. May I suggest a change?" He asked this with the smallest hint of laughter. Something comforting gleamed in his eyes, and Nate knew he could trust him.

Nate nodded. Joshua handed Nate a robe and turned to allow Nate to change. Nate felt the receding pain. The fur fled back into his skin and soon, he was normal again. "Thank you, Mr. Black. I am not sure how we would have finished it without you."

Joshua turned and smiled. "My pleasure. You did a pretty good job of it yourself. He needed a knock on the head, and three was probably less than he deserved."

"I don't think it would be a good idea to return him to prison," said Nate, turning to the figure now sprawled on the ground. He began to wonder whether he should have just killed the man. What if Joshua insisted on sending Gray to prison?

"Oh, I am sure we will take care of the matter here and now, if you haven't already." Joshua glanced at Gray's bloodied form on the ground. "If you would join your friends outside, we won't be more than a couple of minutes."

"Yes, of course." Nate turned and left the cave. It was dark out, and the Moon was in the very center of the sky. It shone its silvery brilliance down, casting a long rippling shadow upon the lake. Nate had never seen so many stars, but soon, the stars were no longer what held his attention.

Hurst stood with Carter in the entryway. Baako and John, also wearing robes, were talking to the two in hushed voices. When they saw Nate, they both ran over and hugged him. Baako had a long scratch across his cheek, and he was holding his arm at an odd angle. John limped as he ran.

"You all right?" asked Baako.

"Easy," said Nate. The multiple places where Gray's knife had penetrated him burned with pain as they hugged him. He immediately turned his attention to Hurst. Nate gave him a look that informed him he had a lot of explaining to do. At this point, they heard a quick succession of gunshots. The four henchmen were led outside where they joined their fellows against the wall. Two Special Police came out next carrying the prone figure of Gray. Nate could see blood spreading from his chest. The sight was satisfying, but he looked away. He knew it was for the best. The rest of the Special Police followed.

Joshua saw them and headed their way. "Well, that cleaned up nicely," he said cheerfully. "John, we might finish all this back at the school. Would you agree?"

Hurst nodded his assent and turned toward something that made Nate's jaw drop. There was a stone pathway almost ten feet wide going straight through the center of the lake from the right of the waterfall to the far shore near the main building.

Nate and his friends set off across the stone pathway. They turned when they were about a quarter of the way across it and saw a remarkable procession following them. First came Black, Hurst, and Carter, not five feet behind them. Behind them, two Special Police carried Gray. Behind Gray's body, two Special Police forced four separate prisoners across. There were black bags over the prisoners' heads. Behind the prisoners, the other ten members of the police brought up the rear. It was quite a sight to behold. Nate looked up at the waterfall behind the procession. It pounded relentlessly down the side of the cliff and made its entrance into the water a majestic show.

They reached the far side of the lake in a matter of minutes. Nate knew it had probably only taken the Special Police three minutes to run over the newly created bridge bisecting the lake. He stepped off the bridge, and the rest followed him. When everyone was off the bridge, it sunk back into the lake, leaving the crisp dark water as though it had never been.

Chapter 27
The Truth

THE FIRST THING that Nate noticed when he entered Hurst's office was that the usual clutter of paperwork had disappeared from his desk. Hurst himself was leaning over the only piece of paper, a letter he appeared to be writing. There was a door he didn't remember seeing before. *It must lead to Hurst's private quarters,* Nate thought. It was odd, however, because the door seemed to open up onto the roof, and there was no visible hallway beyond. The desk and chairs around it were made from cherry. The cherry was so brightly polished that it glowed in the early afternoon light. The desk itself had only a few items on it. There was a large, carved onyx bear in one corner. It had definitely not been there before.

Nate turned his attention to the windows. The view was spectacular. He was always so preoccupied while there, it was the first time he could really appreciate it. The campus of Noble stretched out far below him. The trees swayed ever so gently in a calm breeze. The sunlight shone in an almost perfectly straight line down into the valley.

Since most of Noble was lined with glass walls and this time of day the Sun was shining directly into the building, Nate had not thought to take off his aviators. He found that, ever since his encounter with The Bat, his eyes had become overly sensitive to the sunlight.

There were several people playing Jeka in the warm spring air. Nate watched as his captain made a spectacular play. Others watched as well, cheering and applauding as they saw fit. The leaves on the trees outside were almost fully grown. A cough brought his attention back to the room.

"Nate." Hurst finally looked up from his letter. "I'm glad you came. I know I have a lot of explaining to do."

Nate nodded. There was no point in pretending otherwise. Hurst had lied to him, and Nate wasn't going to pretend he hadn't. Nate was in Hurst's office for solid answers to all of his questions. When he looked at Hurst, he noticed regret in his eyes, and it was this, more than anything, that made him realize he would hear nothing but the truth today.

"Nate, although I would prefer if you did not relay this to your friends, I realize it's your decision. Perhaps it is better that your closest friends do know." He paused and gave Nate a calculating look before continuing. "I was in your parents' class here at Noble. Mr. Black was also in our class. Everyone forms their own groups, as you have done with your friends. My group of friends consisted of your parents, Mr. Black, and several others. When we graduated from Noble, we all went on to do separate things. I became a Mind professor here. Your father and Joshua joined the Special Police. Your mother worked with them. Joshua and your father were very close, so naturally they chose the same career path."

Nate fidgeted as he listened.

"I must fast-forward now almost fifteen years. You were a young child, and your father was now the head of the Special

Police. Your mother raised you but did a considerable amount to help your father with whatever she could. I became the head of Noble, and Black was your father's second in command. Then the killings began. There were so many of them, it was hard to keep track. Finally, the leaders of our society met. We knew that these killings had been done by one of us. Your father and Black agreed to hunt down the murderer, and your mother requested to help."

I already know most of this, Nate thought, getting impatient.

"After several months of tracking him, your father found himself in Texas when he was notified that a murder had just occurred in the southern part of the state. He called for backup and then headed after the murderer. He caught him just as he was about to flee over the Mexican border. This man was Gray. You know that, but I wanted to give you the background first. We caught him and held him for trial, but he was cunning. Within no time, he had escaped, and we were on the chase again. Before any of us knew it, he had gotten to your house. Your mother, father, and brother had been murdered, but there was a rumor that you had escaped. Your body was not in the house, and we searched tirelessly for you for days. Everyone wondered how you had escaped at the age of six—everyone but me. Your father had told me that there was something different about you."

Nate nodded. No surprises there.

"Six! This was completely unheard of. It was eleven years earlier than expected. You had escaped a full-grown, calculated killer and found your way into the arms of one of the most powerful men in the world. Now, Nate, here is the well-kept secret. I would have wished for your father to tell you this, but Desmond Williams is one of us. He prefers to live isolated from the rest of us, like your parents did, but he was two years behind your parents at Noble.

"Desmond found you on the cliff and noticed immediately from your face and the signs on your clothes that not only were you his friend's son but that you had changed that very night. William and Nadea Banks were your real parents.

"They were very well-respected members of our society and will always be." His voice drifted off. "Desmond contacted me and told me you had shown signs of changing. He watched you a little more carefully and noticed subtle signs that you had already unlocked extra-mental ability, even to the degree that we have as fully matured naturals. We realized you were different. Desmond loves you like his son, and you *are* his son. He has watched you grow and mature these past years. He knew exactly what was happening during your coma, but thought it best not to tell Sofia or Emma. He knew the coma probably changed you even further. It is true: We tell students they have full ability, but they do not. I would've liked to keep it that way. I doubt that'll be possible now."

"No, it won't be possible." Nate had no intention of keeping the secret.

Hurst inclined his head. "When I visited you, I watched you. Nate, you are *The* Natural. Gray was not lying or manipulating you in that respect. You have unlocked everything. You have an extraordinary opportunity and responsibility on your shoulders. You have inherited a responsibility that no one has ever had to endure."

Nate looked up. "Gray told me you were responsible for my parents' deaths."

Lines of pain creased Hurst's forehead, and he felt guilty for putting him in such a position.

Hurst regained his composure. "I didn't know he would get there so fast. I waited just a couple of minutes too long to inform your parents that Gray was in the area. I heard about a murder he had committed just two hours before. I thought I would notify the senator in the area before I told your parents. It was the worst decision I've ever made, and I regret it to this day. If I had told them, maybe they would have had time to ..." Hurst's voice caught.

Nate noticed tears in his eyes. "As you said, Gray was an expert. I'm sure it wouldn't have made a difference."

"Your parents were experts too." Hurst tried to steady his voice. "They were the best at what they did. They could have stopped him. I know they could have."

"Don't let things that have already happened bother you, because there's nothing you can do about them."

"Damn good reasoning. We don't have teachers as smart as you." Hurst smiled at him. "Nate, I thought you should know everything and now you do."

Now that Hurst was back in control, all his questions came flooding back. "Gray mentioned that I can do anything. What can I do that you can't?"

"The man is smart, I'll give him that. I can change the weather, the material of this desk. I can read your mind and speak to a bird. I can do all those things, but Nate, you can move to anywhere in the world in a second. You can go back and forward in time. You can manipulate people's lives. There is nothing you can't do. There is no one who can teach you these things. You must learn them yourself. You are the first and you will be the last, so teach yourself well."

Nate had more questions, but for some reason, they had all slipped away. It suddenly hit him what he was. He was probably the most powerful person in the world. There were plenty of positives, but as he thought about it, negatives seemed to pile up by the second. He would now be a constant target from virtually everyone on the planet. People would see him as something of a superhero, and although he enjoyed the attention, he knew it would get old, quite quickly.

"Figuring it all out?"

"Ups and downs." He forced the thoughts to the back of his head and told himself to think about it later. The idea was so daunting that deciding anything now would just make him regret it later.

"Do you have any other questions? You should probably take a walk—maybe a long one."

"One more question. Can I save Imani?"

"You can accomplish anything you set your mind to."

"Thank you, Professor Hurst." He rose and turned for the door.

"In case I don't see you, have a good summer and say hello to your father for me."

"Will do, sir."

When Nate reached the ravine, Baako and John were waiting for him. Without a word, the three of them set off for a long awaited brunch. Nate was planning to eat more than he'd ever eaten in his life ... and then some.

The dining hall was empty. Most people had either eaten or had brought their food out and had chosen to sit by the lake. Nate thought this wasn't a bad idea, so they ordered with a fairy and then went out through the glass door. They found a wooden picnic table under a large oak standing firmly by the water. Nate flung himself down onto the bench.

As they waited for their food, Nate told his best friends everything. They listened patiently. Sometimes frowns or smiles creased their faces momentarily but then were wiped away, to be replaced by a clean slate. When he was done, they looked at Nate in slight, barely noticeable, awe.

Chapter 28
The Natural

LIFE AT NOBLE had been winding down over the past couple of days. The weather had been perfect, and no one spent more time than they needed inside. Exams had been canceled on the pretense that everyone was too preoccupied to do well. More importantly, perhaps, was the fact that they still didn't know whether there were some of Gray's people wandering around the valley. Nate had spent all his free time outside, talking with his friends.

Nate lounged against the same large elm that he, Baako, and John had eaten under just a couple of days previously. The large elm provided more than enough shade. The sky had been cloudless, and Nate didn't expect that to change for a while. Several people were swimming in the lake, and the rest were lounging around under trees, just like them.

Nate sat with the people he cared most about, apart from his family. Jasmine leaned against him. She had been remarkably calm about the whole situation and was now listening intently to Nate's retelling of the night he'd defeated Gray. The others relaxed in a haphazard circle. Olivia was lying with her head in Curt's lap. Rebecca was lounging on her side between Baako and John. Erica nestled up to Baako. Curt and Sam sat with their arms stretched out behind them. None of them moved as the story unfolded. Baako and John had heard it by now, but it was always good to hear it again.

Nate had decided, after much consideration, to tell his friends pretty much everything that Gray had told him. He knew that, somehow, the fact that he was The Natural would leak out, and he knew it was better to tell the story right so rumors didn't make it smaller or larger than life.

All of Nate's friends had heard the story of the fight from Nate, Baako, and John, and got wind of the various other versions that floated around. None of them, apart from the three, knew what Gray had told him. It was this that Nate now recounted to his eager audience. The story was already getting old to him, and he knew he would have to tell it again many more times throughout his life. What he thought about it never got boring. Baako, John, and Nate had spent hours talking about what Nate might be capable of. They just kept spitballing ideas, and by the time they had exhausted the subject, Nate had a sizable list, both inside his head and out.

By this time, Nate knew the story so well that he could tell it without actually paying attention to what he was saying.

The three girls all let out gasps as Nate told of how he had changed when he was just six, attacked Gray, and then escaped. He brought himself back to attention for the last, most important part of the story.

"Gray told me that I'm different. To use his exact words, 'You are *The* Natural. You can do anything you set your mind to. You can do more than anyone else in this world.' "

At this point, Nate stopped. Curt, Sam, Rebecca, Erica, Jasmine, and Olivia, who had never heard this, were sitting up straight, looking at him. They seemed unable to take in what he'd just said. Nate didn't blame them—he was still easing it into his head, letting it sink in bit by bit. When it finally sunk in, Nate would be able to accept it and begin learning things on his own. He was extremely interested in the time travel aspect that Hurst had mentioned. He knew it involved a lot of science, but it would be pretty great if he could travel through time at his leisure.

"So, we all can only use thirty percent of our brains and for some reason, you're special and are able to use all one hundred?" asked Jasmine.

"That's what they tell me."

They all stared at him, then realizing what they were doing, looked down at the grass. After several seconds, Nate laughed and the rest of them joined in.

When they'd finished, a thought came to Nate. "At one point, when I was sure you guys were in the cave, the big man, Horace, I think his name was, left and never came back. I thought he would have found the guards you had subdued and raised the alarm. How did you deal with that?"

"Simple," said Baako proudly. "I followed him out, knocked his head on the rock, and put him with the other one. Then I crept back in there to join John. I can't believe the thug didn't realize what was happening. I was kind of surprised we fooled them. I would've thought they had more experience."

"I guess they're used to torturing helpless old men. They don't have experience dealing with younger, more agile, and astute people," said Nate.

"Like us." John laughed and everyone joined in. "One last scrimmage of Jeka, Nate?"

"You up for that Nate?" asked Baako.

Nate picked up the yellow ball that had been a great back support from behind him and jumped up.

"I'll take that as a yes," Baako said, grinning.

The boys stood and divided into teams. Baako and Nate were

easily the best, so it was them against the other three. Baako and Nate still won, but it was a fun match. At the end, it sort of fell apart, when instead of tackling the ball from Curt, Nate ran right up to the ball and kicked it as hard as he could. The ball whistled off through the clear-blue sky and disappeared in the trees.

"Great, Nate," said Curt, half-annoyed, half-amused. "Now we'll never get it back."

"What are you talking about?"

The ball sped out of the woods and within seconds, Nate had caught it. He grinned.

The coach buses arrived that afternoon. Everyone had packed the night before so they could enjoy the morning before their departure from school. It took Nate three trips to pack away all he had brought under the bus. He then leapt aboard to find a good seat. As usual, Nate and his friends found themselves with two booths directly across from each other: Baako, Erica, Jasmine, and Nate in one, and Sam, John, Curt, Olivia, and Rebecca in the other. Rebecca and Olivia shared a seat. Isabella's parents were picking her up separately.

The coach buses wound down the mountain road. The road zigzagged precariously down the nearly vertical cliff until the buses landed in the valley. Mountains ran along the valley sides, stretching up so far that some of them were capped with snow. Fields and farms were laid out between the bus and the mountains as though someone had painted them in.

Rivers intersected their path, and the road devised ways to cross the babbling water. Most times, the bridges spanned the length of the river. Occasionally, they had to go through tunnels to get through the mountains. Nate always loved the feeling of going through a tunnel. The lights on the side of the tunnel flashed beside him before they entered into a completely different landscape.

The Williams' jet was white with a blue line along each side. On the door was a large, modern family crest. It was a beautiful array of objects on a kite shield. The top right corner of the shield was the biggest and contained the family animal. Fittingly enough, a wolf's head was emblazoned there. They boarded the jet, and it took off immediately.

Chapter 29
The Coast

DESMOND WAS THE first to reach Nate when he descended the jet stairs onto the tarmac. He hugged his son tightly. He had been in contact with Hurst during the entire incident with Gray, and Nate could tell he was overjoyed to see him looking fit and healthy. Nate knew he noticed the glazed look in his eyes and deep cuts that were attempting to heal stretching across his face, but it could've been so much worse. Desmond pulled back and looked at his son.

"I'm sorry," Desmond said quietly.

Nate caught his father's gaze. He knew this applied to everything, and he was very grateful. After leaving his father's arms, Nate felt a crash as his mother slammed into him. He hugged her, breathing in her familiar perfume. Tear tracks ran down her face, and she held him for a very long time. When she finally released him, Nate picked up his little sister and hugged her tightly. He had missed her. He had missed all of them.

Nate introduced Jasmine to his family. They got along very

well in those few minutes, and Nate knew from their instant chemistry that Sofia and Jasmine would become friends. After Nate had kissed Jasmine goodbye and Emma had promised to have her over for dinner that weekend, they headed back to the car. Nate noticed that Sofia was already entering Jasmine's number into her phone, and he smiled to himself. As they closed in on the hulking, sleek black Rover, Nate noticed there was another car hidden behind it. The shadow cast by the Rover made it impossible to see the four interlocking circles on the hood, but Nate knew it was his car. He grinned.

Desmond smiled and gestured for him to take it.

There was nothing like a drive to clear his head. He wondered how much a drive would've really helped had he been able to bring his car to Noble. When he reached the car he opened the door and slid into the leather seat. The keys were elegantly draped over the steel shifter. Nate grabbed the keys, and the engine roared to life. He was just about to pull out when he heard a shout. Sofia ran around the car and slid into the passenger seat.

They drove out through the airport gates, and it was a little while before either of them spoke; Nate was enjoying the silence. There had been a lot of it today, but after the past couple of days, he welcomed the respite.

Finally, Sofia breached the silence. "Any good stories?"

Nate laughed. "A lot."

For the rest of the car ride home, Nate filled his little sister in on everything that had happened since he'd last been home. He spent most of the time focusing on the past week. She reacted much differently than anyone else when she heard what Nate was, because the first words out of her mouth were, "Can you help Imani?"

"I can, and I will cure her."

After a while, Nate breached a topic that had been on his mind. "Sofia?"

"Yes?" She looked over at him curiously. He rarely said her

name.

"If you don't change in a year, I will make sure you're accepted to Noble." He looked at her and saw her face brighten.

"You can do that?" she asked breathlessly.

"Well, I am The Natural. Hurst told me I can do anything I set my mind to, and I want you to go to Noble. What I have lived has been more exciting and amazing than Watson could ever offer any of us. I know you want to go, and I want you to go too."

"Thanks, Nate." She leaned across the car and kissed him on the cheek.

Nate smiled. It was the best gift he could've ever given her.

The house looked exactly the same as when he'd left, except for a new car that sat right outside the garage. A gleaming, gray Bentley Continental convertible sat drawing attention like the Sun, where the Aston Martin had once sat. Nate appreciated his father's taste.

Nate entered the house he loved so much. Everything was neat and clean.

Desmond came in and dropped Nate's bags. He was about to say something to his son, who was still staring out across the city through the living room windows when a member of the Guard slipped in.

Desmond nodded and said something back to the guard in a low voice. The guard nodded and left. Desmond then gestured to Nate. "How about a drive?"

"Sure." Nate pulled his keys out of his pocket.

"I was thinking my car. You want to try it?"

"Course!" He said goodbye to his mother and sister. The two of them were deep in conversation about an upcoming movie when Desmond and he left. Sofia and Emma were almost exactly alike. Sofia had several offers and had the same agent as Emma now. It seemed they talked movie business almost all of the time.

Before Nate could get another good look at the car, Gatsby rushed over to him from the yard. His dog was wagging his tail excitedly and rubbed up against Nate's leg, looking up at him with happy eyes. Nate pet Gatsby's soft coat for a couple of seconds then Emma called Gatsby into the house.

The Bentley was nicer than any car Nate had ever driven. Before they started, he put the top down. He then eased on the gas and sped off down the driveway. The gate had already opened for them. They left the gate far behind and sped off into the hills. At the point where the road forked to go to the city, Nate veered right and headed in the opposite direction, deep into the beautiful countryside.

As they drove, he noticed several cars he recognized had joined the minimal traffic on the road. One was in front of him, and the other two were in back of him. Desmond often attracted the wrong kind of attention, and Nate was comforted by the skill of the Guard.

Desmond was silent for a while. Nate loved the feeling of the air rushing through his hair. He breathed in deeply. It made him feel relaxed and comfortable. He felt a slight twinge of regret that his car of choice had not been a convertible.

It was rare that they took this road. It was a four-lane highway, but it wound through beautiful hills. There were cliffs lining the right side of the road, with waterfalls cascading down them. Some of the waterfalls were thick and thundering, while others were thin and barely noticeable. They all flowed into a river. The river was huge, and it carved its way down between the cliffs and pushed out toward the ocean.

Desmond finally broke the silence. "Nate, I know you must resent me for not telling you that I'm one of you—for not telling you about your brother. I would resent me too. I thought it'd be better if you found out for yourself. I was wrong and so was John. I'm very sorry."

"I don't resent you, Dad. I probably would've done the same thing. What are you?"

Desmond smiled, taking this question as a sign that Nate had truly forgiven him. "Mountain lion."

"That's awesome." He could totally picture his father as a mountain lion. He hoped he would see it in person, maybe even this summer. "Do Mom and Sofia know?"

"Yes I explained it to them a few weeks ago. They weren't too happy at first, but they've gotten used to the idea."

They were quiet once more. Nate was the one to break the silence. "You knew my parents?"

Desmond's face saddened, just as Hurst's had. "Yes. Very well. Your father was my best friend, and I knew your mother well too. I was two years behind them, but I idolized your father and he was a very good role model for me. I never really liked John Hurst, to be honest. I put up with him, but I have gotten over myself in recent years."

Desmond continued: "I knew you were different. Not just that you were different like we both are, but that you were more than that. I knew that you were more than anything I had ever seen."

"Is that why you took me in?" The words flew out of Nate's mouth before he had a chance to consider what he was asking. Now that he heard them, he hated himself for it.

"No! Nate, I took you in because you were my best friend's son. I was legally your godfather before I became your father. I knew you immediately."

Something jolted in Nate's past. His childhood with his parents came rushing back. "I remember you."

"Thought you might." Desmond beamed. "I knew something of that night had affected your memory. Hurst told me it would come back, and I just had to be patient."

Nate remembered his mother. She'd been beautiful, loving, caring—everything Emma was, but something more. He remembered her smile—her eyes. He very vaguely remembered his father, but he knew he had been enamored with him. Every day he would tell Nate bits of his day, and Nate would sit on his knee and stare up at him in awe. Last of all, Nate remembered his little brother. Andrew had followed him wherever he went.

"What do you think of it all? That you are The Natural, I mean."

"It depends on the moment. At times, I think it's awesome, and I think about all the things I want to do. At others, I realize it will be a burden. People will look to me for advice and pretty much everything. I will be a target. I have come to accept that. I still haven't come to a conclusion about what I truly think, though."

"I know it's a lot to take in, but I have watched you grow for seventeen years Nate. I don't think there's anyone more fit for the responsibility. I couldn't handle it. It is natural to feel conflicted." They both laughed at his word choice. "I have a feeling you won't make up your mind for a long time. If you ever need me, I'm always around."

"I know." They fell into silence once more. Then Nate asked, "Can we drive to the coast?"

"Whatever you want."

The drive was remarkably beautiful. Nate was only partially paying attention to the road. Most of his brainpower was focused on his new responsibility. There would be plenty more nutjobs like Gray. He would probably need his own personal guard before too long. Something about what Gray had said was still bothering him. Gray had told him that he kept the balance. Nate had to wonder about that. Something was always needed to keep the balance, but Nate couldn't be sure whether there was already a system in place.

Nate could now see the ocean. It stretched out as far as he could see to where it joined the sky many miles away. The road took a turn and led along the ocean for a while. Nate found a place to pull off, and he stopped the car. He looked out over the pounding surf. The sea air felt good on his face. He opened the door to the car as the three black Audis pulled alongside.

Nate left the car and walked to the edge of the bluff, about fifty feet from the car. The beach rolled out beneath him until it gave way to the lapping waves. The Sun was close to the horizon. A glowing path led from it all the way to the pounding surf.

Gray must've been exaggerating when he'd said there would be chaos if the regular population found out about the Hidden World that was right beneath their nose. Nate found it hard to believe that they would be persecuted. It wasn't the fifteenth century anymore. He remembered extreme historical cases, but the United States had a stable government. In less-structured parts of the world, however, fear could reign. There would be much less chaos if the normals were told, rather than them finding out accidently. The age of tolerance was possible—it would just take time.

ACKNOWLEDGMENTS

I would like to thank my brother, Christian, for making many things possible for me, and for everything he has said and done for me that has contributed to where I am today. My sister, Marielle, for always being there to talk to, regardless of what I had to say, and who has the uncanny ability to make me simply enjoy my time in her presence, no matter what. My father, Charles, for his outstanding personality that has made me who I am and the endless amounts of time he has devoted to me when I needed it most. I would like to thank my mother, Carol, for being who she is, all the time, never backing down, and always being there for me to do anything in her power to make me happy. I would like to thank my entire family for supporting me throughout many difficult years and believing in me. Each and every one of my family members has helped me to arrive at where I am today, and I am very grateful.

I would also like to thank my agent, Leticia Gomez, for believing in me and finding a home for this novel. I would like to thank John Koehler and Joe Coccaro for accepting *The Hidden World* and the entire Koehler Books team for making the publication of this book a reality. Thank you to Jack Pope, for designing and building the website that allows me to connect with readers.

Thank you to Mary Pope Osborne, Dr. James McGoldrick, and Geoff Marchant for being fantastic writing mentors. I will never forget or take for granted what they contributed to my writing career.

Lastly, I would like to thank my friends, the old and the new, for giving me the happiness that allows me to enjoy my accomplishments.

CPSIA information can be obtained at www.ICGtesting.com
Printed in the USA
BVOW07s1854201113

336859BV00006B/241/P